Cloud Hands

The Disclosure Files™ - Book One

Nancy J Nelson

Brown Leaf
Press

Brown Leaf Press

Published by Brown Leaf Press. Los Angeles, CA.

ISBN: 979-8-9919647-4-6 (Paperback)

ISBN: 979-8-9919647-5-3 (eBook)

Library of Congress Control Number: 2025922365

Cover Art by David Leahey

Interior Formatting by Atticus.io

Second Edition (revised) 2025

Author's Note

Thank you for picking up this revised edition of *Cloud Hands, The Disclosure Files – Book One*. Since its original release in 2024, I've taken time to reflect, revise, and expand the story in ways that deepen the characters and sharpen the journey they're on.

This version includes new scenes, updated dialogue, and refined worldbuilding—changes made not only to clarify but to better align with where the series is heading. If you've read the original, you will notice many familiar moments. If you're new to the story, welcome. You're getting the most complete version.

Stories evolve, just like the people who tell them. I'm grateful to have the chance to keep growing this one.

—Nancy J. Nelson

CONTENTS

PROLOGUE

I used to think this story was about me. After all, isn't everyone the star of their own life? It was only later that I realized we are all just bit players in some ever-repeating, cosmic pattern—a fractal pattern made up of love, hardship, desperation, joy, sorrow, and hope.

Let's never forget about hope.

—Victoria Heywood
Excerpt from address to the UN

There was a little cluster of forget-me-nots arranged in a vase on the table in front of Vicki. They had been Beth's favorite flowers. Small and vibrant, so cute they made you smile. Just like Beth herself.

The waitress put a cup of coffee and a pastry before her, and the same in front of the man seated across the table. Kurt Martinsson—she had called him Professor Martinsson when he taught her senior business seminar a decade earlier—added some sugar to his cup before he took a sip. Well-built, dark hair with a touch of gray at his temples. He had aged well. His bespoke sports jacket, manicured nails, and expensive haircut suggested he was also doing well.

"It was kind of you to look me up, Professor Martinsson, especially after all this time. To be honest, I haven't been getting out much." She hadn't been getting out at all. What was the point?

Their parents had died in a car accident several years back, and now Beth was gone too. Per her request, there had been a closed casket; the chemo had ravaged her body and taken all her hair. There was no amount of makeup, no wig good enough, that could have fixed that.

"I heard about your sister, Vicki; I'm so sorry. I understand you left your position at the Department of State to look after her."

Beth had argued against that. *"I'm young and strong; I'll be able to beat this—there's no reason for you to leave the job you worked so hard to get. Mom and Dad were so proud that you became a diplomat—they wouldn't have wanted you to give that up."* She had been wrong about being able to beat the cancer, but right that their parents had been proud. They would have been just as proud to see their youngest open up her own flower shop in a prime location in downtown Los Angeles.

"I took a year's leave of absence when it became clear my sister's illness was terminal. I have another four months before I either return to work or submit my official resignation."

"So, you haven't decided what you'll do?" Professor Martinsson cocked his head to one side and looked at her. He had finished his croissant. She hadn't even started on hers.

"No, I haven't. Every time I start thinking about it I..." She looked down at her coffee cup. It was too hard to think. Too hard to think about the future or anything else. She had officially shut down Beth's flower shop the week after her sister died, although it hadn't been in operation for a couple of months before that. At Beth's urging, her two part-time employees had both found other jobs, and the shop sat dark and shuttered. She supposed she should do something—make arrangements to sell the building or rent it out—but she just didn't have the bandwidth.

"I have an idea that might interest you. I need to do a lot of traveling over the next few months. My two children are more than old enough to stay home by themselves—Brad is sixteen and Jessica is twenty-two—especially since there's household staff. But I'd feel better if someone was around to keep tabs on them specifically."

He paused, then casually asked, "You do still have a Top-Secret clearance, don't you?"

Vicki looked up from her coffee and stared.

Chapter One

A uniformed staff member answered the door and took Vicki's suitcase as she stepped into a marble foyer that was bigger than her condo back home in Washington, DC. She had been prepared for something grand after seeing the manicured grounds and the expensive cars in the circular drive, but even so, she fought to keep her jaw from dropping. White marble, a sweeping staircase, a massive chandelier, and floor-to-ceiling windows soaring three stories in height. Kurt Martinsson had done *very* well for himself in his post-academic life.

He came down the staircase now, dressed as if he had someplace to be. "Vicki! I'm so glad you agreed to spend the summer here. I appreciate the help."

"I'm the one who's grateful, Professor Martinsson. This will give me some space to figure out my way forward."

Hopefully, this would be easier to do when she wasn't feeling numb in the middle of everything. She had been staying in Beth's small apartment just above her flower shop, drinking countless cups of coffee, staring at what seemed to be an endless list of tasks, and procrastinating on doing anything. She needed to clean out all Beth's belongings and decide what to keep and what to donate. She needed to look at the shop and figure out...what? Should she put the building on the market? She needed to...

"No more Professor Martinsson; call me Kurt—I left academia years ago." He glanced at his watch. "And I need to leave in exactly half an hour, so let's talk while I attend to some last-minute details."

She followed him down a hallway to what appeared to be his home office: wood paneling, oriental rugs, and at least half a dozen television and computer screens. On one screen, CNN was covering civil unrest in a foreign country. On another, a business program talked about recent events on Wall Street.

"So, what does your company do... Kurt?" Okay, that felt weird.

"Government contracts. The Partnership for Advanced Technologies Transformation—we just call it the Partnership—is a group made up of some of the world's top companies in aerospace, security, intelligence, and IT. We handle some of the most sensitive issues facing the planet. That's why I needed someone with Top-Secret clearance—someone loyal and trustworthy."

"To look after your kids?"

She was incredulous. She wasn't sure she hid it well. Her ten years with the Department of State didn't seem to be doing her much good. She had once read a quote that said a talented diplomat can tell someone to go to hell and make them look forward to the trip. Vicki jokingly told her colleagues that she had only mastered the part about telling people to go to hell.

"Their mother—my ex-wife—died five years ago. Her death was obviously painful for both children, especially since they were living with her at the time. But while Brad managed to pick up the pieces and move on, Jess became erratic. Therapy didn't seem to help, and it got even worse after she was in a minor car accident a couple of years ago. She's physically fine, but..."

"Does she self-harm? Does she use drugs?"

A sudden wave of anger surged through Vicki—she hated surprises. She and Kurt had exchanged several emails since their coffee shop meeting a few weeks ago, but he had never mentioned any behavioral issues with his kids. She'd assumed he just wanted someone around to keep them from getting too wild while he was gone. Now it seemed like there was a deeper issue at play.

"No, no, no, nothing like that."

Kurt must have heard the anger in her voice because he became apologetic. "Jess is emotionally fragile—she has fears and worries that sometimes paralyze her, but at the same time, she's wildly empathetic. I don't want to see her hurt. I just need someone who will be able to manage a situation should it arise. Someone who will be there when she's going through a hard time."

Her anger died down, the now-habitual numbness creeping back in. So not a babysitter. But not an orderly either, thank goodness. Stepping in as a sort of low-level handler when things got too emotional? She could do that.

"So why the insistence on the Top-Secret clearance?" Kurt had actually checked back with the Department of State to confirm that her clearance was still active before they finalized her stay.

"As I mentioned, the Partnership handles some of the world's most sensitive issues," he said, eyes on his screens as he typed. "We've made incredible scientific breakthroughs—technology that could truly improve everyday life for everyone on the planet. I'm not exaggerating. But it also has serious military potential."

She waited, keeping her expression politely neutral while she resisted the urge to roll her eyes. His words sounded like smooth clichés—empty and meaningless. She'd heard plenty of that in her career, and her internal alarm was going off. The only difference between Kurt Martinsson and the government officials she'd dealt with was his use of business and technical jargon instead of a political vocabulary. Was he hiding something about the company? Maybe this was just the standard spiel for people not cleared for the full story. But it was also possible he didn't fully understand it himself and was using buzzwords to cover his own confusion. Something to consider later.

"The kids moved in with me when their mother died. For the first couple of months, I mostly worked from home while I looked for a larger house and found staff to hire."

Oh my God, *this* was the size of a house he thought he needed for just three people, two of whom would probably move out as they got older? It boggled her mind.

Kurt continued, "But sometimes I had to go to work sites, and a few times I ended up bringing them along. Jess and Brad were good about sitting quietly in the back while I was in meetings or attending technical demonstrations. They saw and heard a lot of things they normally wouldn't have been exposed to."

"You think Jessica learned something classified and is going to leak it to someone?" A scenario that seemed so unlikely she worked hard not to scoff. *Tamp it down, Vicki, tamp it down.*

"Not exactly." Kurt leaned back from his keyboard and ran a hand through his hair. "Jess is sensitive, which doesn't always go well with the kind of advanced tech we work with—stuff that still can't be shared with the public. A few times, she's seen demonstrations and gotten really upset that this technology isn't being used to help people. And she's not wrong—what we've developed could do a lot of good. But we're not ready to release it yet. Jessica's smart, but she's emotionally fragile. Sometimes it really gets to her."

"What are you worried might happen while you're traveling? If everything is still classified, I don't imagine Jessica will be presented with many random opportunities to come across things your firm has developed. Will she?"

"No, she won't; it's just that Jess is overly empathetic, overly compassionate." Vicki raised an eyebrow, and he gave a wry smile in response. He was attractive when he smiled; with looks, money, and intelligence, he was probably in high demand as a dinner partner—and more. "I know compassion is a character trait that parents want their kids to have, but in Jessica's case she gets triggered by news programs covering tragedies."

He nodded at the screen where CNN had finished its story about the civil unrest and moved on to coverage of the aftermath of a hurricane. "Or even by seeing someone asking for money on a street corner."

"What happens when Jessica is triggered?"

"Tears. Crying. Extended periods of ranting. Reactions that are all out of proportion. But it's worse when she goes quiet—she sometimes shuts herself in her room for hours or even days on end, just lying on her bed staring at nothing. It doesn't happen often, but I want someone to be there just in case, someone who is there specifically to notice when she's having a hard day. Hired staff have their own jobs and may not spot it."

"But no self-harm and no drugs."

"No self-harm or any drugs at all."

"You just want her to be safe."

"I just want her to be safe."

"So, how about Brad? You said he's sixteen now, right?"

Kurt's face broke into a grin. "He's funny, easygoing, and a certified genius. Both kids have had private tutors since their mother died, and while Brad is still in high school, he's already taking some university-level courses. He's brilliant with electronics. I confess I don't understand everything my son is doing, but he built his first computer when he was just thirteen."

"How about Jessica?" Time to focus back on the one he considered the problem child.

"Right now, she's concentrating on media studies. She lost a couple of years of education after her mom died, so even though she's twenty-two, she's only at the level of a second-year university student. She still has plenty of time to change her major, though."

He glossed over it so easily. A teenager losing a couple of "education years" after their parent dies is a sign she's going through a major, life-altering, catastrophic experience. And her father wasn't acknowledging it. Another thing to think about.

"She still has plenty of time to change her major? Do you think she'll do that?" Vicki's face was still one of polite attentiveness.

"I just think someone with Jessica's emotional sensitivity is not the right person to be in front of the camera. I've argued with her about it, telling her she doesn't have a strong enough nature to put up with the attention and limelight, but for the time being, she's insistent."

In Vicki's experience, people often studied what they needed in their lives. Maybe Jessica needed to speak—and to be heard. She idly wondered what Jessica might say if given the chance.

Kurt continued, "But despite what I say or complain about, my kids are great; you'll like both Jess and Brad. Let's go meet them."

Chapter Two

Their father had introduced them to Vicki, then immediately left for a three-week business trip. So... a little awkward. Brad wondered what Vicki thought of them—so much depended on her, and he hoped they would get along. More than get along. He was hoping they would become friends.

He didn't worry about his sister; Jessica usually made a good impression on adults. She was slender, with dark brown hair that fell just past her shoulders, and had a certain vulnerable charm. But Brad knew that impression of vulnerability was neither natural nor accidental—Jessica had worked hard to create it.

While Vicki hadn't stared at *him* openly, Brad knew what she saw: a tall, gangly teenager with stretched-out limbs and a face still catching up to the rest of him. The eyebrows, though? Flawless—and he was proud of them. He and Jess both had expressive brows, which they used to full effect when making a point.

Both he and Jessica had been genuinely happy—even excited—to meet Vicki, and he could tell that that had caught her off guard. Most teenagers would have greeted a glorified babysitter with sullen faces, not smiles.

But he and Jess both understood what was at stake. Vicki didn't.

He almost laughed, remembering the stunned look on Vicki's face when their father tossed her the keys to the Bentley as he left.

"But I have a car," she had protested. Brad had seen that beat-up Toyota in the driveway and wasn't impressed.

"These are the keys to the kids' vehicle. Neither of them drives, so they need someone to take them around town: to classes, for shopping, or to visit friends."

He had then driven away in his own Bentley, one that was much sportier and less family-friendly.

Which is why, three hours later, Vicki was behind the wheel of "her" Bentley.

"I feel like James Bond!" she squealed.

"You shouldn't; James Bond drives Aston Martins," Brad piped up from the backseat, not even looking up from his phone.

"That's in the movies. Read the books—the man preferred Bentleys."

Touché. He smiled to himself.

Vicki glanced at Jess beside her in the passenger seat. "So, you've never had the thrill of driving this lovely car?"

"She can't—she's too fraaagile," Brad interjected in a singsong voice before the conversation could get too serious.

That cracked them all up, even Vicki. He liked that she didn't get weird about it. She noticed stuff, but she didn't push. Still, neither he nor Jess had actually answered her question.

He was pretty sure Vicki had noticed that too.

* * *

Following Jessica's directions, Vicki turned into a small parking lot in front of a sprawling hacienda-style building. It was painted a coral pink that reminded her of the color of sandstone cliffs in the light of a setting sun. Beds of primroses and baby's breath—Beth had trained her well—lined the front walk. The sign over the front door read, "Cloud Hands Tai Chi Studio."

She followed Jess and Brad inside. They exchanged greetings with a few other people, then disappeared through a door with them into their classroom. Vicki sat in one of the easy chairs that dotted the reception area to wait. The only other person was a woman seated behind a desk at the far end of the room. With skin the shade of a caramel latté and hair twisted up in tight little corkscrews, she appeared to be in her early forties. When she noticed Vicki, she came over with a wide smile.

"You must be Victoria; the kids mentioned you would be the one bringing them to class. I'm Mona Cooper. My husband, Calvin, and I own this studio. Cal teaches the advanced class that Jess and Brad are in right now," she said, nodding toward the door the kids had disappeared through.

Vicki smiled back. "Call me Vicki. And I have a question—I thought tai chi was something only elderly people did?" None of the dozen or so people who had gone into the classroom with Jess and Brad were elderly; most looked to be younger than twenty-five.

Mona laughed. "This is the last class of the day, and we have nearly an hour until it ends, so let's talk out back by the pond. It's so much more pleasant out there."

Pleasant was an understatement—the back of the property took Vicki's breath away. It was about a third of an acre with white clematis vines twining through and over the fencing. Trees, bamboo, lush foliage, and winding gravel paths surrounded them. Beth would have loved it. They walked along one of the paths to a small koi pond dotted with lotus flowers, then sat on one of the two curved benches at one end.

"So, how much do you know about tai chi?" Mona asked.

"Not much, and obviously less than I thought I knew when I woke up this morning," Vicki replied. "My only experience with tai chi was seeing a couple of YouTube videos of older Chinese people doing tai hi in a park. When Jess and Brad told me that I needed to drive them to their martial arts class, I assumed it was something like Jiujitsu or Krav Maga. Tai chi just doesn't seem as exciting."

Mona laughed softly. "That's pretty much par for the course. To people on the outside, tai chi looks like movement in slow motion; it's often described as 'moving meditation.' However, slow movement is actually a method of creating muscle memory. In the event there's a threat, a tai chi practitioner should be able to react rapidly and instinctively. Admittedly, some forms of tai chi are taught for the health benefits only, but other forms include the use of swords, fans, and canes. It's said there are about five thousand different types of tai chi—and just as many arguments about which type is the 'true' tai chi." She ended on a dry note.

"Which type of tai chi is taught at this studio? The 'true' tai chi?"

"Not even close." Mona snorted. "Cal and I focus on working with the chi—the energy or vital force found in all things throughout the universe."

"How does that help the student fight?"

"We say the best way to win a fight—the best way to protect yourself—is never to have to fight at all. So, our teaching, at least in the advanced class, is about how to use chi to sense paths, and then about choosing the path that would best benefit you and those around you. Tai chi is not just a martial art—at least, that's what you learn if you study it long enough. Tai chi can also be about physical healing, or about maintaining your equilibrium in situations and in a world that seem to make no sense. There are some who translate 'tai chi' as the relationship between yin and yang. The dance of opposites—male and female, heaven and earth, light and darkness, activity and passiveness."

"Not good and evil?"

A philosophical discussion was not what Vicki had expected when this conversation began. She watched as a frog jumped from the side of the pond into the water. It was dusk, and the lotus blossoms were starting to close. Their delicate floral smell was getting weaker, now being replaced by another aroma, something very sweet.

"The universe doesn't recognize good and evil."

"This is what you're teaching in a martial arts class?"

"Advanced class."

But by now, Vicki had identified the sweet scent, which was growing stronger. "Moonflowers?" They bloomed at night.

At this, Mona laughed out loud. "A few years ago, our son James went through a phase when he was obsessed with flowers. He was very insistent we plant them—he chose all the flowers for the studio grounds, being very particular about the variety and color of everything. And then? Then, just as quickly, he lost interest. He's in the advanced class with the Martinsson kids; he and Brad are best friends."

Mona returned to the studio to complete some tasks, and it was full dark when Vicki followed her back in ten minutes later. The reception area was empty, but the door to the classroom was open a couple of inches. She went over to peer in, her curiosity piqued by the conversation with Mona.

To her surprise, there was no one in the room—just a few windows and some mats on the floor. But it wasn't empty. It was full of a light that was... not light. A hazy, ephemeral glow that appeared to have no source. And it seemed to pulse. But that wasn't the right word. Maybe it rippled? She was mesmerized. It pulled at her, and she wanted to be part of it.

But she was wrong about there being no students in the room. At the very back of the classroom, she saw an older student—a very fit, military-looking black man—sitting on a mat in meditation with his eyes closed. She must have made some sort of noise because his eyes snapped open. When he noticed the glow—and realized he was all alone—a look of despair came over his face, and he slammed his eyes shut.

Vicki went back to the chairs in the reception area. She was puzzled. What was all that about? And where were the rest of the students?

A few minutes later, she heard voices from the classroom and looked up in shock as young people poured out of the previously-empty room. She just nodded sharply when Jess and Brad said they'd be outside with their friends; she couldn't speak. It didn't make sense. There was only one door. There was nowhere for the students to have come from, gone to, or hidden.

She could still hear a couple of low voices coming from the classroom. Curious, she walked over and looked through the now fully open doorway. The male student she'd noticed earlier was speaking urgently, his voice rising as an older man—probably Calvin—placed a hand on his shoulder, trying to soothe him. But the student's eyes welled with angry, desperate tears, and he suddenly began shouting, his words spilling out in a rush of emotion and confusion.

"Excuse me." Mona pushed past her and firmly closed the door behind her. Vicki stared at the door as the yelling devolved into loud, wracking sobs, with the soothing voices of both Mona and Calvin as they tried to calm him. The sobbing didn't sound like it would ever let up.

She backed away.

* * *

Vicki waited until they were back at the house, getting snacks in the kitchen, before saying anything. The house was empty, the staff having left for the day.

"Would you care to explain?" she snapped.

"What?" The siblings looked at her blankly.

"You weren't there—the classroom was empty except for a misty light! And then everyone came out of the room no one had been in before! Except for that man who was crying and yelling."

She admitted it—her voice was raised. Maybe she was even yelling. That's how she reacted when she was scared.

Jessica and Brad exchanged a look.

"We didn't think you would notice," said Jess, "at least not yet."

"Not notice?" Vicki was more than scared; she was also angry. The stress was building up in the back of her skull, her head pounding. While feeling angry and scared might be better than the emptiness she had been living with since Beth's funeral, now she just wanted answers.

Instead of replying, Brad took out his phone and dialed a number.

"You were right," he said. "She's already asking questions." He listened for a moment, then said, "Okay," and ended the call.

Looking up at Jessica and Vicki, he said, "We'll meet to talk about it after our next tai chi class in two days."

"I want answers now!"

"It's not our story to tell, and we don't know all of it."

Jessica looked at her brother. "I guess this is the beginning."

The siblings went off to their bedrooms—Brad strangely calm, Jess looking stricken.

Chapter Three

The next morning, Vicki rose early, begged a cup of coffee from one of the kitchen staff, and then wandered the grounds while sipping her caffeine. She spotted at least two gardeners—one thinning out a bed of flowers, the other raking a gravel pathway. Quite a few people were employed in just the maintenance and upkeep of the property: kitchen staff, maintenance, cleaners, grounds people. After a decade as a diplomat, she was accustomed to the idea of household help, but this seemed like... a lot. How rich was Kurt Martinsson? And what exactly did her former professor do to justify the salary he would need to afford all this?

She turned a corner around the back of the mansion and came upon a patio with several different seating areas. She sank into a chair and gazed out over the back of the property. There was a tennis court and a pool/pool house combination, lots of trees, more flowers, and an entire hedge of rhododendrons. If she cared to investigate, she was sure she'd find another patio with yet another seating area tucked away in the greenery, but instead, she studied her empty coffee mug.

"Here you are. Lucia said you'd probably need a refill by now." Brad set a carafe on the table next to her, taking a seat as he cradled his own coffee cup.

"Lucia?" Vicki refilled her mug. It was as if the previous night's conversation had never happened.

"One of the ladies who works in the kitchen."

Unexpectedly, Vicki felt lighter finding out that he knew the name of at least one of his father's employees. She had found truth in the old saying that someone who is nice to you but rude to the waiter is probably not a nice person.

"Are you supposed to be drinking coffee at your age?"

"Mom loved coffee." Brad took an appreciative sniff of the beverage. "And Jess drank it too. I was only seven or eight when I started taking sips from their cups. It was so bitter! But I didn't want to be left out. Now, I love it."

Vicki was wondering if she could ask him about his mother, but the opportunity passed when an older woman wearing an apron arrived with a tray of breads, jams, and fresh fruit. This was Lucia. After Brad made the introductions—something his father had failed to do the previous day—they sat with their coffee and ate breakfast.

"Where's Jess?"

"You won't want to see her yet. She's not a morning person, so she's grumpy until she has a chance to wake up. And that takes at least a couple of hours."

"While you're sweetness and light?"

"Why, yes, yes I am." Brad laughingly waggled his eyebrows. "By the way, I wanted to let you know that you can hang out with us and our friends tonight if you feel like it."

"What's happening tonight? Am I driving?"

"Not driving; it's happening here." Brad's plate was empty, so he reached over, grabbed another roll, and began to spread jam on it. "Just a few kids; there will probably be less than a dozen of us total. Since Jess and I have private tutors, Dad periodically arranges for these get-togethers to make sure we know how to socialize."

"Your dad is arranging playdates for you? At your age? At Jessica's age?"

Surprisingly, Brad didn't take offense. "Playdates with the *right* people," he corrected her in a wry tone of voice. "Except for my friend James, they're all sons and daughters of the people Dad works with—sons and daughters of the Partnership."

"That's even worse," Vicki muttered, immediately regretting the comment.

"It is, but we're used to it. Every month or so, we host a gathering—people come over, we watch movies, eat snacks, and make sure everyone sees we're normal and part of the group. It's all about networking. Jess and I could do it in our sleep."

"Am I to assume you're not normal?"

"Being normal is overrated." Brad grinned at her.

And *that* ended up being the understatement of the year.

* * *

The guests—about a dozen young people—had all arrived by early evening and were snacking on the food Lucia and her assistant Mateo had prepared for them. Although he had given Vicki the green light to hang out with them, Brad noticed she was limiting herself to stopping by about every half hour or so to see if any platters needed refilling. He appreciated that she didn't want to hover. Since the household staff had left for the day, refilling the platters gave her an excuse to check in on things without making it obvious.

"Vicki, come over here a moment." Brad waved one hand at her, the other holding a pool cue. Beside him stood a shorter teenager with heavy glasses and a short afro. It was time to introduce her to another member of the team.

"This is James Cooper—James *Fenimore* Cooper," he said with emphasis.

"You're Calvin and Mona's son? Which one is the frontier wilderness fan?"

"My dad." James glanced down at his feet, then met her eyes shyly. "But it's not like anyone our age gets it."

"Yes, only us old people," she laughed.

"Hey, I'm not old!" protested Brad, pretending to be affronted.

He and James returned to the pool table—they were in the middle of a four-player game, and their opponents had just completed their turn—but he kept an eye on Vicki. She was looking around with curiosity: Jessica sat with four or five guests on a leather sectional in front of an oversized home theater screen, watching a *Star Wars* marathon. Onscreen, a high-speed spaceship chase sent the heroes tumbling under heavy gravity. The young people burst into amused hoots: "Fake! Primitive!" Another three girls—one raven-haired with tan skin, the other two blondes—were talking quietly by the food board.

He wondered what kind of impression this group was making on Vicki. Did she notice how healthy they all were? Except for James, no one wore glasses. No one had acne or other facial blemishes. All of their bodies were toned. Brad had the feeling Vicki didn't miss much.

He turned back to the game—it was his turn to shoot. It was another 40 minutes before he noticed Vicki again, refilling the cookie tray on the food board—and then suddenly freezing as the conversation between the three girls became audible.

"The tests showed the tumor was malignant, so my dad is having it treated next week," the girl with black hair—Aija—was saying.

"Will he have an operation? Or will he have it dissolved?"

"He'll have it dissolved, of course. Surgery on the brain is risky, even with the world's best doctors. And that's even before the chemo. Using frequencies to dissolve tumors or cancer is only an outpatient procedure. Why would he do anything else? Why are you even asking the question?"

Aija sounded annoyed. She took a compact out of her purse to examine her eye makeup and perfect skin. She wore a small gold ring in one nostril.

"Well, you know, some people feel it's not fair to take advantage of treatments if other people can't. Remember Jessica's mom?" The three young women turned as one to stare at the group watching the movie.

It was as if Jessica could feel their gaze because she turned to look at them, then spotted Vicki, and her eyes widened. This caused the girls to finally notice her, and one elbowed the other two.

"What?" grumbled Aija. "She has a security clearance—we can talk about things involving the Partnership in front of her."

Brad thrust his pool cue at James and took a step toward the girls. But he was too late—Vicki had fled the room.

* * *

Vicki didn't hear any more because she was stumbling blindly back to the kitchen. She couldn't breathe. She couldn't think. She realized *this* was the reason Jess became so upset with her father's company. Revolutionary, lifesaving treatments they said couldn't be shared with the public. Cures only they had access to, while other people—while Beth—endured months of painful treatment and died anyway. Beth had *died* while these people were being cured in a simple outpatient session.

She sat down at the counter and started crying—ugly crying. The pain was so raw, so sharp. Anger and grief blew through her, scraping away what little sense of balance she had managed to regain since Beth's death. She didn't know how long she cried, but her sobs had died down when a hand awkwardly patted her shoulder, bringing her back to the present.

Both Brad and Jessica were there, Brad looking solemn and Jessica, her eyes bright, threatening tears. "Everyone's gone home; it's just us now."

Vicki didn't say anything—just wiped her eyes and blew her nose.

Brad said, "I guess you're pretty mad right now; we don't blame you."

She took a breath. The anger had burned off, leaving her a little shaky. "I think you have no idea how I feel," she said stiffly.

"Our mom," said Jessica quietly as she moved to sit down on the opposite side of the counter, "was funny and super smart, the best person I ever knew. She always saw the good in people and loved us more than anything. She was my hero, and I wanted to be just like her. But I failed."

Her expression was bleak.

"Mom came down with some sort of kidney disease," Brad picked up the story. "It was something that could be easily cured with the medical technology the Partnership has, but she wouldn't accept the treatment; she said it was unethical to accept something they wouldn't allow the rest of the world to have. It took her three years to die."

"Dad divorced Mom right at the beginning of her illness," said Jessica. "He thought it would be bad for his career if his own wife refused treatment from the Partnership. So, it was just Mom, Brad, and me."

Divorcing your wife and leaving your children with their dying mother? That was cold. More than cold. Vicki suddenly didn't like Kurt Martinsson very much. "So, you spent three years watching her die," she said flatly.

"We begged her to go and get treated at the Partnership's clinic—she could have been cured in a single visit—but she wouldn't," Brad said. "Even though she loved us, she couldn't change who she was. She was a person who believed that everyone in the world deserved a chance; that everyone in the world deserves to succeed; that it wasn't just for a chosen few." Brad's eyes were distant now, as if remembering a word-for-word conversation from long past.

"That's where I failed to live up to my mother's example." Jessica's voice had a slight hitch in it. "I was in a car accident a couple of years ago."

"Your father mentioned you had been in an accident—a fender bender or something like that. He said you had developed some emotional issues after that."

"It wasn't just a fender bender!" Brad burst out indignantly, his eyes flashing. "A drunk driver broadsided Jess. The ambulance took her to a regular hospital, and she nearly died; they were going to amputate her arm."

Jessica's eyes were haunted. "I'm not as strong as Mom was. It was either to be treated at the regular hospital and lose my arm or go to the Partnership's medical facilities and be perfectly cured. I was weak, so I chose to keep my arm."

She was wearing a sleeveless top. Vicki's eyes went involuntarily to her arms, but there were no signs of past trauma—no scars on her perfect skin. Jessica wrapped her arms around her body in a self-soothing gesture and started rocking ever so slightly. Brad put his arm around her shoulders protectively.

"And that's why they say you're erratic and overly sensitive," Vicki guessed.

"I feel so guilty!" Jessica's voice cracked. "I should have been stronger; I should have been a better person."

"It wouldn't have mattered." Vicki's words were blunt. The siblings both looked at her in surprise. "You can't be sad enough to make another person happy. You can't be sick enough to make someone else healthy. Never fall into that mindset."

"So, you don't think it was wrong to go to the Partnership to get my arm healed?"

"No, I don't. Those who are in the wrong are the people keeping these treatments from the rest of the world."

In the past, Vicki had assumed—cynically—that most information was classified to avoid embarrassing the powerful. She was wrong. It was worse. Things were also classified to keep power and control in the hands of those who already had it.

She yawned as a wave of weariness swept over her. She needed to get to bed before she fell asleep in her chair. Jessica also seemed to be teetering on the brink of exhaustion. It was Brad who got up and herded them off to their respective bedrooms.

Chapter Four

V icki didn't wait in the reception area when she drove Brad and Jess to their tai chi class the next evening. Instead, she made her way to the back garden and the koi pond. It was beautiful in the sunset, with the proximate sounds of frogs and birds, and the more distant hum of traffic. She didn't look up when she heard people coming out.

Mona sat on the bench beside her and broke the silence. "You haven't met my husband, Calvin."

Seated on the bench across from them, a man with mocha-colored skin nodded. He wore a dark gi and sported a stylized yin-yang tattoo on one forearm. Mona inclined her head to indicate the black man sitting beside him. "And this is his older brother, Larry."

Wait, older brother? This was the student who had become so upset in the last class. Calvin appeared to be in his mid-forties, while Larry looked a decade younger. Noticing her surprise, Larry made a wry expression. Jessica, Brad, and James were standing behind the bench where the men were seated; Mona didn't waste any time acknowledging them.

"Why am I here? Why are we having this conversation?" Vicki's voice was tight. She felt as if a part of her had dried up and crumbled away.

"Because we need you—badly. And we need you now."

Okay, she was not expecting that. But she also wasn't in a conciliatory mood. She didn't say anything.

Calvin started talking.

"I idolized Larry growing up. He was eight years older than me, and everything he did seemed cool. After high school, he joined the military, and I planned to do the same. But when I was seventeen, Larry came home for a visit and told me—no, he *ordered* me—not to do it. I didn't understand, but something in his eyes gave me reason to do what he said. So, instead of joining the military, I went to college and double-majored in philosophy and physical education. I got a job teaching tai chi, then five years later, married my best student, and we started this studio."

Calvin looked over at Mona and smiled.

"I didn't want Cal to join the military," Larry said. "By every measure, I was successful. I was promoted, given more responsibility, and worked on many classified projects—codeword and above Top Secret. But I had to make a lot of compromises to do my job."

"Compromises like looking the other way when medical breakthroughs were kept secret for the use of the chosen few?" Vicki muttered, thinking of the girl on game night who had talked about her father getting outpatient treatment for his tumor.

Larry carried on as if he hadn't heard her.

"I retired from the military in my early forties, then began working for the Partnership."

Wait, this involved the company Kurt Martinsson worked for? Vicki glanced over at Jess and Brad, but their faces were expressionless. She turned her attention back to Larry.

"Since the Partnership only handled government contracts—mostly military—they already knew me, and I knew them. But once I became a direct employee, I learned they were involved in far more than the contracts required. And those contracts weren't limited to medical advances. They covered new materials, new energy sources, and new forms of travel. The Partnership gave the government only what it was required to—nothing more. But they used what they learned from those projects to make even greater discoveries, without telling the government a thing."

James noticed Vicki was losing interest in the story and got things back on track. "Uncle Larry was in a really bad accident; he died."

Vicki looked over at Larry, who was beginning to look strained.

"Not quite dead, but not alive either. The Partnership essentially built me."

"Like *The Six Million Dollar Man*?" That had been her grandmother's favorite television program when it came out in the seventies.

"In that television show, the main character has several bionic implants. But that's all mechanical—wires, chips, and man-made materials. I'm a one-hundred-percent biologic construct; I won't set off alarms going through airport security. This technology is the pride and joy of the Partnership's HE—Human Enhancement—Division." Larry crooked a smile at her. "And then after they built this body, they transferred my consciousness into it. I am Lawrence Cooper, but not a cell of my body is truly a human cell."

"You are my brother," Calvin said hotly.

"I am your brother in a single moment of time; you know it. I don't age; I can't change. Yes, more information can be downloaded into me. Yes, I retain my old memories as well as add new ones. But I can never evolve to be more than I am right now."

His voice broke a little at his last comment.

"Wait, stop." Vicki was confused. "I can understand an artificial body, but how can you transfer consciousness?"

"This was something the Partnership developed, but not on its own," Larry said. "We had a contract to reverse-engineer some technology the government had gotten ahold of."

"Like from a spy plane, or a satellite, or something like that?"

"More like from a flying saucer."

Vicki stared at him, completely shocked. And a little incredulous. Was he making fun of her?

"Don't believe me if you don't want to. For most people, it feels safer—more comfortable—to remain ignorant. But that's what it was. And it was so exhilarating to work on those projects."

For a brief minute, Larry's voice sounded wistful, as if he were remembering something very precious. "Like I said, the Partnership fulfilled every requirement of their contracts. But they didn't let the government know that those projects opened up doors to other advanced scientific knowledge. That technology, the Partnership kept for itself."

"Medical technology to cure cancer, to reattach severed arms, to take someone out of their dying body and put them in a new one," Vicki murmured. "Why is this considered so secret? Why can't it be made available to the world?"

"Because soldiers get it. A military force that is biologically altered to be stronger, faster, and smarter would be invincible. But only as long as everyone else—whether other military forces or the general public—isn't getting the same upgrade. It's considered a matter of national security."

Larry paused for a moment, then continued.

"But like I said, the Partnership didn't hand over everything it developed to the government. It built its own security force,—more lethal, more powerful, and more dangerous than the government's military. But what really mattered to the people running it was power. They wanted to be part of the elite—to be the ones in control. For them, it was all about becoming superhuman."

Vicki was feeling sick to her stomach. "This is happening because they like to feel they're superior to other people?"

"But they're not superior," James said quietly from his position behind the bench, once again getting the conversation back on track. "There are downsides."

Mona entered the conversation with a question for Vicki. "Do you know anything about transhumanism?"

"Mmm, no?"

"It's a philosophy that promotes using technology to enhance human physical and mental development. The goal is to extend lifespan and boost intelligence. In many ways, it can be a good thing, but if you go to the extreme, you get Larry."

Vicki looked over at Larry and Calvin sitting side by side. "What's wrong with looking a couple of decades younger than you are? What's wrong with having your body of twenty years ago?"

"Because we humans are more than our physical bodies. And if your body is replaced, you are only as good as the hardware and software that are installed in you. A person can't be reduced to just ones and zeros and then downloaded onto a computer chip. There's no limit to human potential." Mona sounded fierce.

"James told us you saw what we were doing in the advanced class," said Calvin. "That everyone had disappeared except for Larry. I was actually surprised you were able to see the light."

Now, they were getting back to her original concern, and Vicki clutched at it, ignoring the many unbelievable things she had just been told. "What was that light? Where did all the students go?"

"Our planet is going through a vibrational shift," said James, stepping forward. He looked self-assured, no longer the shy teenager who played pool with Brad.

"Like some sort of metaphysical woo-woo stuff?"

"Exactly. It has to do with where the Earth is in relation to nearby stars, nebulae, and solar systems. It's a big cycle. In ancient times, Hindu mystics referred to this pattern as the Yuga Cycle; you can look it up."

Vicki didn't want to look it up; she wanted answers. She glared at him.

"Or not," he hurriedly continued. "The point is people have a lot of DNA, and between 75 and 95 percent of it is considered junk DNA—just sitting there and not doing anything. But science is figuring out that DNA and genes can be switched on and off. What causes this is a mystery, at least to scientists. But we know the answer—it's the vibration."

"And that matters, why?" Vicki was still glowering, arms crossed over her chest.

It was Larry who replied. "When they made this form," he said, motioning toward his body, "they couldn't build build it without first understanding how it worked or what each part did. The Partnership does really well with bones, muscle, cells, fluids, organs, and even the brain, but it was impossible to even guess at the purpose of junk DNA. Well, we're figuring that out now in tai chi class."

At this point, his voice broke down.

"It's the vibrational change," said James. "It's waking up our junk DNA, at least some of it. It will take years, but sooner or later, everyone will be able to access the abilities that come with that. Abilities we now consider supernatural—stuff like telepathy and teleportation."

"And disappearing from and reappearing in a closed room?" Vicki asked, a little belligerently. She was still feeling unsympathetic.

"During our meditation, we were vibrating faster and..." James paused, then started again. "The difference between dimensions is the difference between vibrational rates. If you vibrate at a higher rate, you're no longer visible in this dimension, but you are visible in the next dimension. You only see stuff that's vibrating at the same speed you are. So, we didn't actually go anywhere; we were just existing in a different dimension for a little while."

"I have the physical strength of five men," said Larry. "The database of all human knowledge has been downloaded into my brain. I have reflexes that are too fast to be measured. But I will be left behind when everyone else goes through the shift." His voice was bleak.

"I will not leave you behind," Calvin said forcefully. It was clear they had had this conversation before.

"But all that might not matter," said Mona urgently. She turned to face Vicki. "That's why you're here."

"What?" Vicki sputtered. "What does any of this have to do with me? I'm just here for the summer to ride herd on Brad and Jessica."

The siblings remained silent, watching the conversation unfold.

"You're the catalyst," said James, smiling broadly. "We had to wait for you to complete our group."

Vicki felt the hairs on the back of her neck rise. She was getting some serious cult vibes. "I think we need to go."

She motioned to Brad and Jess and stood up.

Mona reached up, grabbed her arm, and yanked. Hard. Vicki found herself abruptly reseated on the bench. Mona spoke at a furious pace. "An hour, give us an hour to hear us out. We've waited so long, and this is so important—I don't know what we'll do if you don't help us."

"Mom!" James sounded exasperated. That little bit of normalcy, more than anything, settled Vicki's nerves. Kids being embarrassed by their moms were the same everywhere.

"Fine, I can stay an hour," she said. Mona slightly relaxed her grip, but it still hurt; she'd probably have a bruise. It made her wonder whether the Chinese grannies doing tai chi in parks also had iron-strong grips.

"Sorry about that," said James, "but Mom is really worried. I sometimes think I shouldn't have told her anything—or at least not so soon."

"*You* told her? So you're the one who started whatever it is that's going on?" Vicki asked. "How did that happen? And what is this all about? No one has explained anything yet."

Now, Brad and Jess moved forward to stand with James.

"It was the three of us who started it," said Jess, "but James is the channel, so he has been the primary focus."

Seeing Vicki's raised eyebrow, she went on, "A channel is like a pipeline for information or energy from other sources—nonphysical beings, beings in other vibrational dimensions, or even the universal field. James started channeling a few years back, so we've been making plans since then."

"And who or what is James channeling?" Vicki asked. She could play this game for an hour. A branch snapped behind her.

"Meet Melly," said Jessica.

Chapter Five

V icki wasn't screaming because her throat had seized up with terror. She wasn't fleeing because Mona was once again gripping her arm. And let's face it—shock was locking her muscles.

In front of her stood a gigantic—seven- or eight-foot-tall—insect. It had the head and forelegs of a praying mantis and the body of a beetle standing upright. A long cape, four short hind legs, and bulging eyes on either side of its triangular head. The eyes were... iridescent, their polychromatic colors whirling around in no fixed pattern. She whimpered.

Jess stepped toward the mantis with a big smile on her face. "Welcome, Melly. We're glad you were able to come."

She steepled her hands and placed them briefly over the first bend of the creature's forelegs. A greeting, perhaps? James and Brad did the same. The older adults, calm but more wary, remained seated on the benches.

"This is Melly!" James was excited as he turned to make the introduction, then looked at Vicki curiously, noting her lack of response.

"I think she's in shock." Jessica stepped forward and took Vicki's wrist in her hand, then felt her forehead. "Weak pulse, clammy skin, shallow breathing. She's in shock."

"We do not have time for this," muttered Mona curtly.

More conversation burbled up around Vicki, then faded from perception. Her brain was... stuttering. There was an alien standing in front of her! A freaking extraterrestrial! And it was a giant bug! She didn't know how long her mind raced along this existential hamster wheel when a cup of coffee was thrust under her nose.

She looked up as Larry pressed the mug into her hands. "It's a bit of a shock at first," he said with a crooked smile. "Especially for us older ones. Unfortunately, you won't have as much time to assimilate it as we did."

She hunched over, clutching the coffee in both hands. Somehow, Jess was now seated beside her; Mona was having a serious conversation with Calvin on the other bench. "It is? I won't?" Vicki carefully stared at her cup rather than the big, scary monster still standing with James and Brad, and took a sip of the coffee. It had been doctored with generous amounts of cream and sugar, and a little bit of sweet sanity seeped back into her brain. "Why does it matter what I do or don't do?"

"Because you are the fourth, and the pattern is now whole. At this time, we can move forward, if that's what you choose to do."

It was the alien speaking. The sound of her voice (yes, the alien definitely had the feeling of a *she*) was... multilayered. Vicki could hear her words, a bit stilted but clear. But underneath was the feeling of gongs, Tibetan singing bowls, and bells—dignified, solemn, joyful, and ancient. She still felt cautious, but the terror began to lessen.

"If I'm the fourth, what—or who—are the other three?" She took another sip of coffee. She still had zero desire to look at that creature. "And what is the matter or question we're supposed to move forward on?"

"We are the Four," said Jessica from beside her. She still had her fingers on Vicki's wrist—monitoring her recovery from shock, apparently. "You, me, Brad, and James."

"And the adults?" Strictly speaking, Jess was already an adult, but she didn't seem to mind being lumped in as a teenager.

"Their role during the last few years was to keep us safe and help us understand the bigger issues before moving forward," Jessica replied. "But now you're here, so we can move on."

"Me? I'm supposed to replace them in keeping you safe?" This didn't make sense. She was a diplomat, not a soldier. Also, they were being annoyingly vague about what they needed protection from.

Although seeing a giant alien standing in front of her was giving her uncomfortable ideas.

"Not to worry. We are not as weak and fragile as we once were," piped up James. The three young people snickered.

"And your dad? What role does Professor Martinsson have in this?"

Shuttered eyes. Masks in place. "No role whatsoever," Brad said flatly.

"But what are we supposed to be doing?" Vicki asked, darting a quick glance at Melly. The creature's eyes were mesmerizing; she looked away.

It was Melly who answered. It took some effort to focus on the meaning of her words through the overlay of bells echoing in Vicki's head, but finally she was able to hear.

Hear? Looking back, she wasn't sure *hear* was the right word to describe a conversation with this alien being, but it was the only vocabulary she had at the time.

"It will come as no surprise to those who are paying attention, but humanity has had contact with extraterrestrials for a very long time. Your governments—those in power—deny it. Instead, they secretly communicate with alien groups and hide this from the general population. To admit to the existence of extraterrestrials would also mean acknowledging that they—your governments—are not all-powerful, which would weaken their control over the population. But this was a choice they were free to make, and we respected it."

"Until now," Vicki hazarded. It was getting dark, and the scent of the moonflowers was growing stronger. She found it easier to face the alien when she was half-hidden in shadows.

"Until now," agreed Melly. Then, the overlay of her voice took on deeper, more somber tones, like the low, reverberating music of a Bach organ concerto. "You must understand that not all beings in the universe are committed to the well-being of humans. Yes, the vast majority of us have curbed our most violent and destructive tendencies—tendencies that are still given free rein on your planet. But many alien groups are also focused on their own self-interest. We are only human."

"You're only human? Literally or figuratively?" Conspiracy theories involving extraterrestrial DNA manipulation and star-seeding raced through Vicki's thoughts.

She didn't know how she could tell, but Melly was clearly amused. "I will not deny that some degree of the literal meaning of the phrase indeed took place, but now I am speaking figuratively. People are people, whether we look like humans, insects, plants or orbs of light. And people all have their own agendas."

"What's your agenda?"

Beside her, Vicki heard Jess let out a small gasp as if she shouldn't question Melly's motives. Both Brad and James also whipped their heads around to look at her with disapproving expressions. What? Was she not supposed to scrutinize the motives of a freaking extraterrestrial?

At this, Melly laughed quietly. At least, Vicki *thought* she was laughing. The feeling of small bells.

"And this is why you are needed as the fourth. You will question, you will analyze, you will evaluate. Only if you come to a positive conclusion will you be supportive. But it is at that point you will become a powerful ally—an ally who is familiar with navigating the government sphere, which is something that is urgently needed. The young ones just accepted me without question."

Beside her, Vicki felt Jessica relax. The expressions on the boys' faces also eased.

"So, what's your agenda?" Vicki repeated.

"For the people of Earth to know who they truly are."

"What does that even mean? Are you talking about history? About DNA? About humanity's place in the universe? About who we are in relation to non-Earth species? And then—what happens when we find out?"

Again, the impression of small bells as Melly laughed. "This is why you are so critical to the present efforts. When this day started, you believed humanity to be alone in the universe. But already, you are probing and strategizing."

"No one has actually clarified the issue we're supposedly here to discuss," Vicki said pointedly to no one in particular, taking another sip of her coffee.

"We—those of us here—are latecomers to a race in which humanity will go down one of two paths," said Larry, standing close to the bench where Mona and Calvin were seated. It was now full dark, and Vicki couldn't make out his facial expression.

"We can choose technology and live in a future that corporate organizations like the Partnership will design for us. Our lives would be comfortable, predictable, and safe. No one would be poor; people would have all their needs provided for. Everyone would enjoy perfect health and genius-level IQs. But anyone who didn't conform to what's acceptable would be turned off."

"Turned off?" Vicki lifted her head to stare at him.

"Eliminated. Killed," he clarified. "If the Partnership thought I was behaving unacceptably—if I was refusing to follow instructions, or if they decided I was working against what they considered the company's best interests—they could flip a switch, and I would no longer exist. Do you think they would create something like me without the ability to exercise ultimate control? I am a commercial product to them, not a person. The Partnership fully expects—and will demand—to make a profit off my continued existence."

Competing scenarios ran through Vicki's mind. This advanced technology could end illness and poverty—but taken a few steps further, it could lead to full corporate ownership of humanity. A new kind of slavery, where a person's worth depended on how much profit they could generate. And what happened when someone stopped being profitable? If history had proven anything, it was that safeguards were never as strong or foolproof as their creators claimed.

"More importantly," said Mona forcefully, "going down the path of transhumanism means we give up what makes us human. The Partnership thinks it can enhance people—that it can make us stronger, smarter, more beautiful, or whatever. And the Partnership will both control access to that advanced technology and take it away as it sees fit. None of us here are technophobes, but abuse of power wouldn't be a possibility—it would be a foregone conclusion."

"It would cripple humanity," said Larry. "Remember the tai chi class. While my classmates are learning to harness their internal abilities, I can't. It's forever out of my reach. I am alive because of the Partnership's technology—some might even call me superhuman—but I am also stuck in the here and now. The Partnership will ensure that all of humanity not only becomes stuck but stays stuck—that people will never advance. Their goal is to remain in control." His voice was harsh.

"And tell me again why there are aliens?" Vicki risked darting a glance over at Melly. James and Brad were engaged in quiet conversation beside her.

"Certain alien groups—your popular culture refers to them as the 'Tall Whites'—were responsible for the speed with which the Partnership developed the technology," said Melly.

Her eyes were whirling. Vicki didn't know how she knew this, since it was dark and she couldn't see them; she just *knew*.

She continued, "The momentum has been too great, and humanity's technological development has moved faster than it should have. This usually doesn't happen until a population reaches a certain stage of development and moves beyond its violent behavior. We discourage major technological advancements unless there's also progress in spiritual and metaphysical growth. The Council ruled that, since the beings who accelerated humanity's technology are members of the Galactic Federation, we share responsibility—and are therefore obligated to inform humanity of the situation. The people of your planet can then make decisions about their future instead of walking in ignorance."

Then Melly straightened, and her words took on a serious gong overlay. "You can choose to continue down the path of relying solely on technology, or you can choose to develop your innate abilities. You can also choose a combination of the two. We will support whatever path you take. What is important is that the choice be your decision."

Wait, there's a freaking alien Council? And a Galactic Federation? Vicki's thoughts stumbled over those ideas for a bit before she refocused on her original question.

"And why am I here? Why are any of us here?" She glared at the young people. "I can't imagine we're the ideal group to resolve interplanetary disagreements."

"We are, actually," Jessica gently corrected her. "We're all connected to the Partnership, understand how it operates, and have reason to distrust the people who are in charge. James was the original channel—our communicator—as well as historian. He received a mental download of what's at stake and was able to guide us in making initial preparations. Brad is a genius computer guy, both hardware and software." At this, Brad grinned and waggled his eyebrows.

"And I'm the media person—the human face of Disclosure," finished Jessica.

Vicki thought back to how Jess had insisted on studying media despite her father's objections. Now she knew the reason why.

"And me? Why am I here?"

"You're the strategy and policy expert—the government person," said Mona. She sounded more relaxed now that she'd had her say. "Calvin, Larry, and I are support staff when it's needed."

Larry interrupted, "I'm also the muscle and a well-placed inside source."

"And you're all crazy," Vicki said.

"But there's still an alien standing just a few feet away from you," said Jessica with a smirk.

It was hard to argue with that.

Chapter Six

The next morning was bright and sunny, and breakfast was served out on the back patio. Lucia arrived with a full coffee service, followed by Mateo, who pushed a cart loaded with eggs, bacon, pastries, and fruit. Once everything was set up and they'd left, Vicki and the young people started eating. After the stress of the night before, they were all starving—but the coffee came first.

Priorities.

"So, are there next steps?" Vicki asked.

"We"—James gestured at himself and the Martinsson siblings—"already know what we're doing and what we need to work on. So, our next big step is to bring you up to speed."

James had spent the night at the Martinssons' place. He had suggested it in order to give them a chance to "bond and establish trust." He could tell Vicki realized he was referring to her, but she had been too tired to argue.

"Wasn't I brought up to speed last night?" Vicki asked. "That information dump was fairly extensive."

Brad nearly spit out his coffee, laughing. "There's a big difference between being informed and being brought up to speed. Last night, you were just informed. Now it's time to catch you up—our version of up to speed. The first step is tai chi class."

"That's going to be a problem, then," Vicki said. "I've never practiced any martial art, much less tai chi. I barely know what it is. I'll be placed in the beginners' class, and it will take months or years for me to get up to your level."

"Not a problem. Dad's giving us private lessons—accelerated ones," James said. "We're skipping the martial arts part of tai chi and just focus on moving energy and working with the chi. Jess, Brad, and I already know all this, but it's easier to learn in a group, so we'll do it with you. Plus, it'll help with connecting to Melly."

"We're going to be working a lot with Melly?"

James almost laughed as Vicki glanced around nervously, as if fearing the alien might pop out of the hedges. But while he loved working one-on-one with Melly, he knew others might not be as comfortable with it. A case in point was the adults—despite having interacted with Melly for nearly two years, neither his parents nor Larry had ever come forward to formally greet her when she appeared.

"Yeah, a lot," James said. "But most of the time, it won't be face-to-face. It'll be more like how I channel—except instead of just getting info, you'll actually have full conversations with her in your head."

But something was bothering Vicki. "What about Larry?"

The three young people looked at her blankly.

"Last night, Larry said the Partnership has the ability to flip a switch and turn him off if they believe he's doing something against their interests. Wouldn't working to expose what the Partnership is doing qualify? What's to stop them from killing him?"

"Well, they can't do it from a distance anymore." Jessica gave a quiet smile.

"We told you Brad's a genius with computers," James said. "Last spring break, he spent a couple of weeks job shadowing at the Partnership. One of the first things he did was modify Larry's software so no one could shut him down remotely. He didn't disable the program completely—someone in the Partnership's Human

Enhancement Division would have noticed—but now they'd have to get really, *really* close to take him out."

"And since Larry is superhuman, that might be difficult to do," said Brad.

"Spy cameras aren't just something in the movies—they're a thing in the real world," Vicki persisted. "Can they monitor his electronics to see what he looks at or listen to what he hears?"

"Not in the current version of his body," said James. "Larry was the prototype—a very last minute emergency prototype since he was unexpectedly nearly dead. Their original plan had been to carefully build a body and transfer someone into it when it was ready. It was going to be a several-year process."

"Like in *Avatar*?"

"Exactly like in *Avatar*. But then Larry had his accident, and the Partnership decided it was—quote—'too good an opportunity' to pass up." His voice carried a bitterness that sounded older than his years, but he had his reasons. "So yeah, they went into overdrive trying to keep Larry alive long enough to finish his biologic construct. They didn't have time to think about spyware. But now? Software and hardware upgrades are probably out there—and yeah, they'd include audio and cameras."

"But Larry hasn't had an upgrade?"

James scoffed. "Heck no. The HE Division keeps urging Larry to get one, but he just puts them off by saying he has a 'bad feeling' about an upgrade. You'd be surprised at how respectful military people are of superstitions and bad feelings—a lot of times, paying attention to a bad feeling in your gut is what kept you alive in the field."

That visibly cheered Vicki up. But then she shifted gears.

"So, we're the 'Four'?" Her tone capitalized the informal title used the previous evening. "How did that happen? Based on what was said, I understand the different roles and what we each supposedly contribute. But honestly—why *us*, specifically?"

"We need to get a new name for ourselves," muttered Brad to no one in particular as he spread jam on his third croissant. "Calling us the Four is boring. What we're doing is exciting. But the *Fantastic Four* is already taken."

"What say we get back on track. Why us?" Vicki looked at James, who had proven himself willing to clarify several things the night before.

"I need to back up a little bit, but I'll give you the condensed version." James pushed his glasses back up on his nose. "Melly and the Council realized that the Partnership's reverse-engineering of ET technology—helped along by the Tall Whites—was going to put humanity's development out of whack."

"The Tall Whites—are they rogue extraterrestrials?" she asked. Life was getting strange; never in a million years would she have predicted that the words *rogue extraterrestrials* would come out of her mouth.

"Not exactly rogue, but their actions weren't approved by the Council, especially since this technology would be kept secret and used to control humanity without our knowledge. It would limit people before we knew what we were capable of—before we knew what we would be giving up by relying on high-tech rather than high-human."

"So, the Council isn't against what the Partnership is doing," Vicki mused, "just against the part where most of humanity is being kept in the dark."

James nodded. "The Council decided the Partnership and its tech had to be exposed, and at the same time, people needed to learn about the bigger picture—what's really possible when we raise our vibration. It's a free-will universe, so humanity has to be given the choice. But the Council didn't know how to do that without causing mass panic. I mean, aliens can be pretty scary."

"And why us?" Vicki asked again. "Any chance you're going to answer my question."

"It all started with our tai chi class and the vibrational shift the Earth is beginning to go through—I mentioned that yesterday. When our class hit a certain vibrational level, it activated parts of our so-called junk DNA, along with the abilities connected to it."

"Like disappearing and reappearing in a closed room." Vicki was still hung up on that part.

"That's just the start, the very lowest level," James said. "But when we hit that higher vibration in tai chi class, it overlapped with Melly's. It got her attention. She told the Council, and they decided to use us as a kind of access point. Or something like that."

"Why isn't your entire tai chi class here, then? They were able to disappear and reappear in the classroom just like you three. Wouldn't it be helpful to have more people involved?"

Jessica spoke up. "We—and Larry—are the only ones in the class connected to the Partnership. Too many people involved would mean a larger risk of us being uncovered and stopped before we're ready. Also, not everyone would want to do this; it's dangerous."

"But I'm not connected to the Partnership; I'm an outsider. Why am I being brought into this?"

"Because of your sister," Jessica said simply. "She didn't have to die—the tech to save her was already out there. You believe in fairness, in what's right and wrong. So, of course, you'd want to stop others from dying needlessly. And more importantly, you have a role in the government. That kind of connection—Melly couldn't simply download it into someone."

James could see that bringing up her sister hit Vicki hard—she was clearly unsettled. He wondered whether they were pushing her too fast. But then she rallied.

"What? Melly *downloaded* stuff into you?"

"More like she activated a specific part of the junk DNA," Brad said. "James was the youngest and the most open-minded, so it made sense for him to become the channel and handle the first contact with Melly. But I wasn't always a computer whiz. Melly triggered something in my DNA that lets me absorb or attract the tech knowledge I need. I don't really get how it works—but it does."

Vicki turned to Jess. "And you?"

"Melly didn't need to change much with Jess," Brad said before Jessica could respond. "Her role is media—she's going to be the public face. She already cares, looks good on camera, and people believe her." Then, more quietly, he added, "She's the kind of person you trust. I'd follow her without question—not because she's my sister, but because of who she is. And we're going to need someone like that when all of this goes public."

Vicki glanced at Jessica, who smiled faintly, avoiding Vicki's eyes as she took a sip of coffee. Kurt Martinsson had told Vicki his daughter was overly emotional and erratic; he had implied she was unable to cope with modern reality. But her brother had just made it clear—not only would she be the one in front of the cameras when the shit hit the fan, he also believed she'd handle it successfully.

"So, the final step is for Jess to do her media stuff and bring the story to the masses? What needs to happen before that point—and more importantly, what's the actual story we're telling?"

"Actually, the final step is for you to help implement whatever policies and procedures are needed within the *real* government," said James with emphasis. "Not the shadow government run by the Partnership. But for that to happen, everything needs to be public first." He nodded toward Jessica.

"And I'll be working with Larry on getting the evidence for the various technologies the Partnership has developed," said Brad. "We have his body and his experience as proof, but we need more evidence for other things like free energy and advanced materials."

Vicki asked her final question. "If Larry is so involved in what we're doing, why isn't he officially part of this group? Why aren't we 'the Five'?" She made air quotes with her fingers.

"Because no matter what we believe, the fact that Larry is a biologic construct would be used to argue he isn't human. And if he's not human, people would say he has his own agenda—or that someone's controlling him. That makes him a target. Just being there would become a distraction that could derail everything."

James knew his voice sounded bleak—there was even a trace of grief in it—but some things just couldn't be fixed.

CHAPTER SEVEN

"I hate tai chi," Vicki groaned.

It was the end of their special class, and she was stiff from sitting cross-legged on a mat for the past hour. The three young people had gone with Calvin to the kitchenette to find something to snack on—or "a second breakfast," as James called it, quoting a certain hobbit. It was early morning, and Vicki was sprawled out on the classroom floor, recovering—and not very gracefully, either. Larry was tidying up the other mats, getting the room ready for the first official class of the day. After all the talk about the Four, she'd been surprised when Larry joined them, but she hadn't complained. She liked Larry.

"This isn't tai chi," Larry said, his voice oddly soothing. "Right now, you're just learning to move the chi—the energy in your body."

"I have to feel the chi before I move it, I think." Vicki was frustrated. They had been at it every day for a week, and all she was feeling was sore. "I have no clue what's supposed to be happening."

Larry laughed. "It's like that for everyone at first."

"You're not a part of the Four." Vicki spoke slowly, cautiously, as she rolled up into a sitting position. She didn't want to distress him; she had witnessed his pain that first time she came to the studio. "You're also not able to do what the kids do—what they're trying to teach me to do—because you're a biologic construct, and don't have any junk DNA that can be activated. You say you'll never be able to do it. So why do you come to this class?"

"While I'm not part of the Four, I'm part of the team." Larry didn't seem disturbed. In fact, he seemed serene—oddly so. "My role will end before the Four goes public; my presence would be a liability. But in the meantime, we all need to develop a strong working relationship."

"I'm guessing that's your polite way of saying that *I* need to build a solid working relationship with everyone else," Vicki said. It made sense—she was the latecomer to the group.

"Not at all. The kids and I care about each other deeply, but they see me as an uncle, and I see them as my amazing nephew and his close friends. We all need to shift our perspective and start seeing each other as teammates. Honestly, it'll probably be easier for you than for us—we've got years of family dynamics to work through."

"Is that something you want to overcome? I don't see the downsides to having family." Her family—her parents and Beth both gone, and now she was alone in the world. Vicki blinked back tears before they could form.

"Did the kids mention this would be dangerous?"

"I think Jessica might have said something to that effect." Vicki hadn't been paying much attention.

"The Partnership will go to any length to keep their activities and tech secret. Think 'lethal force.' How could I let my young nephew or his friends do anything that might put them in the crosshairs? I can't—they're kids. But if I try to stop them from taking risks, it could cost humanity everything. So I have to start seeing them as they truly are—not as kids, but as skilled members of the team who all have a role. I need to let them do that. And I need to focus on doing mine."

From that perspective, Vicki could understand. They really did have it harder than she did.

"What exactly is your job? The time I first met you—that night I met Melly—you said your role was to be the muscle and get inside information. What does that mean?"

"The muscle part isn't self-evident?" Larry's voice was almost teasing as he flexed a bicep.

"Yes, yes, it is." Vicki reddened a little but persisted. "I guess I'm asking about the inside information part. What sort of information are you looking for? Like who is involved and pulling the strings?"

"The names of the people involved matter less than the technologies they created. And since those devices were developed using U.S. government funds, they were paid for by taxpayers—by everyday people. Society footed the bill for the Partnership, but it's being deliberately denied the benefits. That has to change."

Larry smiled. It wasn't a nice smile; Vicki was glad he was on their side.

He continued, "The federal government is also being kept in the dark, although not as much as the rest of us. The Partnership is legally obliged to report everything to the federal government, but it isn't. Failing to comply with the congressional oversight requirement is considered racketeering."

"So that's why we're exposing this?"

"No, that's just the part that will put these guys in jail." Larry smiled again, that same scary smile.

He continued: "The important part is telling the world what's available to them. We have medical technology that can remove cancerous tumors, replace missing limbs, and make blind people see. We have the science to quickly and easily clean up the environment. We can travel from one side of the planet to the other in just a few minutes with no emissions. We have nonpolluting energy sources that are virtually limitless and don't require tearing up the Earth to produce them."

"I don't understand why the Partnership is so hell-bent on keeping everything secret. Even if they had to hand over their ownership of some of the technology, they would still be rich beyond anyone's wildest dreams."

"Exactly." Larry gave her the approving look a teacher would give to a student who had just stumbled upon the correct answer. "So, the answer is that riches beyond their wildest dreams are not what motivates the Partnership. It's control—control of resources, control of the means of production, control of the future. Basically, it all comes down to the control of humanity."

"So... slavery?"

"Pretty much, although done in such a way that most people won't recognize it. The Partnership already has ownership control of most of the world's media—it decides what people should see, what events they can know about, and what they should think. This is why Melly and the Council are being so cautious about their involvement. If it feels threatened, the Partnership will claim that the appearance of extraterrestrials is an invasion. It would characterize aliens as a violent, warmongering horde. People would be relieved to have the Partnership—with all its high-tech capabilities—come out of hiding and offer to save us. They would insist the Partnership step up and take control."

Larry paused as he considered his next words. "The world would be pathetically grateful to do whatever the Partnership asked of them."

"So, we would essentially put on our own shackles." Vicki felt a little sick. "So how can what we're doing avoid this? I don't understand how exposing the Partnership can prevent this from happening."

"Because of all this," Larry said, gesturing around the tai chi studio. "Helping humanity grow and evolve will give people the tools to think for themselves instead of just reacting out of fear. They'll start to see nonhuman beings—extraterrestrials—with a new awareness. And they'll see their own potential differently, too. Of course, some will always go for the easiest, fastest option, but if we do this right, that'll only be a small group."

Vicki saw a big problem with that strategy. "It will take forever," she said flatly. "I'm getting special classes with people who have already reached a higher level of consciousness, and I'm still not getting it. We don't have the ability to offer the same training for even a few key decision-makers, much less for the rest of the world. At the same time, I'm getting the impression that time is running short."

She swallowed and forced out the bitter words: "We will fail."

"No, we won't." Larry crouched down to where she was sitting on the mat and lifted her face so she was looking into his eyes. "We won't fail." Sitting cross-legged beside her, he smiled crookedly. "I am proof of that."

She just looked at him.

"I am alive because of the Partnership. I owe them my life. I have worked with the technologies they've developed. I've seen all the amazing things they can do. I enjoy every single advantage that the Partnership has to offer. And while I can play an important role in any future the Partnership creates, I can never join the rest of humanity when it evolves. I would be a permanent outsider."

Vicki opened her mouth to make some sort of protest, although she didn't know what, because he was right. But Larry held up his hand, and she remained quiet.

"Yet here I am, putting all my energy into making sure that what the Partnership wants does not come about. Here I am, fighting for a future where I will never belong. If I can see what's best for all of us... If, after profiting so much from the Partnership and knowing this is the only reality in which I *can* excel—if *I* can choose a different path—then so can other people. They just have to know that path exists."

Vicki lowered her eyes. Truthfully, she felt a little ashamed. So much was at stake, and she was arguing for failure? She mentally shook herself.

"So that's why I'm here?" As she said that, it felt like a heavy weight was pressing down on her; the obstacles just seemed so large.

"When the time comes, you'll need to speak from a position of knowledge." Larry spoke gently, as if to a spooked horse that was still deciding whether to bolt. "You are a government official, so you'll be able to say the words our leaders will understand. You know how to play the political game. You will be able to describe what the world looks like at a higher vibrational level and paint a picture for them of possibilities and a future they can barely imagine. Even government officials—*especially* government officials—need to be reminded of the divine within themselves. They'll respond to you if they have proof."

Vicki asked, "You mentioned the government wasn't kept completely in the dark. How much does it know?"

"The Partnership shares only those technologies that the government would be willing to keep secret—devices with military applications."

"Like...?"

"Like travel that is nearly instantaneous. When the Partnership reports on this technology, it emphasizes how easy it would be for someone to bring a nuclear warhead into the country. So, of course, the government wants that technology to be kept secret."

"That... I can actually see the point of that. But what about medical technology? What's the military application of fixing someone's legs so they no longer need a wheelchair? What's negative about curing a person's cancer?" She choked up a little at the last question.

"Because then they'd have a world of people like me, and they'd lose the advantage."

Vicki looked at him curiously, and he continued, "I am stronger than any man alive. My reflexes are hair-trigger fast. I have knowledge of every battlefield strategy ever used in the history of humanity. An army of soldiers like me would be invincible."

She ventured a guess: "But not if everyone was like you?"

"Not if everyone was like me," agreed Larry. "So, they limit the medical technology to a few elite military units. Not the entire military, of course—it would become obvious something was going on, and the secret would get out. But the U.S. military has a couple of squads. The Partnership, unfortunately, has double that."

"So, not good."

"I don't think so," said Larry.

"And the tech to clean up the environment?" she asked. "People would be healthier. Nature would recover. We would all be able to breathe clean air, eat good food, and feel happier."

"Low-level stress is a powerful tool for control—it keeps people from moving forward. A damaged environment only adds to that. When people are facing health problems, struggling to feed their kids, or stressed about polluted air and water, they're too overwhelmed to question what's really happening—let alone resist it. Many governments, including ours, were already using these tactics to control the public—even before the Partnership got involved."

"It sounds so hopeless."

"I feel different. I've seen what the kids have accomplished. I know what Melly and the Council can do. I give our chances of success at better than fifty-fifty, probably something around sixty-forty."

Vicki was thinking about that—sixty-forty was much higher odds than she had expected—when there was a noise at the door, and Brad triumphantly burst in, followed more slowly by James and Jess.

A huge grin split Brad's face. "I've got it! We're no longer the Four; I have a new name for us!"

She waited.

"The Kick-Ass Quartet!"

James face-palmed. Jessica rolled her eyes.

Vicki just laughed.

CHAPTER EIGHT

That afternoon, Vicki was driving Jessica and Brad to another gathering with the "Heirs"—a nickname she'd started using for the children of those who ran the Partnership. James wasn't invited. Although he always came to game nights at the Martinssons' place, he wasn't part of the inner circle. Being the nephew of a biologic construct didn't give him value—at least not enough to be part of their group. The other teens tolerated him at the house—they knew how to act in public—but that was as far as it went.

She turned the Bentley into the entrance of a local park and steered along a curved lane lined with mature oak trees. Eventually, she pulled into the parking lot of the disc golf course. They arrived about half an hour before the agreed-upon start time; Vicki had insisted on starting early because she wanted to get gas. When they got in the car, she had been disappointed—seriously—to find out this was a task taken care of by the maintenance staff at the house. So, no driving up to a pump in a Bentley and having all the other drivers gnash their teeth in envy. She sighed.

"First here?" Brad jumped out of the car and scanned the parking lot. Jessica and Vicki followed more slowly.

"Looks like it," Jessica said.

The siblings both had light carry bags with their frisbees, water bottles, and snacks. Vicki just had her coffee thermos. She wasn't going to follow the young people around the course, but traffic was too heavy to return to the house and then come back to pick them up. It was easier and faster just to wait.

"So, your dad will be coming back tonight for a couple of days." She had received the message just before getting into the car. "Is there anything we should do to prepare for him?"

"Tell James we need to suspend your tai chi instruction until he leaves again," muttered Brad, already on his phone and beginning to text.

Vicki looked at the siblings. This was the touchy part.

"You told me before that your dad has no role whatsoever in what we're doing. What does that actually mean? At first, I thought it just meant he wasn't involved with the Four."

"The Kick-Ass Quartet," corrected Brad, still on his phone. Jessica rolled her eyes.

"But it has become clear," Vicki said slowly, "that you're actually keeping this secret from him. Why is that?"

"You remember he divorced our mom when she refused treatment at the Partnership's medical clinic?" Jessica's eyes were hard—harder than Vicki had ever seen them before.

"Yes, that was a dick move."

"He didn't want her actions to make him look bad. We were just kids, and he left us alone with our dying mom. Our dad's all about money, power, and status. Sure, he likes the idea of Brad and me joining the Partnership someday—as part of some messed-up legacy thing—but we're not naïve. We know exactly what would happen if we ever got in his way. He's not military, and he's not one of the big money guys, so his position is shaky. He won't let *anything* threaten it—not even his own kids."

Okay, that was sobering.

"So, all this networking with the Heirs"—Brad snorted when Vicki used the word but didn't look up from his phone—"is just a façade?"

Jessica didn't respond, but Vicki got her answer as she turned around to wave at a girl who had just pulled up in a Mercedes. Jessica's face—her entire appearance—changed. She somehow morphed into a weaker, uncertain, more vulnerable version of herself. Now that Vicki had lived with them for a few weeks, it was obvious she was doing this deliberately. But how? It would be a valuable ability for an actor—or for anyone in front of a camera—to be able to adopt different personas at will. Vicki suddenly realized how great Jess was going to be in her role as their media person.

Yes, she had used the phrase *"their* media person." She realized she was now thinking of herself as part of the Four. She had finally accepted the reality of every impossible thing that had happened over the past few weeks.

Vicki sat on a bench with her coffee as the group of young people grew to about eight, at which point they headed to the first tee. She watched them take turns tossing their frisbees. Whether they were any good didn't matter—there was something uplifting about watching happy, attractive young people laugh and enjoy themselves.

When Jessica's turn came, she stepped up, paused, and let her frisbee fly. As she stood tall, eyes tracking its arc, Vicki was reminded of a statue of the huntress Diana she'd once seen on a Grecian urn. The frisbee landed, and the group erupted in cheers—her throw was by far the best. Jess turned to face them, and in that moment, Vicki saw her shrink back into a more uncertain version of herself as she quietly accepted their praise.

The group moved on, and Vicki couldn't see them anymore. She thought about Jessica and how she hid herself. Who else was hiding and making themselves less than they were? To be honest, probably everyone on the planet. The desire to fit in—the desire to please others—was a powerful compulsion. There was comfort in being like everyone else and in sharing the same reality. But at the price of hiding their light? Vicki knew Jessica was doing it for a good reason. She wasn't sure about anyone else.

She was especially not sure about herself.

* * *

A couple of hours later, they finished the course. Jessica was eager to leave, but she and Brad had to stick around for the usual small talk before everyone headed to their cars. Appearances had to be maintained.

"I'll be starting in robotics this autumn." This was from Aija, the dark-haired young woman whose father had been diagnosed with a brain tumor.

Jessica couldn't stand her, but she kept her expression carefully neutral.

"With the Partnership or at university?" The black teenager with short dreads was a newcomer to the group—his father had just been hired the previous autumn.

"Two years at Carnegie Mellon, then I'll transfer to the Partnership. I've already tested out of the intro courses and most of the humanities. I can learn the basics at Carnegie Mellon, then get advanced training when I start with the Partnership."

The young woman flipped her hair back and turned to Jessica with a syrupy smile. "Too bad you're not able to take advantage of this."

"Aija!" remonstrated one of the other girls.

Neither Jessica nor her brother showed any reaction. They were used to this kind of behavior. But being used to it—even though she had worked hard to build that very image—didn't mean it didn't still sting. She was so over it, but she only had to keep up the act for a couple more months.

"What?" Aija said, annoyed. "It's not like we don't all know. It's not like pretending will change anything. I don't know why we all keep tiptoeing around her."

"Consider it practice." The taller, dark-haired boy with tan skin was Aija's older brother. He put his hand on her shoulder as if to restrain her, and she reacted with a sullen pout.

"How much schooling do you need to have before the Partnership accepts you for more advanced training?" This question came from the teenager with dreads.

"It depends on the specialty," said Aija's brother. "Some departments, like innovation and forecasting, might take you without any formal university training because it's better if you don't learn any bad habits. For others—robotics, engineering, or computers—you need to have a good grounding in the basics, the kind you get when you go to college."

He then paused and glanced over at Brad. "There are exceptions made for geniuses, of course."

Someone elbowed Brad in the ribs, and he grinned.

"Not fair," muttered someone; Jessica couldn't tell who.

"Hey, they don't bring people on board without making sure you can do the work first," protested Brad good-naturedly. "I spent my spring break in the Human Enhancement Division, shadowing the manager and doing some basic tasks while they looked over my shoulder. Plus, I've been auditing university classes online for the past two years."

"You work so hard, Brad," gushed a girl, putting a hand on his arm proprietarily. She was gorgeous, with green eyes and tawny hair halfway down her back.

"There are a lot of hard workers at the Partnership," said Brad, taking an imperceptibly small step back and loosening her hold on his arm. "Kiran is the one who made it possible for the rest of us." He nodded at Aija's brother. "Without him paving the way—he was the first to be hired by the Partnership without going to college first—we'd all have been required to go the full four-year route, which would have been a bore."

"Yeah, why waste time when we know what we're going to do?" This was the dreadlocked teenager again.

Jessica had stopped listening. She already knew exactly what everyone would say. And she was right—after a few comments about their future roles in the Partnership, the conversation shifted to luxury buys and exotic vacations. She mentally checked out, turning her thoughts to camera angles, interview questions, and how to introduce humanity to the reality of alien life. If she looked spaced out... well, it fit the image she'd carefully crafted.

The group mingled around for a few more minutes, then left in their vehicles.

* * *

They were heading back home and merging into traffic before Vicki spoke up. "So, Jessica, you're playing the fool so others will ignore you? Doesn't that get old for you?"

"I'm not playing the fool," replied Jessica, primly. "I'm playing an emotionally stunted, damaged young woman who will never be a threat to anyone."

The siblings both snickered.

Then Jessica continued, "But seriously, I can't be like Brad; I don't have a naturally happy-go-lucky personality that everyone falls in love with. It's better if I play emotionally stunted; I have the background story to back it up."

"And you, Brad?" Vicki said. "You never mentioned you'd spent a couple of weeks job shadowing at the Partnership before—and with the Human Enhancement Division?"

"How do you think I managed to turn off the kill button in Larry's software?" he asked, smirking.

"But didn't I just hear you say they were looking over your shoulder while you did basic grunt work?"

"I might have exaggerated that part a bit," said Brad modestly. "The truth is, as soon as they realized how skilled I was, they let me loose with a couple of midlevel assignments and just checked up on me periodically. I pretended the tasks were more difficult for me to carry out than they actually were. "When the guy in charge of me left me alone, I poked around the system, found Larry's file, and edited it."

"You did that in just a couple of weeks?" Vicki was impressed.

"Two days, actually. But I had to keep up the pretense of working for the rest of my time there. It would have raised questions if I were *too* familiar with how to find my way around the Partnership's computer systems. It's a super-advanced, proprietary set-up."

She ventured a guess: "Some of the information was downloaded via Melly?"

"The schematics," agreed Brad. "The rest of it—the knowing of computerized systems—came when Melly helped activate the part of my DNA needed to access the information directly from the matrix, or the ether, or from whatever universal knowledge bank exists in the universe. You'll be doing the same thing pretty soon. Probably not with computers, but for whatever issues you'll be dealing with."

Vicki thought about that for the rest of the ride, then pulled into the Martinssons' driveway. She saw Kurt's sporty Bentley parked in front of the house.

"Your dad's home," she said. The kids' expressions both turned blank, as if curtains had been drawn over their faces.

WTF?

Chapter Nine

"**S**o far, so good." That was how Vicki ended her verbal report to Kurt Martinsson. "No meltdowns for Jessica, and everyone seemed to enjoy themselves when they got together with their friends." She referred to the Heirs as friends, though she was pretty sure this wasn't true.

Correction: she was very sure it wasn't true. But she was now playing the game just like Jessica and Brad.

"Any other interactions?" Kurt ran a hand through his damp hair. He had been showering when they arrived back at the house and was now freshly dressed and... attractive.

Get that thought out of your mind, Vicki told herself. *Remember the asshole who left his kids to watch their mother die.*

She schooled her face and smiled. "The kids tell me they have the summer off from studies with their tutors?"

She looked to Kurt for confirmation, and he nodded. She continued, "They say they're doing some internet stuff in the meantime—YouTube videos, blogs, participating in chat rooms dedicated to their interests, et cetera. I'm also taking them to their tai chi classes. Their instructor says they're the best in the class."

Kurt frowned at the mention of tai chi. "I'm not sure going to tai chi is the best way to spend their time. It takes them away from... other things."

By now, Vicki knew exactly what he was referring to.

"It's good practice," she said blandly, unconsciously echoing Kiran's words from earlier in the day. "While Jess and Brad have an *exceptional* path ahead of them, they still need the skills to collaborate and work with people who aren't part of that inner circle."

Kurt's entire face lit up at her words. Lit up like a kid who had just been told he was going to Disneyland.

"I knew you would understand. I knew you were the right person to watch over the kids this summer. There are critically important issues at stake, and the average person wouldn't grasp the significance of what the Partnership is working toward. It was a stroke of luck that I was able to bring you on board. You are exactly the right person to be here with my family."

He put his hand on her arm.

Vicki struggled not to recoil. Kurt was both right and oh so wrong. He was right that she was the right person to look after his kids. He was also right that she could appreciate what the Partnership was working toward. Too bad for him, she was looking forward to helping torpedo it all.

"You said you'll be home for a couple of days?" she asked, casually shifting her position so he had to remove his hand.

"Actually, my schedule has changed—I'll be leaving early tomorrow morning. I'm trying to complete all my travel-related projects while I have someone trustworthy in the house."

* * *

Dinner that evening was served in the dining room. It was Vicki's first time eating there; she and the siblings usually ate family-style in the kitchen, joking with the staff and trading stories about the day. Now, Lucia served them formally, silently apportioning food onto their plates. When she left the room, the conversation turned awkward.

"So, Vicki shared all the details about what you two have been up to since I left," Kurt said with a touch of bonhomie.

Was it forced? Vicki couldn't tell. The mere fact that she was wondering showed how much her perspective had changed since she first arrived.

Jessica stared down at her plate, but Brad jumped in, chatting animatedly about their frisbee game with the Heirs earlier in the day. Clever Brad—he knew exactly what his dad would want to hear.

"Aija said she'll be doing robotics at Carnegie Mellon beginning this fall, and after a couple of years, she plans to start working for the Partnership."

"Oh, yes? Anything more?" Kurt seemed overly interested in what his kids' peers were doing.

"Some complaints about the Partnership saying they'd accept me right after high school with no university training. But Kiran shut that right down; he's a good guy."

Kurt's face registered satisfaction that one of his kids was envied by his coworkers' children. Jessica had mentioned he felt insecure in his position. Maybe he felt that Brad's achievements gave him status? Unfortunately, he now turned his attention to the child he felt was underperforming.

"Jessica, have you done what I asked?"

She bobbed her head obediently, not lifting her gaze. "Yes, I've been researching the different fields you suggested."

"And?"

"So far, I haven't found anything that interests me more than media studies, but I'll keep looking."

Her voice was flat. Brad jumped in with another distraction, and when Kurt was engaged with him, Jessica glanced up at her father, then quickly lowered her eyes again.

Vicki was startled to catch a flash of contempt on her face.

* * *

The next morning, Vicki tried to sleep in. She woke early anyway, roused by a knock at her door.

Bleary-eyed, she opened it to find Brad standing there with a mug of coffee. He thrust it at her, chirping, "Time to get up. Dad has already left, so your tai chi class is back on."

Being bright-eyed and bushy-tailed at oh-dark-thirty should be illegal.

Half an hour later, they were in the Bentley, all of them with coffee in hand. Vicki took a sip, then merged into traffic. "So, how was last night?" she asked.

After dinner the previous evening, she had gone to her room, politely declining Kurt's invitation to watch a movie with the three of them. She had pled tiredness, suggesting they enjoy some private family time. Brad had nearly choked at her words, then covered it with a cough. She had then escaped.

"It was hard," Jessica said, staring out the window. "When all this started a couple of years ago, it was easy. Easy to pretend one thing—and to act as if it were true—but at the same time know something different. But now..." Her voice tapered off.

"But now?" Vicki prompted.

"But now there's a light at the end of the tunnel. Now I can see the point when things will change. And the closer we get to that point, the closer we get to being able to make a difference, the harder it is to maintain the façade." Jessica took a sip of her coffee. "I'm having a hard time holding myself back."

Tai chi was a little different that day. It seemed there had been some discussion between the adults—Calvin, Mona, and Larry—about Vicki's lack of progress with detecting, much less moving, her chi. Apparently, they were just as frustrated as she was. Calvin started class by announcing they'd be adding simple body movements to the practice. Not full forms like regular students learned, but just enough activity "to get the chi flowing."

Yeah, it was embarrassing.

"This movement is called Cloud Hands," Calvin said as he demonstrated—circular, flowing arm motions paired with side-to-side weight shifts. The demonstration was clearly for her benefit. The three kids and Larry were well past this stage, and yet, to their credit, they followed along without complaint.

Vicki did too. They stood swaying back and forth for nearly five minutes, circling their arms. It felt useless.

Then a voice called from the back of the room, startling her.

"Shut your eyes," Mona said. Vicki hadn't noticed when she came in.

"Now imagine you're wearing some sort of long, drapey garment," Mona continued, "maybe a very light robe, and as you move, the fabric follows the movements of your body. Feel the weight of it as it shifts back and forth, flowing along with you."

Vicki tried. She imagined the fabric, and it almost felt real.

"Now," Mona said, "when your hands come close together—just before you change directions—imagine you're holding them over a pile of freshly laundered sheets. You've just taken them out of the dryer, and they're warm and full of static. Imagine your hands are just a few inches above the sheets. Now, feel the tingling of the static."

As she did so, Vicki felt something—the tingling, the static, the warmth running from her hands through her arms and into her body. She nearly stopped to share the sensation, but didn't want to interrupt. Calvin had begun speaking in a low voice, likely guiding them through a meditation, but Vicki barely heard him. She was too focused.

Focused on what was happening inside her.

She was feeling the chi.

It swayed back and forth inside her like water softly sloshing in a cup. It felt peaceful—and oddly, expectant. Which didn't make sense. Chi wasn't sentient, was it? Yet there was a palpable sense of waiting.

And then the waiting ended.

A spot just above her tailbone became warm, then hot. A column of heat surged up her spine, the chi vibrating within her body.

The heat reached her skull and—burst. Burst into light, into stars, into colored ribbons of energy.

"Oh my god," she whispered.

And the world disappeared.

She no longer had a solid body. She was mist—sparkling, weightless, flickering in and out of reality.

There was the sound of bells and Tibetan singing bowls—perhaps even a celebratory gong or two.

"Welcome, Vicki. I knew you would make it."

"Melly?" The alien's form—misty and shimmering—appeared a few feet away. She didn't seem as large or intimidating as she had before, though she was still unmistakably a giant insect.

"Where am I?"

"In a dimension between dimensions," Melly replied. "A meeting location for when we wish to see each other outside the strictures of linear time."

Her words were overlaid with something that sounded like Vivaldi's *Spring*, although it was rendered entirely in bells. "If you need training or instruction, we can do it here, but that should rarely be necessary. Now that you're moving your chi, I can help activate your DNA."

Melly stepped forward, raising her forelegs to hover just above Vicki's head. Vicki stood still and tried not to flinch. The nearness of the alien was unnerving, but Melly didn't actually touch her. Instead, she simply studied her with intense focus.

And then—Vicki could feel it. Her chi swirled, shifting from aimless motion to precise coordination. Although her body appeared to be made of sparkling mist, it retained its human form, and her eyes were still in their proper place. But, to her amazement, she could also see *inside* herself. Her DNA strands glowed with light, rearranged themselves, and settled back into her cells.

A mantle of knowing wrapped itself around her and sank into her being—like Helen Keller at the pump, feeling water overflow into her hand—the first sparks of understanding.

"That is enough for now. We will work together later to help you learn how to use it."

The Tibetan singing bowls sounded satisfied.

Reality snapped back into place as Vicki opened her eyes. She stood frozen, shock etched across her face.

Then, she burst into tears.

"I guess she finally made it," said Mona, clearly pleased.

Chapter Ten

"**Y**ou need to focus, Vicki."

James pushed his glasses up, his expression intent. He, Vicki, and the Martinsson siblings were in the garden behind the tai chi studio, while his parents led their usual daytime classes inside.

"Did you notice that flowers glow?" Vicki was so excited.

"And blood can glow too," James said, his tone serious. "That's why you need to focus—so you *don't* end up seeing too much of it."

He wasn't joking. They'd all gone through this phase after their DNA was activated—seeing colors outside the visible spectrum, suddenly knowing random things like the routes of butterfly migration, how clouds form, or even sensing who was just around the corner before turning down a hallway.

It was that last skill James wanted Vicki to hone. He and the Martinsson siblings had had time. Time to practice, to experiment, to screw up in relative safety. They'd laughed through some of it—testing their limits, pushing each other, discovering shortcuts and pitfalls. But that luxury was fading. The clock was ticking now, and the moment for wide-eyed wonder was over.

James wasn't angry at Vicki. He respected her. But he couldn't allow sentiment to cloud what had to happen next. If she didn't catch up—fast—it wouldn't just be her problem. It would end badly for all of them.

So when he watched her now, struggling with the subtleties of chi manipulation or slipping out of sync during group work, he didn't offer comfort. He offered instruction, correction, and a small amount of pressure. Because she *had* to get there. And because when the moment came, they would all be counting on her to stand firm—and maybe, just maybe, to change everything.

"We were talking about reaching out with our energy to sense other people?" Vicki asked, signaling that she was ready to focus again.

James relaxed. "Everyone has a life force, a sort of energetic field surrounding them. If you reach out with your own energy, you can 'see' other people before they actually come into view. If you want to sneak around without anyone knowing, this is a good way to stay hidden."

"If I'm able to see another person's energy, can I also tell who it is?"

"It takes a lot of practice. Brad is really good at it," said Jessica.

Brad put on a modest expression, then ruined it by comically waggling his eyebrows.

"Hey, it was useful. I had to know who was nearby during my shadowing at the HE Division. If it was just support staff coming into the room, I could keep digging around the system. But if it was one of the design guys or the manager tasked to watch me? That'd be a problem. I had to close the file fast and look busy before they walked in and figured out what I was doing."

"So, not just for sneaking around physically," said Vicki.

"For whenever you're doing something you'd rather no one else knew," agreed Brad.

"You said it was what you needed to know," she said. "Can anyone do this once our DNA is activated? Can anyone access this ability, or is it something we have to need?"

"Picking up on someone else's energy is pretty basic," James said. "We all have some ability to do it. And the more you practice, the better you get. Brad and Jess are actually better at it than I am." He nodded toward the siblings. "But remember—Melly didn't activate all our DNA. If she had, we'd probably be too overwhelmed to focus on what we're supposed to be learning and doing. She only unlocked the minimum—just enough to give each of us the abilities we need."

"Like Brad's technical and computer expertise," Vicki guessed.

"Exactly."

"But what's the harm in having full access?" she asked. "Maybe it would be useful. Isn't it better to have it and not need it, than to need it and come up short?"

James had thought about that too, and he sometimes wished he had access to more. But Melly had been pretty clear about this.

"Because even though the planet's vibration is shifting, we still live in the same world as everyone else. We have the responsibility of helping people discover who they really are—what it truly means to be human. To do that, we still have to *be* human. We can't show up looking like some mythological demigod from ancient Greek legends."

Yeah, while his dad was a frontier wilderness fan, *he* was an ancient history buff.

"I'm not sure what Melly did to me. Did I get any specific activations?" Vicki asked. It was clear she couldn't tell.

"I don't think there was a plan to give you anything specific," James said. "It's more that you needed stronger basic connections than the rest of us. Once Disclosure actually happens, our part"—he gestured to include himself and the siblings—"will mostly be done. But your work will just be beginning. You're the one who'll have to explain everything to the governments and convince them to take the right actions."

Brad grinned. "Yeah, I don't think there's a superpower where you can wave your hand and—*abracadabra*—convince everyone to do what you want."

"Exactly why you need to get familiar with the full range of basic abilities, instead of focusing on just one," Jessica said. "It'll help you understand what it's really like to live at a higher vibration. You're the government person—you'll be the one translating what we know and what's possible into something bureaucrats can actually understand. Always think about your audience and what they need to hear."

When Vicki raised an eyebrow, Jessica smirked. "I'm the media expert, remember?"

"So, if I don't need to do much until everything is over, why do you have me here practicing the fine art of skulking?"

"Because we need you, we really do."

They hadn't heard Larry coming down the path, but they should have smelled him—he was carrying three large pizzas. It was a little early for lunch, but no one complained.

But it became clear this was a working lunch, because as they opened the boxes, Larry continued the conversation.

"We really do need you, Vicki. You need to be a part of everything."

But Vicki's mind was on other things. "You need to eat? You're a biologic construct. Can't you just plug yourself in or something?"

James snorted, then started coughing as something went down the wrong tube. Brad pounded on his back until he got his breath back. Larry laughed out loud.

"To give you the short version—I can go a couple of months without food before it really affects me. But my body is still designed to use food as fuel. Eating is something living beings do—at least in our reality. A body that doesn't need to eat would seem too alien for most people. The Partnership didn't *have* to design the need to eat into biologic constructs—it was a strategic choice. It made the product they were offering feel more... human. It was a nod to the psychological side of what it means to be one of us."

"How many people are 'living' as biologic constructs?"

"The government has a couple of elite squads of enhanced soldiers—about twenty in total. But most of them are only partial constructs. It's more accurate to say they've been augmented with specific upgrades like better vision, hearing, or lung capacity. The Partnership, on the other hand, has twice as many—and they're all full biologic constructs. The problem is, a lot of them are also full-blown psychopaths. The Partnership actually looks for psychopaths because they're more willing to carry out certain missions—the kind that involve manipulation, cruelty, and abuse."

"Many of them are stationed off Earth," Brad added.

Vicki must have let out an exclamation of surprise because Larry gave a wide smile.

"It's the most incredible feeling, Vicki—being in one of those ships out in space," Larry said, his voice full of awe. "They're unbelievably fast and smooth. You can change direction instantly, cross from one horizon to the other in seconds—and there's no sound at all. Just silence. And the stars... they're breathtaking." He trailed off, lost in the memory.

"There's a small outpost on Europa—one of the moons of Jupiter," James volunteered. "But it isn't manned full-time. Right now, the Partnership is there exploring for metal and minerals mining."

James had heard his uncle's stories plenty of times before, but he never got tired of them.

"I was part of a Europa work unit when I got hurt," said Larry. "Back then, we were just starting construction on the base. I understand it has come a long way since. I've been grounded since the accident. Since I was the first to become a full-fledged biologic construct, they want to keep me where they can study me easily."

"I would have thought there would be an outpost on Mars," Vicki said.

"That's initially what the Partnership wanted to do, but they put it on Europa for strategic reasons."

"Strategic reasons?"

"The other side of the asteroid belt," clarified Larry. "Farther from the prying eyes of the government and astronomers, but still convenient for mining asteroids if that proved practical."

"And did it?"

"There are lots of rare and valuable minerals in the asteroids, so yes, it's both practical and profitable. But only for part of the year; they close down operations when Jupiter—and Europa—move too far away from Earth."

Vicki looked like she wanted to dig deeper into Larry's stories, but James needed her to stay focused, so he shifted the conversation.

"So we've been trying to explain why you need to be involved in everything, even though your actual role won't really kick in until the end. It's because you're more than just the government liaison—you're a strategist. And having both those strengths boosts our chances of success big time."

"How am I good at strategy?" Vicki asked, confused. "I don't have a military background."

"But you're a diplomat," Larry said. "You've dealt with tough personalities and found solutions when people were at odds and ready to fight. You've had plenty of practice changing course and finding a new path when the original one doesn't work. And you're good at it—Melly told us so."

Vicki swallowed a bite of pizza and opened her mouth to say something questioning his—and Melly's—assessment, but Jessica spoke up.

"I've always wondered why the State Department was never a part of any of this; it's the federal agency that deals with foreigners. Dealing with extraterrestrials sounds like a natural fit."

It was clear to everyone that Vicki had an easy answer ready. "The State Department has the reputation—well-deserved, I might add—of leaking like a sieve."

"Plus, extraterrestrials and advanced technology have always been framed as national security issues, which means they fall within the military's purview," said Larry comfortably.

"In any case," continued Jessica, "Melly wouldn't have worked to bring you to us if you weren't good at this—if you weren't capable of doing what we need you to do."

"What? Melly arranged for me to be here?" Vicki was shocked.

"She just smoothed the way," Brad said. He and James had already demolished an entire pizza and now he reached for a slice from the box Jess and Vicki were sharing before continuing.

"I don't know how she pulled it off, but Melly somehow identified people who had the traits she was looking for—and who were connected to our dad. You happened to be nearby, so *boom*, you were the match. Then she got the Tall Whites—the aliens the Partnership works with—to create a new project that would keep our dad busy and away from home. He was already looking for someone to watch over us. And then Jessica had a couple of her episodes, which reinforced that need."

James, Brad and Jessica all snickered.

"Wait—the rogue aliens? Melly told them what to do, and now they're on our side?"

"They're not rogue aliens," James said. "The Tall Whites are just an ET group that tends to be really focused on their own interests—and they kind of just lost track of the bigger picture. But they're also very hierarchical. So now that Disclosure is officially a Council project—and the Tall Whites are part of the Galactic Federation—they'll follow whatever orders the Council gives."

"So why can't the Council order the Tall Whites to carry out Disclosure? Why are we doing it?"

"It needs to be a human effort," Larry reminded her. "If it were implemented by any group of extraterrestrials, the Partnership would frame it as an alien invasion."

Brad spoke up, changing the subject. "When Larry brought in the pizza, you didn't notice he was coming, did you?"

"I still can't do that with anyone." Vicki shot him an annoyed look.

"None of us did because none of us can," said Brad.

Vicki looked at him in surprise.

"It comes with being a biological construct," said Larry calmly. "Apparently, the energetic field surrounding a normal human body doesn't form around the biologic construct when a person's consciousness is transferred in."

He chewed a piece of pizza, then added, "If the Partnership's elite soldiers come for us, we won't have any warning."

Chapter Eleven

Jessica admitted it: the following week was fun as they helped Vicki learn how to harness the power of her activated DNA. It was fascinating to watch her practice how to sense other people's energy. Watching quietly from the background, Jess was half-impressed and half-jealous. She'd almost forgotten that early sense of wonder—the thrill of discovery, the excitement of exploring new realities, and the shock of realizing that the world wasn't at all what they'd been taught.

But they didn't have time to waste, so they made a schedule. After their morning tai chi classes, they'd train in the garden behind the studio. After lunch, they'd move on to more challenging places, mostly coffee shops. Jessica insisted on these public spaces not just for the noise and distraction, but for the variability.

And it worked. Jessica could see Vicki starting to get the hang of it. At first, she was nervous. Distracted by the clatter of dishes, the hiss of steam, and the jangle of conversation. But after a few days of practice, something shifted. Vicki could sit with her back to the door, effortlessly identifying who was coming in, where they paused, how long they hesitated at the counter, and where they eventually sat.

Her range was growing. If the place wasn't crowded, she could track up to six people—feel their emotional signatures, sense their attention patterns. Any more than that, though, and the energies became a tangled mess.

James sat back after finishing his hot chocolate. "I guess I was worried for nothing; you're good."

Vicki grinned and teased, "As good as Brad?"

"I'd have to say you're better than me," Brad responded.

Jessica looked at him, slightly amused. Brad seemed so... Brad. Always one to show off, but now, strangely quiet and absorbed in his phone. No smirk, no teasing—just thoughtful.

"Why do you say that?" Vicki asked, her voice light, but underneath was curiosity.

Brad put his phone down and shrugged. "Because you can follow more people at a time than I can. More than three people, and it gets all muddled up for me. Even during my two shadow weeks with the Partnership, I couldn't tell anything specific about the individuals. I'd just get a general sense of whether they were support staff or the computer guys. I have to already know someone to identify them purely by their energy. But here you are, drinking a latté, and describing complete strangers as they walk in."

Vicki grinned. "Aren't I supposed to do that?"

"I guess you are," Jessica said, taking the last bite of her brownie, wondering about the implications. "Melly's just activating the skills we need. Apparently, you'll need to be able to look around a corner and tell how many people are there, along with their ages and genders."

"And whether they're telling the truth," Vicki added.

"What!" The exclamation burst out simultaneously from both Jessica and the boys; Vicki laughed at their identical expressions of shock.

"I guess that's not normal?"

"Well, it hasn't been something any of us have experienced," Jess said carefully. "How does it work for you?"

"I've started feeling the sincerity of people's words like a vibration in my gut," Vicki explained. "If someone says a white lie, like telling someone they look good when they're actually sleep-deprived, I get a little twinge—barely noticeable. But if it's a serious lie... Remember that young couple sitting at the table next to us earlier?"

Jessica nodded, waiting.

"They came in stiff and reserved, but when they left, they couldn't keep their hands off each other."

Jessica had noticed the couple the moment they walked in—both well-dressed, both radiating tension. The woman kept her purse between them like a shield. The man checked his phone three times in the first two minutes.

"They were having a fight, and then they made up?" James ventured.

"You need to pay closer attention than that," Vicki shot back, pulling a face at him. "The guy told his girlfriend it had all been a mistake and it wouldn't happen again. I got the impression he had been cheating on her."

"And he was lying?" Jessica asked. But the question was just for confirmation—if Vicki was bringing it up, she already knew the answer.

"When he said it was a mistake and that it would never happen again, I felt sick. Like I was going to throw up," Vicki said, her face darkening. "He'll be cheating on her again the moment he gets the chance."

Jessica didn't say anything, trying to process it all. The Four could use this, she was sure they could. But, more importantly, why had Melly thought this was something Vicki would need?

James seemed to be thinking the same thing.

"I guess this is good news, then," he said. "I'm sure we'll be lied to sooner or later, and it'll be useful to know when that happens."

But Vicki was tired of being quizzed. "I think we should go outside, spend some time in the park, and practice looking at flowers. I want to see how they glow."

"Flowers? Flowers aren't important," James scoffed.

Vicki raised her eyebrows. "Really? I seem to remember your mom telling me you chose all the flowers for the studio grounds. You were quite insistent they plant them."

"And he chose the flowers for our house, too," Jessica added.

"What? I didn't know that."

"We already had plants in the gardens—we have gardeners who do that," she explained. "But I told Dad I was auditing a botany course, and he gave me permission to change whatever I wanted. So, we got the flowers James suggested, and the gardeners planted them for us."

Vicki looked at James, now fully curious. "You were, what, maybe thirteen? And you were landscaping both the grounds of your parents' business *and* your best friend's estate?"

"I wasn't landscaping," James protested, shoulders hunched. "Just choosing some flowers for them to plant."

"Why?" she asked. "I mean, it's not a bad thing to do. In fact, my sister Beth would have loved to sit here and talk to you about it." She paused for a moment, then continued, "But isn't that a little strange for a kid to do?"

"Strange being relative," Jessica muttered. She had been amused back then by how seriously James took his flower "choosing."

Vicki snorted a laugh. "Okay, I give up. Let's go to a park now."

"Actually, we're meeting Larry for an early supper," Brad said, glancing at his watch. "Traffic will be heavy, so we need to leave now."

"When was this planned?" Jessica asked, surprised. This was the first she had heard about it.

"Just a few minutes ago, when I messaged Larry," Brad explained. "He didn't want to put us in any complicated situations until Vicki had reached a certain proficiency level. It's pretty clear she's there now. The restaurant is popular with employees of the Partnership, so if we're lucky, we'll run into other biologic constructs."

"So... a mystery supper where we might be surrounded by psychopaths. Sounds fun."

Jessica was glad to see that Vicki shared their sense of humor—they were all going to need it.

* * *

The GPS directed them to a restaurant not too far from where the frisbee game had taken place the previous week. It was on a golf course, and after consulting his phone, Brad led them around to a patio in the back of the restaurant where Larry was already seated. They had a good view of the course.

At least some of them did; Larry directed Vicki to take the only chair that didn't have a view. They waited while a waiter filled their water glasses, distributed menus, and left. Larry then lifted his water glass to her.

"Congratulations, Vicki. The kids say you've mastered how to identify people's energy."

The young people also raised their glasses, and they clinked. She smiled; it was nice to finally be good at something rather than struggling to catch up.

"That's not all she can do," Brad said. Larry raised an eyebrow and looked at her.

"Apparently, being able to tell when people are lying is a new thing?" Vicki asked.

A flash of surprise crossed Larry's face; then he smiled—an eyes-crinkling, full-face grin. "This is great—we are going to be able to do so much with that."

They all fell silent as a waitress came to take their orders. When she left, Vicki turned to Larry.

"James said the exact same thing—that having someone who can tell when people are lying will be useful. How, exactly?"

She had her own ideas, but she wanted to hear what he had to say.

"Being able to tell who's an ally and who's not. Finding out how much certain people know. Figuring out who is fully involved and who is just so narrowly focused on their own work that they don't realize how it will be used. Determining how deep the rot goes."

Larry didn't pause, barely taking a breath as he listed the reasons. It was clear he had been thinking about this a lot.

"Allies—we have allies? It's not just us?"

No one answered as the waitress arrived with their food. Vicki's BLT looked and smelled amazing. Once they were alone and eating, the conversation started up again.

"I think Kiran would be an ally if given the chance," said Brad, digging into his mac and cheese skillet. "He's always been a good guy."

"Good enough—and strong enough—to defy his parents? To go against the financial interests of his family? To destroy his future with the Partnership? To have all his friends turn against him?"

Just like Larry, Vicki didn't have to pause when giving her list. She had been thinking about how hard it would be for anyone to break ranks.

"He wouldn't mind having Aija turn on him," said Brad. "She already annoys everybody."

Yeah, Kiran's sister was a piece of work. Vicki turned to Larry.

"Would any of your colleagues be allies? Would any of the people who are biologic constructs be willing to turn their backs on the Partnership?"

"That's a hard no on the biologic constructs," said Larry, calmly buttering a roll. "Anyone who's now a biologic construct volunteered for the job, a true believer. I was the only one who didn't sign up for it."

"How about other employees?"

"A couple of them might be possibilities. I've heard a few comments that could be interpreted as being unhappy with what the Partnership is doing, but I couldn't tell if the comments were genuine or whether they were said as a strategy to root out those who are less than loyal."

Vicki frowned. "So it could be a trap—or it could be fear."

"Or both. That's the problem." Then he looked over at her and smiled. "But now we have you."

"Show Larry what you can do now," urged Jessica. "Close your eyes and tell us about the people sitting at the other tables."

She did so. The couple sitting at a table behind them was elderly, calm, and enjoying post-golf game martinis. The middle-aged woman on the left was lying when she told her husband how much she liked the birthday gift he had given her. Two waitstaff, both young males, were leaning against the door frame, bored, waiting for any summons from a customer. At their own table...

Vicki opened her eyes. "That's strange."

"What?" Larry was looking pretty happy with her performance.

"At our own table, it's easy to tell the kids' energy and distinguish who's who. But when I reach out to where you are..." She felt puzzled.

"We already told you we can't detect the energy of people who are biologic constructs," said James, jumping in to reassure her she wasn't failing. He had ordered breakfast for supper and was scraping up the last of his bacon and eggs.

"But I can."

Everyone straightened up, their eyes locked on her.

"What I mean to say," she clarified, "is that when I reach out to feel a person, it's normally the movement of their energy—their chi—that I detect. The movement is what's important—the patterns and the swirls. I assume that's what the rest of you feel too." She nodded at James and the Martinsson siblings. "But when I reach out to Larry—if I concentrate hard enough—I can feel the chi. But it's as if it's standing completely still, like it's petrified or something."

The young people looked confused, but Larry nodded in understanding. "I can't evolve; I am frozen in time. Likewise, my chi is a snapshot, a single slice of who I was frozen in time."

"If the chi isn't moving, how can you tell the difference between someone who's a biologic construct and some random inanimate object? Something like a tree, for example," asked Jessica.

"Human chi," she said simply. She fixed Larry with her eye. "You might consider yourself to be just a snapshot, a single moment in time, but whatever DNA Melly activated in me still recognizes you as a member of the human race."

Larry took a deep breath, then smiled at her crookedly. "That gives me hope."

"Incoming," said James, low and urgently.

They all looked up as two men approached their table. Early thirties, good-looking, limber, and muscled like Larry. And, Vicki realized, like Larry, they had chi that didn't move. It looked like they were going to meet two more of the Partnership's biologic constructs.

Larry stood up to greet them. "Dave, CJ—it's good to see you." The men all shook hands, and Larry introduced them.

Their eyes pretty much ignored all of them except for Brad, who nodded at them. "Good to see you again. With any luck, you'll see a lot more of me in the HE Division after I turn eighteen."

They murmured some pleasantries, then turned back to Larry.

"We heard you were taking the summer off. You'll be back by the end of August for sure? We have a couple of important projects on the horizon. They're calling everyone in, so we need to be ready."

Vicki thought it was CJ speaking.

"But you should come in for the upgrade beforehand," said Dave.

"You know I have a bad feeling about upgrades," said Larry.

"There's nothing to feel bad about," said Dave. "You won't even notice that anything is different."

"Nothing different, except you'll be performing at a much higher level," said CJ. "You should come in and just talk to the director about what can be done for you."

Vicki could tell CJ was holding back. He knew who the Martinsson kids were, but he didn't know whether he could speak freely in front of her or James.

The three men chatted for a few moments, then Dave and CJ left to make their tee time.

Larry watched them leave. "I think we finally have our timeline; we need to be ready before the end of August."

Jessica leaned toward her. "Vicki, could you tell if those guys were telling the truth?"

"About the upgrade?"

She nodded.

"They were lying," Vicki said. "They were lying like a rug."

Chapter Twelve

V icki was dreaming.

It was nighttime, and she was standing in a field. There were no signs of human habitation—just her, the long grass, and trees in the distance. The stars were shining so sharp and bright it took her breath away. But she felt... someone. And she recognized her.

"Melly?" she asked.

"Yes, Vicki." The feeling of soft bells. Melly seemed to take form about a dozen feet away, still an eight-foot mantis, but more familiar and friendly somehow. Her cloak was a deep burgundy. Vicki hadn't noticed that before.

"Why are you in my dream, Melly?" As soon as the question left her lips, she realized it was foolish. Everyone was responsible for their own dreams.

"I heard you calling," Melly said. "You have questions."

She was right—Vicki did.

"Have you ever been afraid, Melly?" She started out hesitantly, but then her questions began rushing out without pause, tumbling over each other in their eagerness to be free.

"Have you ever been so afraid that you stop breathing, stop moving, and try to wish yourself out of existence? Have you ever felt so terrified that you wanted to go back in time and do everything possible to avoid ever being on the path you're on?"

"It sounds like you're feeling alive, Vicki."

A sudden fury rose in her. "It's too much to ask. They're gambling too much on the hope that somehow we can carry out some amazing, magical, unspecified thing that's supposed to help change the future for everyone on the planet. This is an impossible task. The burden is too great. I can't do it, but I also don't know how to get myself out of the middle of all this."

Melly sighed—the feeling of muted gongs. "Your reality is so very dense. The burden will ease as the vibration rises, but we understand the challenges you're facing now. We'll help when we can—but only if the support can't be traced back to nonhumans."

"Wait, how—?"

But the dream faded, and Vicki woke up with tears on her face.

* * *

Brad noticed that Vicki was in a funk. They were eating breakfast on the back patio, a practice they followed whenever the mornings were nice enough—and in California, most mornings were nice enough. That day, Lucia had made quiche. Vicki had a slice on her plate but just stared at it while sipping her coffee.

"Not hungry?" Brad spoke with his mouth full. He was nearly done with his first piece of quiche, and was planning on having a couple more slices before breakfast was over.

"I had a dream last night; I talked with Melly." Vicki toyed with her coffee.

Both Brad and his sister looked up.

"You do realize," Jessica said slowly, "that when Melly appears in your dreams, it's usually not just a dream—or at least not a regular one. Parts of your DNA have been activated, which means you're now open to kinds of communication you weren't before. So if Melly shows up, you should assume it was real.

"That's what I was afraid of," Vicki said morosely. She pushed her plate away.

"Do you want to talk with us about it?" Brad asked. He cocked her head to one side, waiting for a response. People told him that he looked just like his dad when he did that, which he hated hearing. But as much as he tried, he couldn't break the habit.

"We can't do it," Vicki burst out. "The Partnership is too powerful; they've had half a century of preparation—half a century working in secret—and we're just getting started. Half a century! And they have what amounts to unlimited wealth and resources. And hey, they also have an elite force of superhuman soldiers, plus technology that is so advanced the rest of humanity can't even begin to dream of it. We're supposed to somehow prevent them from doing what they're doing by the end of August?"

Her voice was getting higher and louder. She took a deep breath, poured herself another cup of coffee, and hunched over, unwilling to look at their faces.

"When you put it that way, it does sound hopeless," Jess said calmly.

Brad just served himself more quiche—you snooze, you lose.

"Wait, this doesn't bother you guys? I just explained why we are going to be a total failure—a total failure that will probably get us all *killed* if I didn't already make that abundantly clear—and you just sit there calmly eating breakfast?" Vicki looked at them, confused by their reaction. Their expressions held no dismay; they looked... understanding.

"We've all gone through the this-will-be-a-total-disaster phase," said Jessica.

Brad nodded, chewing. "All of us."

He didn't like to dwell on that—his own dark night of the soul. Everything had felt heavy and directionless. Getting out of bed had been a struggle. Conversations had drained him—it had taken him nearly a month to shake it off. And now it was happening to Vicki.

Brad knew that even though she was strong, there was no guarantee she'd bounce back quickly. But she *had* to. And they didn't have the luxury of a month—what lay ahead wouldn't wait for anyone to recover.

"What happened to move you out of your disaster phase?" Vicki asked.

"It helps to remember that the planet's vibration is already rising," he said. "A lot of people are going to reach higher levels of consciousness no matter what we do, so the momentum's in our favor. Whatever we manage to do—big or small—will just speed things up."

"So even if we only manage partial success—even just a small shift in how the Partnership operates—it'll still make a difference," Jess said. "We might not stop them completely right now, but we can slow them down. If we throw enough obstacles in their path, the planet's vibration will have time to rise before they can fully take control."

"When the Partnership draws up schedules and makes its plans, are they taking the rising vibration into consideration?" Vicki asked dryly.

Jess laughed. "I'm pretty sure they're not. They're probably completely unaware of it. Keep in mind the Partnership is an organization that worships technology. So even if someone there understands vibrations and how they could affect the Partnership's plans... and then they try to alert upper management? They'd be ridiculed—slapped down. It would be an absolute career killer."

Brad nodded. "And Melly and the Council are supporting us."

Vicki sat up alert. "I want to hear more about how—I'm really not interested in some random 'even if we lose, we win' philosophy."

She continued. "In my dream last night..." He and Jessica both glared at her, so she amended. "Last night in my conversation with Melly, she told me something similar—she said the Council would help us as long as it couldn't be traced back to an extraterrestrial source?"

It was clear she desperately wanted to believe this.

"That's right," said Brad. "If there are ETs involved, the Partnership would call it an invasion, and people would panic."

"Larry said something similar to me," Vicki said. "The Partnership would frame any involvement by aliens as an attack. And then the Partnership would step in and offer to protect the planet."

"At which point the Partnership would take full control," Brad agreed. He, James, and Jessica had already had this conversation—more than once—with Larry. But the fact remained: this had to be a human-led effort.

"How can Melly help us?" Vicki asked. "I'd like specifics—a list. I want to see a way forward that won't involve death for all of us."

"Getting our DNA activated was a good start," said Jessica.

"What we can do so far is really amazing, but that's not enough to keep us alive," said Vicki. "Being able to see around corners won't make us a match for superhuman soldiers."

"You don't know that. You still don't know how to work with whatever DNA has been activated in you—there are probably things going on you're not even aware of," said Brad.

He looked at his sister, and they both smiled.

"What?" Vicki asked, looking between them.

"You haven't noticed?" asked Brad.

She frowned at him. "If you would just please tell me what you two are talking about?"

"Look at the flowers," Jessica prompted. "Look at the flowers that are near you and the ones that are farther away. Compare them. Do you notice any differences?"

Vicki looked startled, but did as she was asked. The patio was surrounded by purple monkshood and orange lilies. She took a moment to enjoy them, then compared the flowers near her with those blooming on the other side of the patio.

"The flowers are all glowing, but the flowers near us are glowing more brightly," she said, surprise in her voice. "*Much* more brightly."

Brad and Jessica burst out laughing.

"You didn't notice—you didn't," said Brad, chortling.

"No, I didn't. But why do we care? Does it mean something?" Vicki asked, her expression confused.

"Vicki, the flowers aren't glowing more brightly around us; they're glowing more brightly around *you*," said Jessica, smiling. "In fact, you're glowing yourself."

"Like a lighthouse," said Brad.

Vicki stared at them in shock, then glanced down at her arms.

Brad saw her expression shift, the wheels turning in her head, as she noticed the slight luminescence radiating from her skin. Then she looked back at them, narrowing her eyes. Brad knew she could also see them glowing, albeit more faintly than she was.

"Would you care to explain?" she asked tightly. She appeared determined not to lose control.

"It's because of biophotons—photons of light in the ultraviolet and low visible light range. All people have them. Plants and animals too—all living things," said Jessica. "Normally, we can't see them at all."

"But since our DNA has been activated, we can? Just like we can now see colors that shouldn't even exist? Just like how we can see the flowers glow and the pigeons light up?"

"Exactly," said Brad, reaching over to take the last piece of quiche.

"Why didn't I notice this earlier?" Vicki asked. "I've been working with my activated DNA for a week. Wasn't this something I should have spotted?"

"Probably because we were having you practice so much with the chi," said Jessica, unconcerned. "Until you figure out exactly what a person's chi or energy looks like and feels like, you wouldn't be able to distinguish between chi energy and biophoton energy. It took me over a month."

"So why am I glowing brighter than you guys? And why did you say the flowers were reacting to me, not to you?"

"You're a lighthouse," repeated Brad. He'd said his piece. While he *could* say more, he didn't think it'd be useful.

Vicki scowled at him.

Jessica was more helpful. "Your biophotons are more visible because you're resonating at a higher level. We told you Melly hadn't planned to activate any special abilities in you, and she didn't. But she did make sure you had a stronger foundation in the basics."

"Which means...?"

"Energy and vibrations naturally sync up. That's what will happen during the Earth's vibrational shift—as the planet moves through a higher-vibrational part of the galaxy, it will begin to resonate at that same higher level. In the same way, just by sitting near these flowers while you're vibrating at a higher frequency, you're affecting their environment. The flowers are syncing with your energy and vibrating higher too. That's why they're glowing more brightly."

"That doesn't explain why you're not glowing more brightly even though I'm sitting right next to you," she said. "Doesn't this work on humans?"

"We're a more complicated life form; I'm sure it takes longer," said Brad. "But if we weren't operating on such a tight schedule, it'd be a cool experiment to send you into crowded movie theaters and see what happens."

Vicki stuck her tongue out at him.

He looked over at her still-untouched quiche. "Are you going to eat that?"

Chapter Thirteen

It was obvious to Vicki that Jess and Brad had mentioned her breakdown to the adults because after tai chi class, they went off with James, while Larry took her somewhere in his car—a bright blue Corvette. He was driving, and she didn't know where they were going.

He spoke first. "Just so you know, we are trying to find a way through all of this that does *not* include us dying."

"Glad to hear one of our goals is to stay alive. Do you have any idea how to do that?" she asked.

He steered around a corner. "Well, you're supposed to be our strategy expert."

"The strategy expert who is saying what we want to do is impossible," she snapped. "Maybe you guys should start listening to me."

He changed the subject. "You said you could detect my chi energy even though it's not moving; it's frozen. That you can still recognize me as human. Does your energy detection also include biophotons? Can you look at me and see me glow?"

She looked at him and concentrated. Concentrated hard, because he sounded so hopeful. "Sorry," she said, "I can't."

He shrugged, seemingly indifferent. "It was too much to expect. My cells were one hundred percent created by the Partnership, so there's no reason they would emit light. You can't have every-thing."

They drove in silence until he turned onto a tree-lined lane marked private. A tall, serious-looking fence was partially hidden by the trees, and she was pretty sure she saw a camera or two. Even-tually, they pulled up to a gate with a sturdy-looking guardhouse. Larry stopped and popped the hood without being asked, allowing a guard to check the engine. Another guard crouched down with a mirror device to inspect underneath the car. Larry rolled down his window as a third guard, carrying a clipboard, walked over.

"Larry, it's been a while since we've seen you here."

Larry was taking out his ID—it looked like a Partnership em-ployee identification card—so Vicki took out her driver's license. He handed them both over to the guard, saying, "I'm taking leave until the end of summer, but my friend"—he gestured at Vicki—"has never seen this before."

"Victoria Heywood." The guard read her driver's license sus-piciously and compared it against his clipboard, which she now saw was actually some sort of electronic tablet.

"She's with the Department of State, part of Kurt Martinsson's household this summer. She should have been cleared earlier; I think the paperwork was submitted a few weeks ago."

"Here she is." The guard made an entry on his tablet, handed their IDs back to Larry, and gave the sentries a thumbs-up. The gate opened, and they were motioned through.

"Is this where the Partnership has all its offices?" she asked, noticing a large warehouse as they drove up a long lane.

"Most of them. The compound spans 15 acres and includes corporate offices, research facilities, engineering labs, and several warehouses and showrooms. But they're well spaced out and have their own entrances, so everything is fairly well siloed."

She raised an eyebrow, and he clarified, "The programs and workgroups are physically isolated from one another, which means in-depth knowledge of the advanced technologies is restricted to the people who work on them. And, of course, there are other facilities in some very inaccessible places."

She didn't say anything but thought about the Partnership's base on Europa. Were there production facilities in space?

Larry continued, "Right now, we're going to an official exhibition space where the Partnership can show its devices to the government reps who draw up the contracts. They also give demonstrations to potential buyers or investors."

"And today," he said as he maneuvered into the parking lot, "is Family Day."

"Like, Take-Your-Kid-to-Work Day?" she asked.

"Pretty much. This is the first step in accustoming the kids to what they can expect if they choose a future with the Partnership. Makes it a lot easier to recruit internally."

"I'm not a government rep, a buyer, an investor, or a family member," she pointed out as they approached the door.

"But you have Top-Secret clearance, and you're looking after Kurt Martinsson's kids," Larry said. "He had you cleared for this ahead of time, after Brad and Jessica mentioned it might make a good outing. They're not actually interested since they've seen it before—but they knew you'd need to see it eventually." He opened the door for her.

And they stepped into a wonderland.

"It's magic," she said, awed.

"Weird science and freaking magic," confirmed Larry. "That's what they call it."

And it was.

The space—showroom—wasn't overly crowded. Small family and friend groups were moving from demonstration to demonstration. She turned to Larry.

"It's Family Day, but I don't see any children younger than their mid-teens?"

"Just a precaution," Larry nodded. "This is secret, after all. The Partnership doesn't want to risk the youngest kids talking about what they've seen. In families connected to the Partnership, Family Day is a rite of passage for when the kids turn thirteen. By that age, they're old enough to hold their tongues when they're lectured about the importance of secrecy."

Turning to watch a group of well-dressed young teens laughing and joking as they watched a presentation, he added, "It's also the age when they're old enough to enjoy feeling superior to everyone else."

Vicki barely heard him. She was heading over to an area where a man was demonstrating healing devices.

"This..." The lab-coated man waved a gadget over his head, ensuring that everyone watching had a clear view. The device was slightly larger than a mobile phone. "This is a pulse harmonizer. It oscillates at the same frequency as your body's subtle energy force. If something is wrong with your physical body, the pulse harmonizer can restore it to its original pattern."

Then people—Vicki included—screamed in shock when he took out a knife and plunged it into his hand.

"See my hand?" The man removed the knife and held his wounded hand up for everyone to see. Blood dripped down his arm, staining his white lab coat. For the most part, the audience was appalled.

"This is another reason why the little kids aren't allowed in," said Larry under his breath.

The man pushed a button on his pulse harmonizer gadget and held it over his hand.

It was amazing. Something flared, and there was his hand, whole and uninjured. He took a cloth and wiped the blood away. There was no mark where the knife had gone in. Astonished exclamations came from the young people. Their parents just looked on, smiling. The man took off his lab coat, threw it in the corner, and put on a new one. Vicki noticed a pile of bloodstained lab coats in that corner.

"I guess this wasn't the first time he gave that demonstration today," she whispered to Larry.

Now, the man was working with a volunteer from the audience—a young teenager with a serious case of acne. He stood in front of her, blocking their view while slowly moving his device over her face. Then, the big reveal: he stepped back so everyone could see. "Ta-da!"

Perfect, blemish-free skin. The girl's mother burst into tears. Members of the audience oohed and aahed.

"Let's see something else." Larry steered her to another booth.

In this station, the demonstrator—an upbeat woman wearing a blue jumpsuit with the Partnership's logo—cheerfully sliced a clean swath through a square of cloth. The cut edges fluttered briefly before she passed a shimmering, wand-like device over them, and the fabric knit itself back together with eerie precision, threads realigning in a ripple of gold and silver light. Without missing a beat, the woman then grabbed a section of her own hair and, with theatrical flair, chopped it off. Vicki's eyes widened. But again, the wand traced the break, and the severed hair—still limp and lifeless in the demonstrator's hand—rejoined her head, seamlessly reintegrated strand by strand.

Larry whispered, "It's called the quantum threader. Realigns atomic structure using sacred geometry protocols. Works on matter. Some say it even works on memory."

Vicki didn't respond. She was too busy watching the woman shake out her glossy, fully restored ponytail, trying to decide whether she was impressed—or unsettled.

At the next booth, Vicki saw someone she knew.

"Kiran!" She said, surprised to see Aija's brother leading demonstrations by himself. Wasn't he too young for this? Kiran looked at her curiously. "I'm staying with the Martinssons this summer," she reminded him.

His face cleared. "That's right, Vicki. I can call you Vicki, can't I?"

"I'm not that much older than you," she said, grumbling. He just grinned. "But I didn't realize you already worked with the Partnership. Aren't you still in college?"

"They took me right out of high school," said Kiran. "I was the first—the guinea pig."

"That's right, I remember Brad saying something about that."

"He'll probably be another one they take right out of high school. After how well he did during his shadowing, they'd be happy to take him now. But he's still a minor."

"How's your father doing?" Seeing the healing device jogged her memory of game night and his sister's mention of their father's upcoming treatment for a brain tumor.

"It went perfectly—in and out in an hour, no follow-up needed."

"What are you demonstrating today?" Larry interrupted, deftly changing the subject. Just as well; it wouldn't achieve anything for her to start obsessing about who did or did not have access to life-saving medical treatment.

"My department is working on a photonitron mechanism." He pronounced it photon-ee-tron. He motioned to a square box thingy sitting on the table in front of him. "Look at what we can do with it." Stepping toward her with a small object just a little larger than a cigarette lighter, Kiran asked, "May I?"

Vicki nodded.

Kiran took the device and... scanned her from head to toe, front to back. Then he inserted it into the box on the table and flipped a switch. At a desk and chair in the corner, "she" appeared. "She" sat down at the desk, opened a book, and began reading.

"What? How?" Vicki stuttered. She walked around the image—it was a full, solid-looking 3-D image of her, front and back. She put her hand on "her" shoulder, but it went right through.

"It works like a hologram projector." Kiran patted the box with a possessive gesture.

"But now you can manipulate the image to move independently of the original object?" Larry asked. "To do things the original object never did?"

"It took us two years, but we finally worked it out."

"Multiple images at a time?"

Kiran nodded, grinning, and indicated the desk and chair. "We set up this demonstration to show the kids how they can fool their parents into thinking they're studying."

Vicki laughed, but Larry's expression remained serious.

"What about the radar signature?"

At this, Kiran's face lost its cheerful expression. He looked straight at Larry. "Radar signature, too," he said.

Vicki's gut told her he was speaking the truth—and that he felt uncomfortable about it.

They moved on. There was a demonstration of an invisibility cloak that almost worked. The person wearing the cape wasn't completely invisible like in *Harry Potter*, but he did become less noticeable—if someone wasn't paying attention, they might not see him.

"Didn't the Japanese make one of these a few years back?" she asked Larry as they moved to the next exhibit.

"The Japanese did it with cameras and wires. This is done with metamaterials." In response to her unasked question, he added, "The material of the cloak was modified with nanostructures to move light around the cloak rather than reflecting it back to your eye. They still have a lot of work to do on it, though."

Of course, no tour of "weird science and freaking magic" would be complete without a free energy demonstration. Surprisingly, there wasn't much to look at—just rows of lightbulbs and spinning wheels with no visible power source. The presenter went on about "energy from the ether." But after witnessing bloody hands and watching one's own body seemingly walk around and sit down to study, this felt oddly underwhelming.

Chapter Fourteen

L arry thought Vicki had taken it pretty well—much better than he had hoped. He knew from experience that everyone went through a discouraged phase when facing this new reality, but there hadn't been time to let her work through it on her own. That was why the trip to the Partnership's Family Day had been the right call. It had snapped her out of it, and given her the push she needed.

Now, sitting in the passenger seat beside him, she looked like herself again. Her posture was upright, her eyes alert. She wasn't sulking, and she wasn't staring blankly out the window. Seeing her this way, Larry felt a wave of relief. The funk was gone, and he couldn't help but feel grateful—so much was depending on her.

Traffic on the highway moved steadily, sunlight flickering across the hood as they headed toward the Martinsson's place. For a while, Vicki was quiet. Larry kept his focus on the road, not asking questions. He didn't push—sooner or later she would voice whatever she was turning over inside.

"Flying saucers!" she suddenly said, breaking the silence. "Why didn't we see any flying saucers?"

"Those are demonstrated in a different location," said Larry. "One that isn't so heavily populated. Flying saucers require a lot of privacy."

"Privacy from the general population or from the government?" she asked, her tone sharpening.

"Now you're catching on." Larry smiled.

He thought it strange how vivid it still felt, even after all this time. Traveling in a flying saucer had been both thrilling and terrifying—those brief moments of weightlessness, suspended between worlds before the gravity field stabilizer kicked in. He could still picture the view through the ports—Earth below, small and breathtaking in its fragile beauty. There was a deep peace up there.

But that was in the past. He cleared his throat and forced his focus back to the present.

"What did you think of the tech we saw today?" he asked.

Vicki drew in a breath, as if sorting through all the demonstrations in her mind. "Pretty amazing, all of it, and it pisses me off. This knowledge and these devices would benefit everyone in the world. Instruments that can heal. Nonpolluting, limitless energy. Holograms... well, I'm not sure what we'd use Kiran's holograms for."

"I don't know what the world would use the holograms for, but I can tell you what the Partnership *will* use them for," Larry said evenly.

She turned toward him, one eyebrow raised.

"Think about it," Larry continued. "They can scan a single object and move the resulting hologram independently of any movement the original object has completed. And they can do multiple objects at the same time."

"I'm drawing a blank here," Vicki admitted.

"They also have a radar signature," Larry added, helpfully.

Her expression shifted as she remembered. "Kiran wasn't very happy about that," she said slowly. "But I don't know what it all means."

"It means," said Larry, his jaw tightening, "the Partnership can stage a false-flag event—not even a 'real' false-flag event; it can be an entirely imaginary false-flag event."

She shook her head. "You've lost me."

"The Partnership can scan one of their flying saucer vehicles—one that they reverse engineered from an alien craft. Then they can multiply it, project as many as they want, and make it look as if there was an entire fleet of invading extraterrestrials. Even our radar wouldn't be able to tell the difference. From the outside, it will look like we're being attacked. And when the panic sets in, the Partnership will step forward as humanity's savior. They'll 'defend' us, and take control of everything."

Vicki sat back in her seat, staring out window. Her mind was racing. "I think we just figured out what the Partnership plans to do at the end of summer," she said.

* * *

I've finally made it.

Those words ran through Amanda's head as she stepped through the wide entry doors of the Partnership's warehouse, her media badge swinging from a lanyard. The badge wasn't official press clearance—it had been arranged with a quick phone call from her uncle, Colonel David Riley, who worked in the Pentagon's Office of the Secretary of Defense. He had even provided her plane tickets and booked the hotel.

She hadn't really understood what she was coming to see, or why it mattered so much to her uncle. What she *did* understand was the crazy amount of effort he had put into making her realize how exclusive the event was, making sure she knew only a handful had the chance to be there. For that reason, she had spent the whole morning rehearsing how she would carry herself—how not to stand out, how not to look like an outsider. She had chosen her clothes carefully: a fitted blazer over a plain blouse, dark slacks, and low heels. Professional, not flashy. The way she imagined established journalists dressed when covering serious assignments. She had even taken extra time with her hair and makeup, aiming for polished instead of glamorous. Every choice was careful and deliberate—meant to show that she belonged among the insiders.

But the moment she stepped into the massive warehouse, all her anxiety vanished, and in its place came the rush of possibility. The sheer scale of the room—the sense that she was on the threshold of something extraordinary—strengthened her conviction that she was exactly where she was supposed to be. For Amanda, this wasn't just access—it was the beginning of taking her media career to the next level.

Rows of tables stretched across the floor, each one displaying some new piece of technology. Some looked like advanced medical devices. Others resembled weapons or specialized military equipment. Screens glowed with data, diagrams, and images. Scientists in lab coats and executives in tailored suits gave demonstrations to small family groups—her uncle had cautioned her this was an in-house event. The entire hall buzzed with restrained pride, the confidence of people who knew they were being shown knowledge denied to the outside world.

Amanda's heart raced. She was inside that circle now, seeing what the rest of the world couldn't. That thought alone gave her a surge of satisfaction. This was the kind of access that built reputations. The producers and bureau chiefs who had tried to dismiss her—they weren't here. She was.

She wandered past a demonstration where a man used a diagnostic wand on a volunteer's arm. The monitor displayed bone density, blood flow, and even highlighted an injury. Amanda leaned in closer, fascinated. If she so much as hinted at this in an article, it would explode across the media. Editors wouldn't be able to ignore it. But her uncle's warning stayed with her: the Partnership blacklisted people who leaked. For now, she had to play it safe, observe, and take careful notes. This event wasn't about breaking a story right away—it was about preparing her. Her uncle had wanted her here so she would have the background knowledge to draw on later, when the time came to report on the Partnership in a way that mattered. The thought thrilled her. He wasn't just indulging her ambition—he was grooming her for something bigger, something that would set her apart from every other journalist still scrambling for crumbs.

She moved on, her notebook in hand, writing down descriptions in shorthand. The word *breakthrough* appeared again and again on the display placards. She imagined how it would look in her future columns: "The Breakthrough Generation," "The Breakthrough Society." Already the phrases rolled around in her mind as potential headlines. This was exactly the kind of inside access she had dreamed about. Other junior reporters fought for scraps at city hall meetings or charity events. She was standing at the front edge of history.

She stopped in front of a device called the photonitron. A young man—about her own age, maybe a little older—was giving a presentation to a small crowd. He explained that it could create multiple images of the same object, indistinguishable from reality. He didn't even use a screen. In the space behind his table, a single desk multiplied into three, then five, then ten, until it appeared there was an entire classroom ready. From any angle, the images looked real. The audience gasped. Amanda scribbled furiously. The implications were obvious—entertainment, politics, deception, warfare. She thought again of headlines, of talk show panels, of herself as the voice of a new era in journalism.

Amanda straightened her shoulders. She was already part of it. She was here, inside the Partnership's warehouse, seeing what billions of ordinary people would never know existed. They would go on with their small lives—commuting, paying bills, sitting in waiting rooms hoping for medicine that didn't yet exist—while she was here, inside the real future. She felt a surge of superiority. Those people didn't matter.

They were the audience, while she was stepping onto the stage.

A group of engineers walked past, laughing quietly at some joke. Amanda imagined herself walking with them, one of the insiders who knew what the Partnership was capable of. She glanced at her notebook again, and a flush of pride rose in her chest. This wasn't just luck. This was the result of ambition, persistence, and her uncle's belief in her potential. Colonel Riley had told her that Disclosure was a reckless idea pushed by people who didn't understand the risks. He had said that keeping control of information was what kept societies stable. Amanda didn't care much about the philosophy of it. What mattered was that he had opened the door, and she had walked through it.

She paused near another table where two men in suits—clearly higher ranking—were talking about deployment schedules. She caught only fragments of their conversation, but it was enough to confirm what she already guessed. The Partnership wasn't just experimenting. It was preparing. Everything here would eventually be put to use, and she would be one of the first to tell the world, or at least the part of the world they chose to let in on the secret.

Amanda's thoughts quickened. She could be more than just a reporter. She could make herself indispensable to them. She could offer them favorable coverage or help shape public perception about whatever story they wanted told. She knew how to frame things—what to emphasize, what to bury, and what to spin into a narrative that would look good on the evening news.

If they wanted to maintain secrecy, she could do that too, feeding the public only as much as the Partnership decided was safe. That way, she wouldn't just be reporting on them; she would be guiding the message and controlling the conversation. The thought made her pulse quicken. She pictured herself standing beside the very people shaping the future. She would be the woman who knew everything and parceled out pieces of the truth on her own terms.

And if she made herself useful enough, they would keep inviting her back. She would have a seat at the table, access to what no other journalist—or politician—would have. And from there, her name wouldn't just appear on bylines. It would be remembered long after others were forgotten.

Chapter Fifteen

The young people skipped their advanced tai chi class that evening. Instead, they gathered with Larry and Vicki on the Martinssons' back patio to hear the debrief about the visit to the Partnership's showroom.

Debrief? Vicki supposed she was now looking at this as some sort of military campaign.

"I'd like Vicki to give us her impressions first," said Larry. "She's the newcomer and might notice something that is so everyday to us that we take it for granted."

"Weird science and freaking magic," Vicki said, nodding.

Everyone grinned. Yes, it was being used for destructive purposes, but it was hard not to be delighted these things actually existed. It was a reminder that the universe was totally amazing—something she'd lost sight of this past year.

"Anything else?" Larry asked dryly.

"There was a lot of security—a lot of emphasis on keeping everything secret. But I was surprised the guards weren't carrying weapons."

"They were," said Larry. "Do you remember seeing those silver rods attached to their belts?"

She nodded. She recalled thinking those were the thinnest flashlights she had ever seen.

"Those were actually weapons—serious weapons. They disrupt blood cells in the organs. If a guard pointed one at you and discharged it, you would bleed to death from the inside out within a few short minutes."

"Oh," Vicki said, a bit subdued.

"There were also cameras all over the property, all of them monitored in real-time. And the things on the ceiling in the showroom that looked like a sprinkler system?"

She nodded again.

"They're nonlethal weapons—sonic broadcast devices. If they had been triggered, everyone in the showroom would have been knocked unconscious and dropped to the floor like rocks."

"Maybe not you," said Brad, sotto voce. The young people snickered.

"Maybe not," Larry agreed calmly. Evidently, there were advantages to being a biologic construct. "What else, Vicki?"

"The invisibility cloak—we could still see the man who was wearing it. I was surprised the Partnership hadn't figured that one out yet. After all, you guys can disappear in a closed room while doing tai chi."

"They'll probably never be able to perfect invisibility," said Brad with confidence. "It requires shifting into another reality or dimension. That's tough to pull off with tech alone. But people—we can do it when our vibration is high enough."

"So, the super-soldiers won't ever become invisible," added James.

Vicki had to fight not to glance over at Larry.

"And Kiran's photonitron mechanism was cool," she continued. "I wouldn't have known the hologram wasn't real had I not seen it myself—and if the hologram had been of anything else but me."

"It's now capable of broadcasting multiple images, all moving independently and all giving off their own radar signatures," interjected Larry.

There was a quick intake of breath by the three young people. Apparently, Vicki was the only one in the group who couldn't figure out the military implications without having them explained.

"Kiran was not feeling happy about the radar signature thing with his hologram device," she felt honor-bound to add. "He told the truth about it but felt guilty."

"Kiran is a good guy," said Brad. "I'd feel guilty too if I were helping to develop a product I thought was going to be made into a weapon—one that would be used against the rest of the world."

"Is there any way we can use—?" Larry began, when Vicki sat up straight, suddenly alert. Was she sensing a presence? She noticed Brad, Jess, and James had also sat up. Not so much Larry, but seeing their reactions, he jumped to his feet and spun around—fast. The man's reflexes were lightning-quick.

"Melly!" said James, excited.

The extraterrestrial being stood several feet away, wearing her usual burgundy cloak. Vicki got the impression of soft gongs.

The young people and Vicki went over to welcome Melly. She noticed Larry remained where he was.

"Larry, why are you standing there? Why aren't you coming forward to greet Melly?"

"I can't," he said, watching Brad steeple his hands over the first bend in Melly's forelegs. There was longing on his face. "I don't deserve to; I'm not human."

"Umm, I still recognize your DNA as human. Didn't we have this conversation earlier? And Melly herself is definitely not human. Is it some sort of law that a person who is a biologic construct can't say hi to an alien?"

Vicki almost didn't hear his reply, so low and quiet was his voice: "I don't have that right."

Enough of this. Been there, done that—she recognized a pity party when she saw it. She reached over and yanked his arm. Larry was unbelievably powerful as a biologic construct—she couldn't drag him anywhere against his will. However, her action was so unexpected that he had to take a step forward to keep his balance.

"Come with me," she hissed. Her hand was on his arm.

She didn't think he heard her; his eyes were focused on Melly. Two more steps, and Vicki was the next one to greet the alien. "Melly," she said, steepling her hands over a foreleg. This was the first time for her. Melly's skin—was it skin?—felt cool, textured, and leathery.

"Vicki," said Melly with a quiet overlay of bells. "I've been happy to observe your progress."

Progress? What progress? Vicki asked as much.

"You haven't run away—you chose to persist despite the challenges. To arrive at that decision, you had to define who you are—you had to decide what you believe in and how you want to live. This is the most important decision anyone can make."

Vicki was going to ask her how that would help in a battle against an all-powerful consortium with super-soldiers and technology that was literally out of this world, but Melly turned to Larry. She couldn't smile, but the bells felt joyful.

"Larry, I am pleased to meet you properly at last."

Larry stepped forward, a poker face on, and carefully steepled his hands on Melly's foreleg. "Melly."

"Like Vicki, you have decided how you want to live your life. Welcome."

"But I'm not truly alive; I'm just a construct." His voice was so soft, Vicki barely heard him.

"Yes, you are damaged," said Melly. Larry wilted a little bit hearing that. "But all humans are damaged. That is what we are striving to overcome—to bring humanity back to wholeness. You have an important role to play if you so choose."

These words about choosing to accept a role took Vicki back to her first meeting with Melly when she had been told the same thing. Were they all just trying on different roles throughout life, like outfits they eventually outgrew or tossed aside? Could it really be that simple? Did people stay stuck because they didn't realize they *had* a choice?

She thought about her own life—what she'd done, what she hadn't, the choices that had led her to this moment, sitting here talking to an alien. At what point had she started to go down this path? At what point had she decided to become herself?

By this time Larry had stepped back. He looked... calmer, more at peace. James casually edged up to his side and gave him a one-armed hug.

"See? We all told you—you've been stressing for nothing," James said, a bit of a smile creeping in. He looked more relaxed, also, now that his own worry about his uncle was fading.

"Melly," said Jessica. "We think the Partnership is planning to launch activities at the end of summer. Can you tell us whether we're right?"

"You are correct," responded Melly. "It's time to get ready."

All of them wore identical expressions of confusion.

"Isn't that what we've been doing?" asked Brad. Truthfully, he looked a bit put out, as if his efforts to date had been overlooked.

"There are specific things we need to discuss today," replied Melly. "First of all, I must direct Vicki to remove her shoes."

"Now?" Vicki asked, disconcerted.

Melly continued on as if she hadn't heard the question.

"A part of your DNA that's been activated is tied to Earth energies," she said. "It's important for you to open up to that knowledge—and then go even further, strengthening your connection to the planet itself. A physical connection will help with that. Tapping into Earth energies will be crucial when the Four face the Partnership."

"The Kick-Ass Quartet," Brad corrected under his breath.

Melly turned toward Jessica. "We need to begin work on the presentation you spoke of earlier. It's a good plan. When the time comes, you will have it ready."

Vicki's mind drew a blank. She looked over at Jess. "What presentation?"

"Finally!" Jessica pumped her fist in the air. "Finally, it's my turn!"

"Jess?"

"What Melly calls a presentation will actually be a series of videos where I interview her, ask questions, and invite her to talk about extraterrestrials and how they view humanity." Jessica looked excited, and confident, like the person she was meant to be.

Vicki didn't want to throw water on her plan, but it had some serious flaws, chiefly that this would be an amateur production and the audience would be limited.

"The mainstream media won't air it. Are we seriously counting on YouTube and Facebook to get the word out? I doubt the viewership will be enough."

Jess was in such high spirits she laughed out loud. "I'm sure Brad can help with that."

Brad was smiling too. "Computer expert," he said, pointing to himself. "Computer expert who has accessed information through my activated DNA, teaching me how to broadcast these videos on all the major networks without anyone being able to do a thing to stop us."

"Hacker," Vicki said, smiling approvingly.

"Super-hacker," James corrected. He and Brad bumped fists.

The others gathered around Melly and Jessica as the two talked about their plans to film the interviews. Vicki watched them, not paying attention to what was being said. Why was she supposed to take off her shoes?

She left the patio and walked over to a small group of trees. She wasn't as good at tree identification as she was with flowers, but these were clearly willows. She sat down against one, removing her shoes and digging her feet into the dirt. How was she supposed to connect with Earth energies? There was a distressing lack of instruction manuals surrounding all of this.

Maybe meditation? She closed her eyes, sank into herself, and slowed her breathing. After a few minutes, she got that floaty feeling and tentatively pictured herself sending out a beam—a radio signal—to the Earth. She sensed a faint feeling of a question, but before she could figure it out, the energy of the tree grabbed hold of her and drew her *into* itself.

She was now that tree. She could feel her feet—her roots—digging deep into the dirt, anchoring her and bringing her the energy she needed to stay healthy. She could feel her leaves spreading in the sun and soaking up everything they needed. She could feel her trunk and branches—strong conduits between the Earth and the air.

She suddenly realized that communication wasn't a narrow radio beam, like she had first imagined. It was more like sunlight—always present, surrounding and enveloping everything. Just as sick leaves absorb less sunlight than healthy ones, stunted DNA couldn't take in as much knowledge as DNA that was open and resonating. All the information anyone could need was already swirling around them, every second of every day. Once people raised their vibration, they'd be able to access all of it.

She stayed there sitting with the tree; everything she needed was inside her.

Chapter Sixteen

B y the time Vicki got up and went inside, it was dark. Apparently, she had spent several hours communing—or something. She went hunting for whoever was still at the house.

She stuck her head in the entertainment room. Brad and James were playing a video game.

"Hey, guys." They didn't notice. She spoke up louder, "Hey, guys!"

Startled, they both looked up, and Brad paused the game. "You're back," he said. "What'd you think?"

"I'm not sure what to think," she said. "I have questions. Who would have the best explanations?"

"I'm pretty sure Melly is still here. She's with Jess in the studio."

There was a studio in the house? Another perk of being rich, she supposed. After getting some general directions from Brad, she wandered down a couple of hallways and eventually found it. Even though it was just an amateur setup in a private home, it had a *Recording in Progress* sign on the door, complete with a red light bulb next to it. The light wasn't on, so she knocked gently and stepped inside.

Jessica and Melly both looked up.

They were seated on what was clearly a set, with cameras aimed at them and a bland, neutral background behind. But were they really both *seated*? Jessica was definitely in a chair, but Melly... how exactly did a giant insect sit? She was more *inclined* on a short, upward-tilted divan, which made her seem just slightly taller than Jess instead of towering over her by a couple of feet. It worked well for the cameras—and probably helped ease viewer anxiety, too. Between them was a desk with a computer setup, and they were both focused on watching a video.

"Vicki," said Jessica, waving her over. "Come see what we've been able to do."

"We have three forty-minute programs so far," Jess added, pointing at the screen. "We're using a talk show format."

Vicki bent forward to take a better look. Sure enough, Jess and Melly were having a discussion, looking for all intents and purposes like a talk show host and guest.

"Three, just tonight?" she asked.

Jessica nodded. "The first video covers why extraterrestrials are here—the current situation, including what the Partnership has been doing and why the Council isn't happy with them. In the second video, we discuss the shift in vibration and what abilities humans will be able to access via their DNA—all without using technology controlled by the Partnership. The third program is more of a human-interest segment, covering Melly and her people, a few other ET species, and the history of extraterrestrials on Earth."

This third episode was what was playing on the computer. Vicki leaned in closer to hear it.

- **JESSICA:** Melly, you previously stated that the Galactic Council frowns upon other species interfering in the development of a specific planet. Despite this, there has been considerable extraterrestrial involvement in human history on Earth. How did that happen?

- **MELLY:** The catalyst was an accident. Nearly three

hundred thousand years ago, a research expedition from the Alpha Centauri region came to Earth—research expeditions are permitted within strict guidelines. But while they were here, something catastrophic happened to their vessel, and it crashed into the sea just off the southwest corner of Australia. Of course, it wasn't Australia back then, but it's still there a mile or two beneath the ocean floor. You could still find it if you looked.

- **JESSICA:** Oh my gosh. Did everyone die?

- **MELLY:** Not everyone. About five hundred researchers and scientists were living at a base camp set up on an island on your planet when the vessel was destroyed. While they had technology, shelter, and a few small scout vessels capable of flying around the planet, they no longer had effective communication—that had been destroyed along with their main ship. It took decades for the message with news of the disaster to reach their home planet and many more decades before a rescue could be launched—this all happened before many of our more advanced travel methods were developed. But by the time rescue arrived, some of the Alpha Centaurian survivors had integrated themselves into life on Earth. They looked very much like humans, you see.

- **JESSICA:** Just to clarify, the beings from Alpha Centauri were not members of your own species; they were not insectoids.

- **MELLY:** No, they very much resembled the humans

who already lived on Earth, but taller. They were also, to a certain extent, biologically compatible. Please keep in mind that during the years they awaited rescue, most survivors continued to live in the camp. However, the wait lasted several generations, so they had to enlarge the camp over a number of islands and build permanent structures. Other individuals, however, decided to live with humans, and this had a major effect on human development, both technically and genetically.

- **JESSICA:** I'm getting serious Atlantis vibes here.

- **MELLY:** No, this was what you now refer to as Lemuria—it was in an area northwest of Australia, not very far from where the original expedition ship crashed. After the rescue ship finally arrived and took the survivors on board, all evidence of the camp was destroyed in accordance with Galactic Federation guidelines. However, many of the survivors and their descendants who were living in human societies preferred to remain on Earth. This was not allowed, but the rescue ship was not equipped to track down and capture fugitives. After first attempting to persuade these survivors and then unsuccessfully trying to force them, the rescue ship returned to Alpha Centauri.

- **JESSICA:** This story is amazing, but we're out of time. Can we revisit this topic in another episode?

- **MELLY:** The Council anticipated that humanity would have many questions. To ensure everyone is able to obtain the same factual information, the

Council has issued a document that will be made available to anyone who wishes to read it: *The Book of Disclosure: Project Earth.*

Vicki's first impression was that it seemed pretty strange to hear Melly talking because, in the video, there was no overlay of bells and gongs. Maybe that was something that just happened in person? It also seemed as if she had been practicing for this—her words were less stilted than when she spoke to them face-to-face. Melly's eyes were still normal, though, with their whirling iridescent colors. Vicki laughed to herself at what she now considered normal.

The video contained a few more minutes of Jessica chatting with Melly; then it ended. Jessica turned to Vicki.

"What do you think?" She looked happy. She looked complete.

"I think I'd appreciate a pre-release of your programs." Vicki smiled at her. "Could you send them to me? Would that be possible?"

Jessica glanced at Melly. "Can we? Would there be any security risks if I emailed them to Vicki?"

"As long as she views the videos while staying in this building, there will be no problems," said Melly. "Brad has installed a very secure network here."

Once again, Vicki felt the overlay of bells and gongs. It was somehow reassuring.

"Melly, I have a few questions. Can we talk?"

"We're done here, so if you two want to stay here and talk, have at it. I'm going to bed." Jessica switched off her laptop and a couple of other devices, then left the room.

Vicki looked over at Melly. She was still reclining on her divan; it was nice to have her at eye level rather than looming overhead.

"Yes, Vicki?"

Now that they were alone, Vicki was having a hard time putting it into words.

"You told me I needed to be barefoot—that I needed to establish a stronger connection to Earth energies. So, I meditated under a tree for a couple of hours."

"And what did you experience?"

"I sensed movement—it was like the entire planet was breathing. And I could see energy lines, gravity wells, and the magnetic field!"

She was almost hyperventilating. While in meditation, this had all seemed normal—amazing but reasonable. Now, after the fact, she was spooked.

"Instead of saying you 'saw' something, use 'observed' or 'detected.' This will help normalize your experience."

Vicki mentally substituted the words as Melly suggested. Melly was right— it really helped her see things differently. She took a breath to settle herself and asked the big question:

"Melly, is the Earth alive?"

"Not in the way your scientists define life, but yes, the Earth is conscious."

"Conscious, like a person is conscious?"

Melly paused for a minute, carefully choosing her words. "Your planet does not think as humans do, but it does know itself. Imagine Earth as the largest whale in the universe, swimming slowly through the cosmos, singing its song as it goes along its way. This is your planet as it experiences itself."

Goodness. Vicki had not realized Melly had the soul of a poet. Melly continued in a more practical vein:

"By observing your planet's energies, you are learning about the natural forces that exist here in your reality. As you establish a better connection with your planet—as you are able to better communicate with Earth—you will become capable of handling or directing many of these energies yourself."

Vicki was sure Melly had just given her some very important information, but she was still focused on consciousness and thought.

"So, are other things conscious? Trees? Mountains? Water?" She didn't bother asking about anything in the animal kingdom; modern science was already conducting research on animals that were able to recognize themselves in mirrors.

Melly laughed, the feeling of small bells. "Consciousness is not an attribute possessed solely by those who move and breathe. Yes, trees are conscious. Water is conscious. Mountains are conscious. Not entirely in the way humans are conscious—for example, a rock does not ask itself whether that strip of granite makes it look fat—but they have a self-awareness of what they are and how they connect to all things."

Okay, a poet with a sense of humor.

"You said our planet doesn't think like humans do, but does it have any impressions of us at all? Is it aware that people are living on its surface?" Vicki almost didn't want to hear the answer; human beings had been rather cavalier about how they treated the Earth.

"Your planet is aware of humans as sparks of life that exist within its energies. That life is valued. But it is also aware that some of these life sparks act in ways that are destructive to its energies. That problem will be resolved soon enough."

"Really, how? Can some of the Partnership's technology be used to clean up pollution?"

"It can," replied Melly, "but the problem would still be resolved even if it were not. The Earth will soon experience a change in vibration."

"Yes, I've been told."

"Listen to me, Vicki; the Earth itself will go through a change in vibration. Your planet is conscious, and when it changes its vibration, just like humans, it will discard that which it no longer finds beneficial."

"Earth will discard humans? Will it shrug us off, attack us somehow? We'll die?" Vicki was suddenly horrified.

"Some will," Melly seemed unworried, "but no more than if the Partnership succeeds in continuing on its current path."

Okay, the soul of a poet, a sense of humor, and in possession of an amazing amount of sangfroid.

"When humanity changes its vibration, it must do so in cooperation with the Earth. That is what will help more people survive. Otherwise..." Melly didn't complete her thought.

That wasn't ominous, thought Vicki. *Not ominous at all.*

Chapter
Seventeen

The next morning, Brad, Jessica, and Vicki arrived early at the tai chi studio. Each carried a travel cup of coffee. The door was still locked, so they sat on a bench out front. Larry pulled up in his Corvette and came over to where they were sitting.

"The Coopers are running late; they should be here in a few minutes."

Brad held up his phone. "We got the message."

Larry looked at him. "So, about Kiran..."

Brad suddenly tensed up. "He's a good guy; I don't want to ruin his life."

Brad knew that having Kiran on their side would be a big help, but he wasn't sure whether approaching Kiran felt more like a betrayal or a job requirement—maybe it was both. Kiran had always been a friend, but he was also part of the machine they were trying to take down—the Partnership. Even so, Brad couldn't shake the feeling that Kiran was still reachable, that the friend he'd known for years—the one who believed in honor, in doing what was right—was in there somewhere.

"You say he's a good guy," said Larry, sounding a little exasperated. "Don't you think a good guy would want to help us?"

"It's just that it will cut him off from his family. They immigrated to the U.S. only a decade ago and are very tight-knit. His parents' entire lives have been dedicated to improving their kids' lives and helping relatives back home—he talks about it all the time. Both his parents work for the Partnership, and his family believes they owe their success to the company. To break away from the Partnership—to join in our fight—would be seen as a betrayal not just of the organization, but of everything his family has worked for."

Brad shuddered, "If Kiran does something that will destroy his family's finances and status?" He'll be cast out from both his family and his community. The cost for him is very, very high."

Larry took a deep breath, and Brad saw the shift happen. Larry often said they all needed to move past their family roles to do their jobs effectively, and Brad realized that moment had come. Larry wasn't seeing him as his teenage nephew's best friend anymore—he was seeing him as a colleague, a teammate with a critical role to play.

"Brad," said Larry, no trace of emotion on his face. "You need to step up to the plate. If Kiran doesn't assist us, we could fail. And we could fail disastrously. Keep that in mind."

Brad hunched his shoulders, and stared unhappily at his coffee.

"Exactly what do we need Kiran to do?" asked Jessica.

Brad knew she was deliberately taking the attention off him so he'd have time to pull himself together.

"That photonitron device his office has developed," said Larry. "We need one."

"What would we do with it?" asked Vicki, now interested.

"So very many things," said Larry, almost talking to himself. "We could use scanned images to confuse, mislead, and hide."

He looked at them. "The Four can detect the energy of people. The Partnership can't. They won't be able to tell the difference between holograms with a radar signature and a real person. We can use a photonitron device to make it look like we're somewhere else. We can create an imaginary crowd out of thin air and hide within it."

"Is there any chance we could get scanned images of Partnership employees?"asked Vicki.

Larry's head whipped around to look at her, and his expression became thoughtful. "That's an interesting idea. Can we do it, Brad?"

By this time, he had squared his shoulders and was sitting up straight. He was no longer a gawky teenager; Brad was now a person who was figuring out how to do his job.

"I don't think I'll be able to manage it immediately; I'll need a few days of lead time. But I'll put in a request to shadow Kiran starting next week. Actually, maybe I should make it more official and request an internship."

"Does his office want you to intern with them?" Vicki asked. "And could something be arranged so quickly? I would have imagined an organization like the Partnership would be wallowing in red tape and bureaucracy.

"Genius computer expert," teased Jessica, lightly bumping Brad's shoulder." All the departments fought over him when he was there during spring break."

Brad smiled weakly. "The Partnership is always looking for talent—talent they can trust. The fact that Kiran and I are friends will make it easier to arrange. It wouldn't be totally out of line for me to want to spend part of my summer break gaining work experience in the same office where my buddy is working."

Larry gave a quick nod, as if it were a done deal. Brad hoped he was right.

* * *

The sound of a horn announced the arrival of the Cooper family in their minivan. After some horseplay between Brad and James, Mona retired to the office, and the rest of them went to the classroom. In deference to Vicki's rookie status—and her rookie tai chi abilities—Calvin was still leading them in simple movements.

She didn't know what the others thought about that, but personally, she had no complaints. She liked the movements; they helped her focus on her chi. Calvin began with cloud hands.

"Close your eyes and start slowly shifting from side to side." They did so. "Now begin circling your arms, holding in your mind the feeling of chi flowing down your arms and into your hands."

The tingly feeling quickly developed, and soon, Vicki was once again in the mist. The first time she had traveled there, Melly had described this space as a dimension between dimensions—a gathering place outside the strictures of linear time. She was expecting to see Melly, but instead, saw James, Brad, and Jessica. Their "bodies"—like hers—were misty, sparkling replicas of their physical forms.

What actually constituted a body? Did it matter whether it was physical or energetic? Maybe reality was a misty, sparkly essence, and physical bodies were just temporary shapes used to have adventures. Vicki wondered whether there really much of a difference between Larry and the rest of them.

"The Four, all together for the first time in the cloud plane!" Jessica sounded delighted.

"The Kick-Ass Quartet," said Brad in a singsong voice. The rest ignored him.

Vicki looked around. "What are we supposed to—" But then the shape she identified as Melly took form, and she didn't finish her question.

"I give welcome to the Four." The feeling of gongs with a soft overlay of bells.

"The Kick-Ass Quartet." But this time, Brad said it under his breath. He seemed reluctant to let his snark out in front of the extraterrestrial.

They all approached and steepled their hands over one of Melly's forelegs in formal greeting. There was no leathery feel to her foreleg in this state. Instead, Vicki could "feel" energy and chi moving together in some agreed-upon pattern that gave shape to the form they were identifying as Melly.

Interesting. Strange.

"Will you be available for more episodes soon?" Jessica was still riding high on yesterday's experience, and rightly so. The night before, Vicki had watched the first three videos in their entirety; the interviews were informative, professional, and reassuring. She wasn't sure how Jess had achieved the reassuring part of it, but it would go a long way toward calming down whatever panic people felt when the existence of ETs and their role on Earth was disclosed.

"I will come to your studio this evening. We need to have several more episodes ready to help carry out Disclosure." Melly's eyes were doing their polychromatic whirling thing. Vicki was actually growing fond of it.

"Are we here for more training?" asked James.

"More training?" Vicki mouthed to Jessica.

Jessica moved to stand beside her. "The boys and I have been here together a few times already. We were each here separately when Melly activated our DNA, but from then on, it was together, so we'd all have the same information."

Vicki nodded.

"Today is for demonstrating what can be done in this state of existence." A soft echo of Tibetan singing bowls. "Previously"—Melly glanced at the three young people when she said this—"we used this space to practice and train. Now, we will learn about the possibilities this space offers."

The others looked as clueless as Vicki felt, but then she sensed a presence forming. She looked at the sparkling mist condensing, then—"Beth!" she screamed.

Vicki was sobbing as she rushed over to where her sister stood and threw her arms around her. Beth's form was whole and healthy—exactly as she had appeared before the cancer had taken her life. Long hair held back in a ponytail, her face no longer cadaverous.

She returned Vicki's hug. "It's all right," she murmured. "I'm fine, we're fine."

Vicki couldn't stop crying. Melly turned to address the astonished young people. "We are in a meeting place outside of linear time. The rules for reality in your dimension do not apply here."

Jessica and Brad looked at each other. It was Jess who stepped up, her face suddenly hopeful. "If Vicki's sister can be here..." She swallowed and continued, "Our mom?"

Melly's voice, when she answered, was gentle, the feeling of soft gongs. "Vicki's sister had a role in this." Their faces fell; they understood they would not be seeing their mother. "Beth's part has been completed, but she agreed to appear in her energetic form to demonstrate the possibilities of nonlinear time."

Vicki had stopped crying by now, but had slung her arm over Beth's shoulders. "Guys, meet my little sister, Beth—LA's most talented florist." Then it registered what Melly had said, and she looked at Beth in disbelief. "You were working with Melly on all this? You never mentioned it!"

Beth smiled. "It was complicated—is complicated. And confusing. I'm not sure what happened when, or if it's still happening now as we speak. Back in real-time," she put air quotes around 'real-time,' "I've just gotten the news there's nothing more that the doctors can do for me, and you're rushing to get your leave-of-absence approved. So, in my reality, I'm alive. In your reality, I've already died."

Vicki walked with her a little away from the others. "You look great, Beth; healthy, like before you got sick."

"We're both sparkling mist forms, and you're telling me I look like I did back then?" she laughed.

Her laugh. Suddenly, Vicki's chest felt tight, and she was having a hard time breathing—she had missed her so much.

"You know what I mean."

"This is who I am, Vicki. Cancer changed me, but it wasn't me."

"What were you doing with Melly? She said your role–whatever you were doing—is complete. If you're done working with her, will you be able to come back here again?" Tears threatened, but she held them back.

Beth reached over and touched her cheek. "Unlike you—and I am so proud of you for what you're doing now—I didn't do anything different. My contribution was only to give my permission to Melly to rearrange the timing of something. And no, we won't see each other regularly here, at least not now. But keep in mind that a vibrational shift is coming."

"We'll be able to see each other then?" Vicki wanted a promise.

"More like our energies and vibrations will meet. It will be different, but you'll know."

"Beth, I miss you; I need you here. Energies and vibrations—that's too 'New Age-y' for me. I need you."

Beth gave one last smile and stepped back. Vicki felt tears threatening again, but she held them back—she didn't want to blur the final moments she had with her sister. She had a sense of what was coming. Sure enough, Beth's sparkles began to fade, and soon her form disappeared entirely. Vicki stood silently, staring at the misty space where her sister had just been. After a few minutes, she turned back to the others. They had been studiously ignoring Beth and Vicki as they talked, giving the sisters their privacy.

"So, can we use this space to time travel?" It was Brad who was geeking out. "Maybe we could go back to the moment when the Partnership was just getting started and derail it somehow."

"But this is not time travel," said Melly. "This is a pocket out-of-time, a crossroads; neither we nor Vicki's sister inserted ourselves into the other's timeline. Even Council members rarely do it, if ever. The danger of mismanaging the situation and making things worse is recklessly high."

"But what did Beth do?" Vicki was still focused on her sister. Her emotions were lurching between joy and anguish, with a touch of despair thrown in for good measure.

"She did nothing more than live her life, but she allowed me to carry that to another time. James had a role in this, although he was unaware."

The Martinsson siblings and Vicki turned as one to look at James, who, in turn, was looking confused. He held up his hands in a gesture of surrender. "I swear I have no clue about any of this. I don't know what she's talking about."

Vicki looked at Melly, still feeling a little raw. "Could you clarify?"

"It will become clear at a later time. Today's demonstration was about possibilities and was intended to stimulate your thinking. Vicki, you are an excellent strategist, and now is a good time to plan ways to not only move forward, but also backward and sideways. Disclosure must be carried out by humans. Even so, it doesn't mean you should continue to think as if your reality is all there is."

"Well, that's clear as mud," Brad said as the mist faded.

Vicki blinked and found herself—and the others—still in the classroom doing cloud hands with Calvin and Larry. Had any time passed at all? She stopped moving and looked at everyone.

"I want to punch an alien in the mouth."

Chapter Eighteen

Vicki was in her dreamscape again.

"Melly?"

"Yes, Vicki."

"Is Beth really dead?"

There was a brief silence, as if Melly were choosing the right words. "One of your famous physicists said, 'Energy cannot be created or destroyed; it can only be changed from one form to another.'"

Vicki recognized the Einstein quote. Was it applicable to her question? If Melly brought it up, it probably was. But she wanted something more specific, more definitive.

"What happens when we die? For that matter, how are we actually born—how do we come into this life?"

"Vicki." The feeling of far-off gongs. Melly seemed to be trying to be patient. Although Vicki was no longer seriously considering punching her in the face, she still wanted her old reality back.

No, actually, she didn't. What she wanted back was the reassuring knowledge of "this is how things work." She wanted to understand the rules of this new paradigm before she started moving down a path she hadn't known existed just a few days ago.

Melly continued, "Already on your planet, you have the saying 'We are all one.' It conveys the idea that separation between people is an illusion."

"Yeah, that's a saying I really dislike," Vicki said. "It always gives me the creeps—I picture a bunch of people melting into each other, with nothing to differentiate one person from another. We would all be the same—replaceable. I would hate for my best friend to feel I was interchangeable with that annoying guy who works in the next cubicle. If we were truly all one, I don't think we would be ourselves anymore."

She stopped herself. She hadn't expected to rant. Well, maybe she did, but not about this.

Melly laughed—the feeling of faint bells. "Rather than thinking of it as melting into a featureless mass, imagine joining something bigger than yourself. Think of it as if you were just one person on a bus full of others, all of you traveling together for the same purpose—still yourselves, but larger, more powerful, and resonating together. This takes nothing away from the connection between you and your friend."

Okay, she could see that; maybe she would even think about it some more. But it didn't answer her question.

"Melly, why are we talking about this?"

"Because your limited view of the universe will hinder your progress. When the vibration changes, humanity will resonate at a higher level. This does not imply your life and personality will be washed away to become some nameless cell of a bigger thing. Instead, it's an act of creation—a joining of forces to better express life and consciousness in the Universe."

"And again, how is this answering my question?"

"I once told you the Earth and everything else in material existence has consciousness. Everything—not just humans—will go through the vibrational shift. Consciousness, life, and energy are indistinguishable. Think of a cosmic wave with ebbs and flows.

Energy, life, and consciousness expand in a never-ending fractal pattern; the interconnectedness of all things is the constant."

Vicki felt the dream slipping away. She tried to keep hold of it but found herself waking up in bed.

Had Melly ever answered her question? She wasn't sure.

* * *

It was late morning. Brad had been right about the ease with which he had arranged an internship with Kiran's office. Only five days after their original conversation, he was already back at the Partnership. They began scheduling their special tai chi class for even earlier in the day so Brad could arrive at Kiran's office on time. They were still adjusting to the schedule change, relying on endless cups of coffee to power them through. They were all sleep-deprived and feeling a bit tense.

Today, Jess had asked James to come back to the mansion with her and Vicki to help review the eight interviews with Melly. They were good—she knew they were good—but it was always best to have a second pair of eyes.

So now the two of them were huddled over a computer, reviewing the interviews, but Jess could feel Vicki pacing around the studio, restless and anxious—like an itch she couldn't scratch. It was a relief when she finally spoke up.

"Guys, how are we going to pull this off? I'm supposed to be the strategy expert, but I don't have a game plan for how to get from here to there."

Jess looked up at Vicki, feeling genuine surprise.

"You'll do it. Melly chose you because you can do it," she said. "She wouldn't have brought you in if she thought you would fail."

"I thought there was a good chance we'd all fail, anyway."

"There is," she agreed. "But Melly still wouldn't have brought you in if she thought your chances of failing were higher than the rest of ours. We've been at this for a couple of years. You only became involved a few weeks ago. You have a huge learning curve; it'll come to you soon enough."

Simple faith. Maybe it was misplaced—they had only about a month to pull this off. But for Jessica, it was the only way to keep going.

Could they really take down the Partnership? She wasn't sure. It had resources, influence, and the kind of power that could wipe out entire populations without blinking. The Partnership was a juggernaut—built to last. Built to crush anything that stood in its way.

Jess pictured what failure would mean: a world controlled by those who thrived on fear and deception, twisting the truth to maintain power. People wouldn't just be trapped physically—they'd be stuck mentally and emotionally, locked in a system with no escape. The truth would stay hidden. The world would remain blind. And the price of that failure would be more than any of them could bear.

Simple faith. Jessica took a deep breath and came back to the present

James was now looking over a summary list of the interviews, his brows furrowed in concentration.

"Is this the order in which you're going to release them?"

"The first three, yes," said Jessica. "But I haven't decided on the rest. Melly said the first three are the foundational ones; after we broadcast those, the order of the rest is up to us as long as we release one per day."

"Will you be making more, or is this all of it?"

"Melly suggested we film two weeks' worth of interviews to be released, one each day, for a total of fourteen. I asked her if we could keep interviewing her afterward as a regularly scheduled weekly program sort of thing. She hasn't answered definitely—she's checking with the Council—but she's in favor of it so far."

Vicki stepped forward to look at the document she and James were studying

Interviews with Melly

1. What extraterrestrials are doing on Earth, current and

past cooperation between humans and ETs, and why the Council is unhappy with the Partnership's plans and actions, including the probable disruption of human evolution.

2. The upcoming shift in vibration and what it means for humanity: an overview of abilities that ordinary people will be able to access after the shift (i.e., after the activation of junk DNA) and an explanation of how this differs from what the Partnership would be able to offer. Personal freedom vs. being indebted to the Partnership.

3. A short survey of different extraterrestrial species, focusing on Melly's people and those groups that have been most active on Earth, along with a brief summary of the ETs and their activities on Earth throughout our history.

4. An explanation of the Galactic Federation and its charter, the codes and regulations applying to interstellar species, what constitutes good behavior, what constitutes bad behavior, and what happens to a species when it flaunts the Federation's regulations.

5. A synopsis of technology and devices developed by the Partnership that the Federation agrees should be made freely available to human society—what they are and how they can be applied in our current reality in the spheres of a) medicine, b) energy, c) agriculture, d) environmental remediation, and e) transportation.

6. A deep dive into the practical implications of the vibrational shift: long-distance communication, the declining relevance of the nation-state, the economic ramifications of change, and the challenge of elite groups that will lose rank and prestige.

7. How humanity's relationship with the planet and everything else in our physical reality must change after the shift
in vibration.

8. Going forward: how humanity will or will not participate
in the Galactic Federation and interact with the Council.
The need for humanity to speak with one voice in the
Federation.

"That's a fairly extensive list," Vicki said. "And each episode is
only forty minutes?"

Jessica nodded. "More or less."

"How can you cover everything in such a small amount of
time?"

"Do you remember Melly said the Council would release a
book?"

"Vaguely. She referred to it as *'The Disclosure Book'* or something?"

"The Book of Disclosure: Project Earth," corrected Jess. "The
idea is that the book will be a reference guide of sorts—a collection
of background materials. I think it will be made available to people
after the first three sessions are broadcast. Also, at the end of each
interview, we'll provide download links with additional information
related to the topics we discussed. Melly said she'd take care of that."

"You have at least six more sessions to tape. What else are you
going to cover?"

"That's what we're here to figure out," said James. "Melly has
a couple of items she believes we should cover, but at least three
sessions are up for grabs."

"I have a suggestion," said Vicki. "Instead of interviewing Melly about what we can do, why don't you have a session interviewing
her about what we *can't* do? Like a list of *'Danger—Don't Cross This
Line'* rules."

"You're thinking of something specific," guessed Jessica.

She was right. Vicki was remembering a conversation in the misty pocket out-of-time.

"While I'm sure there are other items you could add to this list, something a lot of people will have questions about is time travel—it's a common theme in science fiction literature. Melly told us time travel was discouraged, that even Council members rarely did it. If there's a solid reason why it's taboo—and, even better, if there's a really horrific example of what can go wrong—you should include that."

"I have a horrific example," said James. "When I first came into contact with Melly, we talked a lot about Earth's history."

Vicki raised an eyebrow.

"James is our channel, so he was the first one to connect with Melly—several months before Brad and I were able to," explained Jessica. "She didn't start talking about the Partnership and the vibrational shift until after Brad and I were brought in. So, they just talked, and James likes history."

Vicki turned back to James. "What about Earth's history?"

"You watched the third episode?"

She nodded.

"Then you heard Melly talk about how a bunch of extraterrestrials from Alpha Centauri were stranded on Earth for generations and how this was when ETs originally began interfering in human society."

Vicki nodded again.

Jessica already knew where this was headed. She turned away, pretending to focus on her videos, but she was still listening.

"Not all of them returned with the rescue ship; they wanted to stay living on Earth. This angered the Council because it was in violation of The Federation's policy of noninterference with pre-contact peoples—so they sent a small force to track down and bring back the ones who had refused to leave. But the Council hadn't realized how complicated it would be or how intertwined the human and Alpha Centaurian societies had become."

"Lots of people died?" Vicki's breath hitched. She had finally realized how bad this was going to be.

"It was pretty much a mop-up operation. By then, a couple of centuries had passed with the Alpha Centaurians living among humans. The Council forces had to erase evidence of entire civilizations. They used time travel to weave in and out of Earth's timeline, cherry-picking which events or interactions to delete, wiping out signs of technology we shouldn't have had, and even ending entire bloodlines. Tens of thousands of people died."

Vicki looked sick. Jessica didn't blame her—she had hid away in her bedroom for three days after she found out.

"But that was just the beginning. They hadn't realized how many holes it would leave—holes in our history, holes in our economies, and even some physical holes in our geography. This caused mass starvation, wars, plagues—whatever bad could happen, happened. So now we're talking about several hundred thousand people dead. The population of Earth back then wasn't like it is now—it was a lot smaller—so that means over half the population died. Humanity nearly went extinct."

"It became known as the *Earth Incident*," Jessica said, taking a deep breath as she turned back to the conversation. "Apparently, it led to an entire branch of pre-contact studies in their learning centers. People wrote dissertations. Some even built careers off it. And while Melly's been too polite to say so, I'm pretty sure the fiasco also sparked a whole new genre in whatever kind of entertainment industry they have."

Yes, the whole thing was appalling. Vicki looked numb. But that didn't stop her from blurting out a crass question.

"Oooh—do you suppose they're going to live-stream us when we confront the Partnership? I'm sure the ratings for that episode would be great."

James and Jess stared at her in shock for a couple of seconds, then burst out laughing. By the time they finished wiping their eyes, their moods had lifted.

Chapter Nineteen

Vicki spent the next week working with Earth energy—or at least trying to. Much of the time, she behaved like a tourist. She would sink into meditation and then reach out to the elements. She followed ley lines around the globe, plunged into fissures at the continental divides, played with magnetic anomalies, and explored cave systems hundreds of miles below the Earth's surface. She was stunned at what she found there.

What? There are people down here?

She had been wandering through a cave system located somewhere below the New England states. Okay, she was just guessing; she wasn't sure. As she roamed through a series of caverns, she was surprised to see light shining through a narrow opening. She ducked through and found herself in a small grotto. A human-shaped figure stood in the center of it as if waiting for her. The person was about five feet tall, wearing a light-colored shift, and had bare feet and deep brownish-red skin. Vicki wanted to reach out and stroke its arm—it looked like the softest, most amazing suede she had ever seen.

"Vicki," it said.

"Wait, you can see me in this form?" Her jaw would have dropped if she had been in her physical body. And then what the being had said finally registered. "How do you know my name?"

"Yes, I can see you. And I know your name because the Earth crystal told me. My name is Junia, and I'm pleased to meet you." The small figure gave a slight bow and smiled. Vicki got the impression of female and youth.

"How can you see me?" she asked while looking around the grotto. It was lit, but there was no visible light source.

Junia giggled. Yes, definitely young—maybe about fourteen or fifteen. "We are both vibrating at the same level, so, of course, we can see each other. Look down at yourself."

She did. She half expected to see the same sparkling form she had worn in the misty pocket out-of-time. Instead, she saw what appeared to be her everyday physical self. She was dressed in the clothes she had put on that morning. She took a finger and poked herself in the arm. Yes, she felt solid.

"You see, we are both very real." Junia was clearly amused.

"Can you explain?" Vicki looked at Junia and examined her properly this time. Still the bare feet, the light-colored shift, and brownish-red skin that looked like suede. But now she saw hair—coppery dark hair falling in ropes just past her shoulders—and facial features that, while human-like, could never be mistaken for human. Her eyes, a beautiful topaz color, were shaped like a cat's.

"I was told you already knew about the change in vibration."

"Yes, but in the future. What's happening right here, right now?" Vicki looked around the space they were in. Granitoid walls and ceiling. Light with no visible source.

"Fits and spurts—the vibrational shift will happen in fits and spurts. Major changes don't happen all at once. First, it starts slowly at the edges, then gets faster and faster, until—*whoosh*—we're living at the next level."

Junia threw her arms up to emphasize the immensity of it all.

"It seems to me you're already living at the next level," Vicki told her seriously.

"No, not yet." Junia dropped her arms and adopted a more formal demeanor, although it looked like she was fighting to keep an expression of delight from taking over her face. "We can go through small uplifts and downshifts in vibration without living in the next dimension. Most people, both you who live on the surface of the Earth and us here down below, do this several times a day without noticing."

"What about when I see myself as a misty, sparkly body?" Vicki asked. It felt like a stretch—bringing up something that had happened in a different part of the world, with people Junia couldn't possibly know. But since Junia already knew her name, Vicki figured she might know everything else too. Apparently, she did.

"Definitely a different dimension, but it's only temporary; you're just visiting—you and your friends. The shift in vibration we are all waiting for is the big one with the entire planet."

"You just said *we* are all waiting for the big one," Vicki said, feeling her way forward cautiously. "Are you the only one living here"—she waved her hands to encompass the grotto and the cave system she had been exploring—"or are there more people like you living inside the Earth?"

A wide grin split Junia's face. Vicki hadn't realized she had pinkish teeth.

"Lots of us. Tens of thousands. We have communities, towns, and an entire civilization. I am not some solitary hermit who wanders around the depths of the planet scaring miners and blunting drill bits."

Okay, that was oddly specific. It made Vicki wonder whether there were those who *did* make it a practice to scare miners and blunt drill bits.

Junia continued: "But the Earth crystal thought you'd be too nervous if a whole group of us showed up, so here I am all by myself." Junia began spinning around, her arms held out.

That was the second time she had mentioned the Earth crystal.

"Who or what is the Earth crystal, and why does it have an opinion on how I feel?"

Junia stopped spinning and turned to face her. "We have an appointment. *You* have an appointment. Let's go."

Junia stepped forward and took Vicki's hand. Her first impression had not been wrong—Junia's skin felt like suede. Then she pulled Vicki along behind her as she walked through the granite wall.

Vicki was proud that she didn't cry out, but she did flinch, majorly so. Junia, however, had a grip and muscles that were much stronger than hers. At first, Vicki resisted and was pulled stumbling behind her, but after a few disorienting minutes, she pulled herself together and started walking under her own power. Even so, she didn't let go of Junia's hand. She had an irrational fear of getting lost and being unable to find her way out from underneath miles of rock, clay, and sand. Now they walked through them all, as well as deposits of petroleum, water, and different minerals she couldn't begin to identify.

Were they actually walking? Probably not, but they were definitely moving forward and deeper—*through rock!*—to a destination. The stone was denser than air, like pushing through heavy, dark clouds, but with less condensation. When Junia started speaking, Vicki realized sound waves could also operate in these conditions.

"The Earth crystal is the heart of our planet, of course."

"Isn't the Earth the entire planet? Why do I need to visit the crystal?"

"Communication is easier at the crystal. You need to talk to it, but you were exploring your Earth energies so carefully that we were afraid you wouldn't find the crystal until it was too late. That's why I'm here." She turned and grinned with her pale pink teeth.

Vicki didn't speak again for the duration of the journey. She was too busy worrying about what "until it was too late" meant. Too late for what? And exactly when would it be too late?

Eventually, they stepped out from their rocky environment into a giant, air-filled cavern that, like the small grotto where Vicki had met Junia, was lit with no discernible source of light. In the center lay an enormous, oblong rock, the length of three or four city blocks. Junia had referred to it as a crystal, but it didn't look like any crystal Vicki had ever seen before—it was a dark grayish-brown. Maybe it was composed of some sort of metal? There were half a dozen beings—obviously Junia's people—who stood with foreheads pressed against the crystal.

"We're here!" Junia's voice called out, happy and proud. The others turned and gave small smiles and nods as they saw them. Okay, not as exuberant as Junia, then.

One of the beings, taller than Junia, approached and gave a shallow bow. "We appreciate your willingness to come with such promptness." His voice was quiet and grave.

Vicki didn't think her willingness had been taken into consideration when Junia dragged her there, but she kept her mouth shut.

"The crystal has been eager to speak with you. We understand there has been confusion regarding possible paths forward."

Vicki continued to keep her mouth shut but gave him a sharp nod. How had Junia's people learned about her confusion regarding what she was supposed to do? It didn't matter. Anything that addressed this had her full support. And maybe, along with clarity, she would be given hope? A girl could dream.

"Alun is the Earth crystal's keeper," said Junia in a stage whisper. While doing her best not to interrupt the conversation, it was clear she thought Vicki needed to understand his importance.

Alun glanced at Junia briefly, and the ends of his mouth twitched slightly. "And also, the uncle of this young one," he said, amusement in his eyes.

That made Vicki smile. Glad to find out Junia's people didn't totally lose their sense of humor as they grew older.

"Please." Alun motioned toward the crystal, making it clear she should approach. Vicki shot a brief look at Junia, who nodded encouragingly, then started forward. Alun accompanied her while Junia remained where she was.

"As Junia has probably explained—or maybe not," began Alun dryly. Apparently, he knew his niece. "The crystal has been restless.

It tells us you have been given access to Earth energies, but you are ignorant about how to use them."

"I didn't know I *was* supposed to use them," she replied honestly. "This was pretty much dumped on me, and I was told I needed to practice, but I don't know what that means."

"But you are one of the Guides who will be instructing humans about the vibrational shift!" Alun was startled.

"And I don't have a plan forward." It was embarrassing to admit, but she saw no benefit in downplaying her ignorance.

"There's not much time." Concern, worry.

"Not much I can do to fix that. Is this supposed to help?"

They had now stopped about a foot of the crystal. It towered above them, its grayish-brown surface covered in flowing lines and seams. Vicki could feel warmth radiating out from it. And a throbbing of some sort? Alun motioned her to place her forehead on the surface.

She cautiously stepped forward and did so. And then her reality exploded.

She had anticipated feeling a bit of static, like when doing cloud hands in tai chi class, but this was several magnitudes of energy greater. Her entire body felt electrified. She could feel the blood cells pulsing in her veins, her DNA sparking and tingling. Ribbons of power surged from the crystal into her, exploring her from head to toe. Her stomach gave a couple of flops, but then something clicked in her head, and the communication started.

How could she describe the impression she got from the Earth crystal? Noble, brilliant, honorable, magnificent, impossibly ancient—there were no words to describe the feeling of greatness. And although the crystal itself was dark, she also got a sense of light—a dazzling light steeping into the entire planet, saturating all things with movement and life.

She was still reeling from the initial contact when the crystal began delivering information—information about Earth energies and their movements: tides, volcanoes, storms, seismic faults, and plate tectonics. It was amazing. It was sobering. Honestly, she was surprised humans had managed to survive thus far.

Larry once told her he estimated their chances of success at sixty-forty. She was sure he'd been overly optimistic when he said that.

That had just changed. Things were looking up. *Her* new estimate was seventy-thirty.

Chapter Twenty

The cool stone walls of the Community Hall seemed to close in around Junia as she sat quietly at the far edge, tucked into the shadows. The meeting was already underway. The elders' voices rose and fell. For generations, the Suede Nation had chosen to live hidden from humans. Today, however, they were facing a new truth: the world above—humanity—was beginning to see them.

The air was thick with tension as her uncle, Alun, stood at the center of the gathering, the traditional quartz spire rising up to the ceiling behind him. He was always calm, always composed, but even he couldn't entirely mask the unease that gripped the room.

Junia listened hard, her eyes darting between the elders as they spoke, their voices full of doubt and worry. She felt a rush of disappointment. The day had started off so full of *fun*—and now the elders were fighting against any kind of change. It had been exciting to meet Vicki—to feel that little spark of possibilities. But the elders? They just wanted to keep everything stuck in the past.

One elder, a woman named Morcan, broke the silence. "This was a mistake," she said sharply. "Allowing a human to visit the Earth crystal—what were you thinking? They do not understand the sacredness of it. The Earth crystal is not a relic for the curious, especially not for a species as destructive as humans."

A male elder, Tarran, nodded. "I agree. We have hidden ourselves from humanity for millennia. It is our only protection. And now—now we allow one of them to come so close? What if they tell others? What if they—"

"There are already those who know of us," Alun said flatly. "What's been set in motion can't be undone. The request for the meeting didn't come from the humans or from Suedes—it came from the Earth crystal itself. We did not make that decision; *it* made the decision."

The room fell silent. Junia could feel the energy shift as the elders processed Alun's words with seeming shock. They looked flustered.

Junia rolled her eyes, biting her tongue to keep from saying something in frustration. They were pretending. They *knew* this already—every single one of them. The elders were just acting like if they ignored the situation for long enough, it would disappear. But everyone knew the Earth crystal had asked for the meeting—and that *she* was the one who had brought Vicki. Pretending they didn't know that? It was dumb. That's not how leaders were supposed to behave.

A third elder, a wiry man with a mouth twisted in skepticism, crossed his arms. "But why Vicki? Why this human? The crystal could have chosen anyone, but it chose her. And now she knows about us. She has seen what we are. What does that mean for us, for our safety?"

Morcan spoke again. "We have lived in hiding for so long. The humans have never understood us, and when they did find us, they were often deceitful and cruel. Look what happened to Junia's parents. Remember what they did to them."

Junia's chest tightened at the mention of her parents. The memories flooded in, uninvited—of the night they didn't come home after going herb-gathering on the surface. The humans had grabbed her mother first, and then her father when he tried to protect her. They'd both been caught, judged, condemned, and burned as demons. She knew just how cruel humans could be. Hearing those words felt like a knife twisting in her chest.

But she was older now, and she knew something that the elders did not. Vicki wasn't like those others.

Alun let out a deep sigh, his gaze softening as it briefly met his niece's before returning to the circle of elders. "I understand your fear," he said quietly. "I feel it too. The history between humans and our people has been marked by bloodshed. I haven't forgotten—nor has Junia. But we can't stay hidden anymore. The vibrational shift we've felt approaching for so long—it's here. The surface world is changing, and the veils between our worlds are thinning. Our time in the shadows has come to an end."

The elders exchanged uneasy glances, quickly looking away like they were trying to dodge the truth of Alun's words. "We have always been safe in our secrecy," one elder murmured, her voice trembling with doubt. "How can we trust that humanity has changed? That this Vicki is different?"

Because she is, Junia thought, but kept it to herself. Junia had seen the way she looked at the Earth crystal—like she actually *got* it, like she could feel its power deep down. It wasn't something Junia saw often, not even with her own people.

Alun continued, undeterred by the murmurs. "We have no choice but to confront this now. The Earth crystal has chosen her for a reason. She may be the key to something much larger than any of us can see. Hiding from humanity is no longer an option. The world will know us, whether we like it or not."

His words hung heavy in the air. For generations, the Suede Nation had kept its distance, staying apart from humanity. But now, the walls were crumbling, and nothing would be the same.

Alun's voice quieted, but it was full of determination. "We must prepare for the surface world to see us, for the truth to be revealed. This is not just about Vicki, or the humans she represents. It is about the future of our entire people. We cannot remain in the shadows forever."

Junia's heart raced. This was it—the moment everything could fall apart. But... it was also the moment where everything could change.

Finally!

She wouldn't be just a bystander anymore; she had a role in all of this, whether the elders liked it or not. The future was happening right now, and no one—not even the elders with all their endless warnings—could stop it.

Not this time.

* * *

"Seriously? You believe our chances are seventy-thirty?"

The relief in Larry's eyes made clear that his previous estimate of sixty-forty had been, as Vicki had guessed, more based on hope than fact. A figure plucked out of thin air to keep the rest of them from panicking.

"Yep." She smiled broadly. "Of course, that doesn't mean any of us will get out of this alive; just that we'll be successful in exposing the Partnership and launching Disclosure. The universe doesn't care if we live or die."

"That's all right; I really hadn't expected to still be alive at the end of this." He said this quietly.

That was a fairly shocking admission. Good thing he hadn't confided in her at the very beginning, or she would have cut and run.

It was the weekend, just after their early morning tai chi class. They were sitting in the garden behind the studio, waiting for the three young people to bring them coffee.

"We are older and should be respected," Vicki had told them.

There was some good-natured grumbling, but the teenagers had left to brew up a pot, and now she saw them making their way toward the group with mugs in hand. James handed her hers. She took a moment to inhale the aroma of coffee and vanilla.

"I'd like to hear more about your Earth crystal adventure," said Jessica. "None of the rest of us"—she motioned to herself and the boys—"received a strong connection to Earth energies when our DNA was activated."

"Are there really people living down there?" James's eyes were alight with curiosity.

"Yes, they have an entire society."

"What are they called?"

"I asked them how they referred to themselves. Like many indigenous cultures here on the surface, it's just a variation of 'the people.' So, because of their physical appearance, I'm calling them the Suede Nation—I asked what they thought about the name, and they said they were okay with it."

"Suede Nation has a cool ring to it," Brad said.

"And they knew about the Four—they referred to us as 'the Guides.'"

"Kick-Ass Quartet," corrected Brad.

"Are they native to Earth or are they aliens?" asked Jessica.

"Apparently, they're from Earth."

"If they're from here, why haven't we ever heard about them?" demanded James.

"I can't say for sure, but it's probably a combination of vibrational level and them just not wanting to interact with us. The Suede Nation lives at a slightly higher vibrational level than we do, so it's difficult to see them or their communities. I was only able to see Junia because I was deep in meditation, and my vibration was higher. And then I walked through rock!"

She said that last sentence with a hint of glee—she still had difficulty believing it.

"So, the Hollow Earth conspiracy theories are true?" asked Brad.

"*Not* hollow. Didn't I just tell you I walked through rock?"

"Well, at least there are lots of hollow spaces."

"I'm pretty sure geologists already knew this. But what they didn't know about was the ability to travel through rock and other materials—all the things humans have to tunnel through or go around. When people first speculated that the Earth might be hollow, they were imagining corridors connecting massive cavernous spaces. But corridors aren't needed if you live at a slightly higher vibration. And if they can walk through stone as easily as we do through air, maybe the cavernous spaces aren't needed either. I was honestly too excited to notice."

"So, all the stories about advanced civilizations and lost kingdoms are made up?" James looked disappointed.

"Many, but not all."

Four pairs of eyes looked at her, waiting. "Vicki?" This prompt came from Jessica.

Vicki continued. "The Suede Nation isn't the only group living in the inner Earth. They were the ones sent to find me because they're the Earth crystal's caretakers—apparently, the crystal told them it needed to speak with me. After my session with the crystal, they brought me to meet another race—tall, slender beings. They had an entire city that looked like it was made of crystal."

"Was there treasure?" asked James, leaning forward. "Did they use hieroglyphics like the Egyptians?"

"Were they Nazis?" This came from Brad.

Seriously? Vicki glared at him.

"No—no Nazis and no Egyptian treasure. These beings weren't *Homo sapiens*, though they looked more human than Junia. Aside from their height—anywhere from six to eight feet tall—and slightly elongated heads, they could easily pass as human, especially if you weren't looking too closely. Or if they wore hats or some other type of headgear.

"Just how different from us are they?" asked James.

Aside from having buildings out of crystal, I'm really not sure. There was music. And there were homes, shops, public buildings, and gardens. And a lot of people, from young children to the elderly. I was told this was one of their three main cities."

"Apart from the Suede Nation? Are they totally separate groups?" This sensible question came from Jess.

"Totally separate races and societies, except for some trade. We passed by a couple of the Suede Nation communities while traveling to the crystal city—these were more natural and earthy. Picture small villages from medieval times, but cleaner, better built, and more light-filled."

"Light," said Larry slowly. "You've mentioned light a couple of times. What was its source?"

"There wasn't one. At least not that I noticed. But what weirded me out was that I didn't have a shadow when I was in the interior. No one did—not me, not Junia, no one from the Suede Nation communities, nor anyone in the crystal city. And the buildings didn't cast shadows either. There was just a total absence of shadows."

"Then some sort of natural luminescence emanating from all objects—or bioluminescence in the case of the people. You had mentioned they glowed?"

"Yes, much more so than humans do." Vicki focused on her companions. Larry still appeared to her as people did before her DNA activation; he had never had a glow, but the kids... "You guys are glowing more than usual," she noted.

The young people snickered.

"We were wondering when you'd notice," Jessica laughed.

"What do you mean?"

"Remember when we were having breakfast on the patio, and Brad and I pointed out that the flowers closer to you were glowing more brightly than those farther away?"

"Yeah, so?"

"Since your biophotons were resonating at such a high level, they turned you into a type of lighthouse, beaming out your higher vibration to everything around you. Since frequencies harmonize, just by being near the flowers, you were raising their vibration—and they began to glow more brightly. Then Brad suggested you should sit for a few hours in a crowded theater to see what would happen."

Vicki didn't say anything. She just waited for Jessica to continue.

"Simple life forms change vibrations fairly easily. People—and animals—are complicated, and it takes longer. But because we've spent so much time with you..." Her voice trailed off.

"I'm the reason you are all glowing more brightly?"

"Pretty much."

She wanted to take some time to think about that, but then James spoke up.

"Vicki, look at me," he ordered.

She looked over at him. "What?"

"Do you notice anything different about me?" All the young people were grinning. Larry looked as confused as she felt.

"Something other than you're glowing more brightly? No."

At this, James put his fingers to his face to push his glasses up his nose, but...

"James! Why aren't you wearing your glasses?" All the kids burst into laughter.

"I don't need them anymore," he replied smugly. "My vision is now twenty-twenty."

Vicki was shocked. Larry looked stunned.

Chapter Twenty-One

A fter lunch, Vicki told everyone she needed a nap and retreated to her room at the mansion. It was actually an entire guest suite with a private bathroom and a separate sitting room. If it had included a kitchen, it would have been bigger than her condo back in DC.

She took her post-lunch cup of coffee out to her balcony (because *of course* there was a balcony) and looked out over the grounds. She had never thought her life was boring, but now she was finding out there was much, much more to reality than she had imagined. Aliens! Out-of-control military contractors! Otherworldly technology! DNA activation that gave people magical abilities! A different species living inside the Earth! A plot to take over the world!

And she had walked through rock!

Vicki sipped her coffee while running recent events through her mind. She had been fairly upfront when she briefed Larry and the Four about Junia, the Suede Nation, and her experience with the Earth crystal. Originally, they had all assumed that, as a political strategist, she wouldn't need to get directly involved until their operation against the Partnership was either completed or well underway. And she was good with that.

But she had learned they were all wrong.

The information given to her by the Earth crystal made clear that her DNA-activated abilities were crucial to their success. She hadn't gone into detail about all the knowledge the crystal provided; she just told them she had been given a crash course on how to use Earth energies. She may have implied it had a lot to do with manipulating ley lines and magnetic fields.

Left unmentioned was that she was now capable of generating sinkholes and triggering small earthquakes—at least in theory. It wasn't something she'd be able to practice without causing a lot of collateral damage.

And she had totally glossed over the crystal city and its inhabitants. Yes, they had talked about the natural luminescence and even discussed the possibility of using crystals as energy sources in the future, but she had left them with the impression that these people were, like the Suede Nation, native to Earth.

They weren't. Not even remotely. They were descendants of some of the survivors from Alpha Centauri that Melly had spoken about—the ones whose spaceship had crashed and who had then made themselves at home while awaiting rescue. They were the ones who had intervened in human civilization and had ultimately been the cause of so much death and destruction. When the Galactic Federation sent forces to hunt down the survivors who had refused to leave, they had hidden in the planet's interior.

They hadn't expected to live inside the Earth long-term but discovered they could create a civilization that was comfortable and—more importantly—hidden from the Federation's eye. They had only revealed themselves to the Council a couple of millennia later, and had received permission to remain on Earth as long as they limited themselves to the interior—apparently, the Council had more pressing problems than punishing the descendants of rebels long dead.

They apologized to her.

Vicki didn't know how she felt about that. They apologized to her for their ancestors' role in bringing so much death and destruction to the world, for being responsible for botching humanity's development, and for nearly driving humanity extinct. While it was gracious of them, she didn't think she was the individual they should be apologizing to. But who would be more appropriate? She didn't know; this was something that concerned all of humanity. Maybe Jessica and Melly could make a video about it—this was a story everyone had the right to know. But it would be a catastrophic confession, and she was pretty sure people would not take this new information calmly.

She took another sip of coffee. Something more to think about.

* * *

The flickering light from the large TV screen cast shadows across the sectional in the entertainment room. While the space was designed for comfort, right now it felt like a war zone. The three of them—Jessica, Brad, and James—were locked in a fierce battle in their favorite multiplayer video game. The characters on screen were a blur of motion, explosions lighting up the darkness of the virtual world as they fought their way through a horde of enemy drones.

"Take cover!" Brad shouted, his voice sharp as he rapidly tapped on his controller, his fingers flying across the buttons.

Jessica responded quickly, moving her character behind a nearby barricade. The screen shook as another explosion rocked the battlefield. "We need more power," she said, her eyes glued to the action. "James, you've got the long-range weapon—cover us!"

"On it," James replied, totally focused. His character, a lean, agile fighter, crouched down to get a better view. He picked off enemy after enemy with precise shots, each one falling in a burst of sparks and debris.

"I'm not sure how much longer we're going to last in this match," Brad muttered, sweat beading on his forehead. "It's getting pretty chaotic."

Jessica threw him a quick glance. "You say that every time, but we always pull through."

Brad grinned, his eyes flicking back to the screen. "That's because I'm awesome." He waggled his eyebrows before diving back into the game.

James rolled his eyes but didn't say anything. He was too absorbed in keeping their position secure.

The background music grew faster and more intense, a signal that a major enemy was about to appear. Jessica's fingers tightened around her controller. "We've got a something major incoming," she said, her voice low. The screen filled with a massive figure—an oversized war machine with glowing red eyes and a huge energy weapon.

"Great, just what we need," Brad muttered as he switched to a stronger weapon. "How many times have we fought this thing already?"

"Too many," Jessica said, grinning. "But it's fun to see if we can take it down quicker each time." She launched a barrage of rockets at the machine, watching as its health meter slowly ticked down.

The game demanded strategy, teamwork, and quick reflexes. For the moment, it felt like a relief to focus on something other than the constant pressure building outside their virtual world. As they exchanged quick comments about their strategy, Jessica's mind drifted back to the more serious thoughts she had been trying to push aside.

It was hard not to think about Vicki. They had all seen how quickly she was improving in using her abilities. While this gave them hope, there was still so much they didn't understand about what she could do. Vicki had quiet focus, even when everything seemed to be falling apart. The way she adapted to new situations... it was almost like she was made for this kind of pressure. Jessica wondered whether this was typical of diplomats.

She knew the others had been thinking the same thing—and worrying about it. They'd been having conversations—both serious and casual—about Vicki. But in this moment, in the middle of the game, it was easier to pretend they didn't have so many questions.

Brad suddenly spoke up. It was as if he'd been listening to her thoughts.

"Vicki's really come a long way with her training, hasn't she?" he said, eyes still locked on the screen. "I mean, a few weeks ago, she was barely able to sense anything. Now it's like she's tuned into everything." He grinned. "And that's before she had her session with the Earth crystal."

"Yeah," Jessica agreed, her eyes still focused on the game, though her thoughts were also on Vicki. "It's great how quickly she's picking it up. I can't even begin to wrap my head around how she does it. I mean, we've been at this for a few years already, and she's almost at our level—she's already surpassed us all in the chi-sensing category."

James gave a quick nod as he cleared out a few more enemies. "I guess Melly made the right choice in picking her."

Brad smirked. "Not that we're jealous or anything. It's just... kinda weird, right?"

Jessica laughed, but her smile faded as she considered what he said. "I'm glad she's making progress. But the more she learns, the more I wonder if it's enough. I wonder if we'll actually be able to beat the Partnership. I wonder if any of us will be ready."

Brad's fingers paused on the controller, his eyes narrowing in thought. "I don't think our abilities are going to be the deciding factor," he said finally. "The Partnership is big and has plenty of money. They've got resources we can only dream of—advanced weapons, alien technology, and strong ties with people in power. They have super soldiers and flying saucers. They've embedded themselves into every part of society. We're not just dealing with a group of people; we're up against a whole system that protects them. I'm not sure that our abilities—Vicki's and ours combined—will be enough to bring them down."

"Yeah," James agreed, his voice uncharacteristically serious. He lowered his controller for a moment and turned toward the others. "We're not just fighting a group of bad guys. The Partnership is like a spider with its web spread across the whole world. It's everywhere. It's in our governments, our businesses, our technologies. Taking them down won't be as simple as just showing up and hitting them with the big guns. Not that we have any guns at all."

Jessica nodded, biting her lip. "I know. But we can't let them win. They've already done enough damage by keeping technology hidden, and now humanity's future is at stake. We can't just sit back and let the Partnership keep pulling the strings."

Brad looked at her, serious now. "We're not going to let them win. Not if we can stop it. But it'll take more than our abilities. It'll take everyone. We'll need a plan, and we'll need to use everything we've got."

James looked over at Jessica, his expression grim. "It'll be important to stay ahead of them. The Partnership won't go down easily, but if we can get to them first..."

"Yes, if we can surprise them..." Jessica swallowed, "we'll have a shot. Just one shot. We'll have to make it count."

Brad grinned, his finger hovering over the button to launch another attack. "It'll be like a real version of this video game."

Jessica let out a half-smile. "Yeah. But this time, the stakes are a little bit higher than beating some random war machine."

The three of them laughed, and the moment passed. On the screen, the game's final challenge appeared. Jessica lifted her character's weapon for the last hit, her stomach twisting.

What lay ahead was real. Jess hoped their efforts would be enough.

Chapter
Twenty-Two

Tai chi class was definitely getting easier. Not that they were practicing tai chi in a way other practitioners would actually recognize. Instead, they were still focused on moving the chi—the energy. Vicki could now follow Calvin's instructions as they raised their vibration up a few levels, then back down to waking consciousness. Up even higher, then down to the slightly raised level. Up back higher again, then returning to physical reality. The young people and Vicki seldom met in the pocket out-of-time. The focus was on getting them proficient at raising and lowering their vibration, and recognizing what it felt like when they were in those states.

It reminded Vicki of practicing scales on the piano as a kid—sort of boring, but the foundation of everything else to come.

Although Calvin was the one leading them in the vibrational level exercises, Vicki had never seen him in the pocket reality. Maybe it had to do with need? Or maybe he was being intentionally excluded because, deep down, he couldn't see the young people as full team members. Not when it came to real risk. Sending his only child—and his child's friends—into battle would be nearly impossible for him.

Larry attended every single class and doggedly practiced with them. From conversations with the kids, Vicki knew that he was only able to manage the lowest of the vibrational changes—a level he had achieved prior to the accident that resulted in him becoming a biologic construct. There was no hope, yet still, he persisted.

Respect.

Afterward, Vicki would drive them to the Partnership's offices to drop Brad off for his internship. In response to Larry's prodding, Brad let them know he was working on Kiran, but there had been no progress yet. He was unhappy and hunched over when he told them this, but he no longer protested about how this might ruin Kiran's life. They were all buckling down to do their jobs.

Vicki was in a good mood this morning. With such a beautiful car to drive, any time she had to take the young people somewhere, she was happy. Now, on her way to drop Brad off at the Partnership, her mind naturally turned to happy thoughts.

"James, explain to me better how you no longer need to wear glasses." James was hitching a ride back to the Martinsson mansion so he could help Jessica edit more videos.

"I thought we had? Remember biophotons and being a vibrational lighthouse and all that?"

"Yes, but I'm interested in what else it can do. Are there any other effects? How can we use it?" Vicki turned on her signal, cut across two lanes of traffic, and took the on-ramp to the highway. Maybe she was driving a little aggressively, but hey, she was at the wheel of a Bentley. No one bothered to honk at her, so all good.

Unsurprisingly, it was Jessica who responded. She was still distressed by the Partnership's refusal to release any advanced medical technology and tended to laser-focus on anything related to health.

"I'm pretty sure that's something for the future. First of all, it's not a talent or skill that will help us in our present situation. The fact that people who spend time with you become healthier will do nothing to help us make the Partnership's activities public." Jessica raised a finger as she ticked off her points.

"Second, you are only one person, so any outcome is extremely limited. Unless you want to start a business where people pay big money to spend time in a room with you."

Brad snickered.

Jessica raised a third finger. "Therefore, we need lots more people who are vibrating at a higher level and who have had their DNA activated in the area of Earth energies. Since Brad, James, and I are glowing more brightly, it shows this quality can be spread among people. But *we* already know how to move our chi. We already have a lot of practice reaching states of higher vibration. We already have had parts of our junk DNA activated by an alien."

"So slow going?" Vicki had been following a semi-truck for a couple of miles. Now, she took the off-ramp down to a leafy boulevard.

"Something for when the vibrational shift happens," Jessica said, sinking glumly into her seat.

"But it's important that people know it's possible," said James earnestly. "My eyes are perfect; that means something."

"How about you guys?" Vicki addressed this question to the siblings.

"Our health?" asked Brad. "We've had all our medical needs taken care of by the Partnership for the last few years. I'd be surprised if there was anything left to heal."

Jessica sank even lower in her seat.

"How about you, Vicki? Have you noticed your health improving?"

Vicki thought about it. She was only thirty-two, so she didn't have many health issues yet. But didn't she often get hives from eating tomatoes? They were in season, and Lucia had been preparing a lot of dishes and salads with tomatoes in them, but she hadn't noticed any hives.

"Maybe?" She pulled up to the curb in front of a luxury office building. Brad opened his door and hopped out.

Another thing to think about.

* * *

Brad tried to hide it, but he knew that anyone who saw him would realize he had news. He was already waiting when Vicki picked him up that evening, and he pretty much bounced over to the car—buoyant, animated, and full of excitement.

"Is there anything you want to tell me?" Vicki asked as she steered into traffic.

"I'll wait until supper so I can tell everyone at the same time." He couldn't stop grinning.

Jessica and James had stayed back at the house when Vicki had left to pick up Brad. They were planning on eating together before Larry came to take James home.

"Maybe we should ask Larry to come a little early and have supper with us?" he suggested.

"That's a good idea. Why don't you see if he's free? Then let Lucia know we'll have one more for dinner."

Brad took out his phone and began texting. "Done," he said.

They ate on the patio again. Being so close to the coast, there was always a pleasant breeze, even when it was hot. Lucia and Mateo set out several dishes—stir fry—then left them to serve themselves. The first few minutes were busy with people passing platters and doling out their food.

Vicki took a sip of water and addressed the table. "I think Brad has something to tell us all."

The clinking of silverware halted as everyone stopped eating and turned to look at Brad, who was grinning widely. He loved having an audience.

"Well, I don't want to get too far ahead of myself," he began.

"Don't act differently now, just for our sake," muttered James, putting another forkful of rice into his mouth.

"Over the next two days, our office"—he was referring to the office where he was interning at the Partnership—"is sponsoring an event. Employees have been invited to come and be scanned with the photonitron device our office developed. Next week, we'll start manipulating the images. In a couple of weeks, we'll invite everyone back for a performance of themselves doing highly unlikely things."

"Funny things?" James perked up.

"Of *course*. This is an event suggested by and run by the two youngest people in the office, so anything serious would be out of character."

"The Partnership is letting you do this?" Jessica seemed surprised.

"My office is really, really hoping I'll choose them to work for when I turn eighteen." He smirked. "Kiran told me he overheard a couple of the managers gloating about how this project will keep me at their office for at least another three weeks, so that's almost a month and a half compared to the spring break I had with the IT folks in the Human Enhancement Division. They want to keep me happy."

The IT Division had already made their pitch with shiny smiles and promises of advancement. They'd shown him their world of servers, security systems, and high-tech surveillance, all while selling him on the idea that he could make a difference by shaping the future of technology. It would have been tempting if he had been anyone else. The Partnership wasn't about making the world better; it was about control. And Brad had a different agenda.

Similarly, the Product Development Office—where he was interning with Kiran—wasn't just focused on the next big innovation. They were designing tools to tighten the Partnership's grip on the population. The tech was built to track, manipulate, and steer human behavior on a massive scale. He'd seen it firsthand in the presentations—how their "smart" products could monitor habits, predict choices, and more. It wasn't just about convenience. It was about creating dependency and asserting control through devices that looked harmless, ordinary—and even helpful.

As an intern, Brad had been assigned to these "smart" products. Kiran, however, was a full-time employee, and his special project was the photonitron.

It was everything Brad had feared. And it was everything he needed to know.

Larry interrupted his reminiscences with a question.

"How's Kiran coming along?"

Brad stilled but looked Larry in the eye. He felt like a soldier reporting to his commander; the situation was beginning to feel real to him.

"He's not there yet, but he's coming along. I'm not pressing him too hard right now because obtaining the images is our priority—without them, we have nothing."

"Will you be getting images of the bosses and the top executives?" asked Vicki.

This was one of the main reasons they wanted access to the photonitron technology. Images of the C-suite executives would give them enormous flexibility in figuring out their way forward.

"*Of course* we're getting images of the managers and the top brass. It was pitched to them as a morale-boosting exercise that might encourage other young people to come on board. There are also some other key people we're encouraging to come—a few of the guards, some heads of section, et cetera. I don't know what we'll need, but it's always good to have options."

"It sounds like Kiran is actually helping you quite a bit right now," said Vicki. "Do you think he'll refuse to step up when the time comes?"

"Maybe. The tradition of family obligations is really strong. But he's going out of his way to help us in other ways. Did I tell you that Kiran has been approached to bug our car and our house?"

"*My* Bentley?"

Brad almost laughed at Vicki's reaction—it seemed she was feeling possessive of the car. But her shock was mirrored in the faces of everyone at the table.

"My office is giving me a lot of freedom—access to information and projects that are way beyond top secret—projects that are considered "beyond black." Since our dad already works with the

Partnership, no one suspects me of being disloyal. They just want to give themselves plausible cover for what Kiran literally called 'handing me the keys to the kingdom.' He told me he'll be pushing for an invitation to our house soon. That's when he'll plant the bugs—and yeah, he'll show me exactly where he puts them."

More shock.

"Where in the house?" asked Jessica.

"Kiran and I talked it over—probably the entertainment room and my bedroom."

"The entertainment room won't be a problem," said Vicki, "but what about your bedroom? Don't you have all your computer equipment in there?"

"Computer genius, remember? And I put in all the security for our network. I can isolate the computer background noise and switch in something else...a combination of AC ducts and music or something."

"Video games would be another good one," suggested James. The rest of them nodded.

"So," said Brad in a theatrical tone, "company is coming to dinner."

Everyone rolled their eyes.

Chapter Twenty-Three

Vicki turned into the parking lot and pulled into one of the spaces reserved for customers of the Uptown Blooms flower shop. The lot, situated behind a row of 1950s-ish commercial buildings, served the entire block. The buildings were pretty much identical, with a commercial space on the ground floor and two single-bedroom apartments above. Beth had converted one of the apartments into a plant workroom and greenhouse, living in the remaining apartment. Living where she worked had been heaven for her—Beth had loved it that much.

"Do you mind if we come in too?" asked Jessica.

She was more sensitive than the boys, who were already clambering out of the car. They froze at the question, all eyes directed toward Vicki.

"Come on in, I don't mind."

She unlocked the outer security door, then the wooden back door. When she pushed it open, an odor of moldering and decay greeted them. She wrinkled her nose. When the shop had closed, she had gifted the already-cut flowers to a nearby hospital and the potted plants to a nursing home. Had she missed something? Looking around, she found a trash can full of decomposing plant cuttings. There were also a couple of bowls in a sink she had set aside to soak before washing but had forgotten about. She dumped out the water and began to scrub.

"Can one of you take that bag to the dumpster? It's on the far side of the parking lot."

Brad went to do that. Jessica and James wandered around curiously.

"So, this is Beth's shop?"

Jessica's question was cautious. While inviting Vicki to talk, her tone made clear that if she didn't want to, that was fine too.

"Yes, her pride and joy." Tears threatened to well up in Vicki's eyes, but she shook her head and continued on.

"Actually, she owned the entire building. Upstairs is her workroom and the apartment where she lived. Go ahead and explore if you want."

The two of them went upstairs as Vicki eyed the main shop. Beth had been so proud of it, but now it looked sad and lonesome. What should she do with it? What did she want to do with her life? She still had a few months before she either had to resume her job with the State Department or hand in her resignation. Did she still want to be a diplomat? She had loved her job before Beth fell sick, but since then her priorities had shifted. Now? Now she wanted to explore paths other than those conventional wisdom told them were open.

All this was assuming she would survive her adventure with the Partnership and space aliens. Maybe she didn't need to worry about deciding whether to sell the shop and return to her life as a diplomat—at least not yet.

She went upstairs to find the kids and pick up some clothes from the apartment. She had packed a suitcase when she went to the Martinssons', but she could use some clothes that were more appropriate for the California weather. Jess and James were poking around the workroom. Vicki opened the door to the apartment and stepped in.

At first, she felt like she was surrounded by Beth—her furniture, her books, her knickknacks. She walked over to look at a collection of photos on the wall and blinked back tears at the chronicle of Beth's personal life—pictures of their parents, their family, celebrations, and family pets. The most recent photos, however, were of only Beth and her.

And now it was just her.

But the longer she stood around, the more she got the feeling of emptiness. Beth wasn't there anymore—just dust, stagnant air, and things. She quickly stuffed some clothes into a bag and joined the young people in the workroom area.

"This is amazing." Jessica gestured at the enlarged windows and skylights, which had totally transformed the originally dark apartment. "This is almost a greenhouse—in the heart of downtown Los Angeles!"

Vicki smiled. It had taken Beth a year to complete the renovations, and she had inaugurated them with an open house for all the shop owners on the block. This turned out to be the start of... not quite an alliance, not quite an association, but definitely increased cooperation and friendship among all the shop owners. Beth had been like that, bringing people together.

"Vicki, why is this plant still alive?"

James was pointing toward a pot of chrysanthemums, their white blooms bright among the other pots that were brown and wilted. No one had been in the building since Vicki left over a month ago, and nothing had been watered, so it was a legitimate question.

"No clue. Did you know chrysanthemums are a symbol of life and divinity in the Far East?"

"But I thought they were just funeral flowers," said Brad as he joined them.

"Different cultures, different meanings." Vicki reached out to touch the silky blossoms. "The beauty and transience of life."

Then she paused and frowned. The soil in the pot was slightly damp as if it had been watered a day or two earlier. She glanced up, but there was nothing leaking from the ceiling, no gaps in the window sealant. She shook her head and mentally shrugged; this would have to remain a mystery.

"We should bring this with us," she said. "Can someone grab it for me?"

They all headed back down the stairs, Jessica bringing the pot. Vicki wanted to check the mail before they left. There were several envelopes piled up by the door. She was confident they weren't bills because Beth had automated her utilities when she started her business, and Vicki had closed the rest of her accounts after she died. She leafed through them: a few advertisements and several condolence cards from customers and neighbors. She stuffed them in her bag to take along.

"Vicki, what's in all these boxes?" James stood next to three large cartons that had been delivered a few weeks before Beth died. There had originally been four boxes, but Vicki had opened one, then taken its contents and distributed them among Beth's fellow shopkeepers and the hospice where she spent her last weeks.

"Copies of the book Beth wrote. She finished it when she was in the middle of treatment; I was able to get it printed and delivered a few weeks before she passed. She had intended to sell it in her shop. Beth worked so hard on it—I'm glad she had the chance to see it before she died."

She took a knife and sliced open one of the boxes. Tossing aside the packing material, she took out a couple of copies of the book: *Expressing Yourself with Flowers* by Elizabeth Williams Heywood.

"You guys can all have a copy if you'd like."

James took a copy and looked at it closely. "Beth's name was really Elizabeth? And you're her sister?"

Vicki nodded.

James sounded surprised, but then he flashed her a big smile. "I don't need a copy; I already have one. It was the book I used when I was doing all the planting at the studio and at Jess and Brad's house. I love that book. I used it to decide which flowers to put in."

The siblings turned and looked at him in shock. Vicki did the same. James' eyes darted between the three of them.

"What? Why are you all looking at me like that?"

"James," Jessica said slowly. "You're sure this is the exact same book? Not one that's similar?"

"Yes." His voice was filled with certainty. "She had two last names—Williams and Heywood. I wondered whether Williams was a middle name or if it was her last name before she got married."

"It was her middle name—Williams was our mother's maiden name. Beth never married." Vicki's voice was tight, an octave higher than normal.

"James," said Brad urgently. "It's not possible. You did the plantings three years ago—and it's only been a few months since this book was published. It didn't exist when you were planting flowers."

Brad looked to Vicki for confirmation, and she gave him a sharp nod.

"But it's the book I used; I know it." James' brows knitted into a frown.

"Vicki," said Jessica, her voice coming as if from a distance. "Vicki, look at me."

Vicki slowly turned her attention from James and the book he was holding to Jessica. Her forehead was creased with worry.

"I'm not going to lose it," Vicki assured her. "I'm just kicking myself at how dense I've been."

The three young people looked at her in surprise.

"Yes, I've been dense," she said, her voice harsh. "After Beth finished her manuscript, I acted as her beta reader. I went through all of it several times before it was sent off to the publisher, looking at language flow and punctuation, and checking for misspellings. And I didn't see it."

Jessica still looked concerned.

"And then—then she came to us in the pocket out-of-time and told us Melly had asked her for permission to do something that would help."

Their faces were still blank.

"Melly asked Beth," she said heavily, "for permission to use this book, then she took it back in time. So, the book appeared to James three years before it was published."

"How'd you get the book?" asked Brad, looking at James.

"It was on a shelf?" James couldn't remember.

"Why are you feeling so...dense, you said?" Brad addressed this question to Vicki.

"Look at the title of the book—*Expressing Yourself with Flowers*. It's all about sending messages using flowers. James used the book to make gardens at both the studio and your house."

She turned to James. "Did you choose those specific flowers for a reason, or did you just feel like they were the flowers that should be planted?"

"I just paged through the book and looked at the photos, then chose the flowers that felt right," agreed James.

"Oh," said Jessica. "I think I'm beginning to understand."

The boys glanced at her, still puzzled, then turned their attention back to Vicki.

"The flowers at the studio," Vicki said slowly. "Primroses and baby's breath—they're used for safety and protection. The clematis vines in the back—wisdom. Lotus? That represents spiritual enlightenment and transcendence. And moonflowers signify psychic abilities, shape-shifting, and transformation."

"And our house? What about the flowers that were planted at our house?" Brad was fascinated.

"They tell an entirely different story altogether," she replied grimly. "Rhododendrons—that's caution and danger. Monkshood conveys the same message. Orange lilies mean pride and disdain."

"So, what does all that mean to us?" persisted Brad.

"They're both confirmation and a message—probably intended for me. Not only is Beth my sister"—Vicki swallowed a lump in her throat when she said that—"but I'm also the one who has had the most doubts about what we're doing. I'm the one who still needed to be convinced. Think of it as a road sign showing us we're on the right path. The flowers tell us the tai chi studio is a safe place. What we learn there, especially the woo-woo stuff, is valuable and—for lack of a better word—good."

"And the flowers at our house?" Brad didn't take his eyes off her.

"They're a pretty clear message about the owner of the house and where he stands."

Both Jessica's and Brad's faces stilled.

Vicki continued. "Danger and caution, that's pretty clear. Pride—you've told me how proud he was to be a part of the Partnership. And disdain—contempt for the needs of not only his children but for anyone else in the world. This isn't rocket science."

"And these flowers?" Jessica was still cradling the pot of chrysanthemums in her arms.

"Life. Life that flourishes even when everything else in the room has dried up and died."

They all turned to head out the back door.

"And it's hope," Vicki continued. "Let's never forget about hope."

Chapter Twenty-Four

Vicki was once again holding on to Junia's hand as she was led through rocks and earth. When she started out that day, she had only intended to explore—she wanted to try and figure out what she could do with Earth energies and what might be available to her—but Junia had been waiting for her when she stepped into her... Territory? Dimension? Sphere of existence? Vicki didn't know how to describe it.

"They want to see you again."

Junia hadn't bothered with social pleasantries like "How are you?" or "Good to see you again." She was a girl on a mission and just grabbed Vicki's hand and plunged through the rock, the damp, dense feeling once again enveloping her as they moved forward. Vicki did better this time and prepared for it, but she still didn't let go of Junia's hand.

"Your uncle wants to see me? Why?"

Junia glanced back at her, her topaz-colored cat's eyes wide, her expression incredulous. "Why would you think Alun wants to talk with you?"

"I don't know. Maybe because you said he wanted to see me again and you're leading me there now?"

"No, Alun doesn't want to talk to you." She shook her head so forcefully that her dark, ropey hair went flying from side to side. "It's those people in the city."

Those people in the city. The colony descended from the survivors of the Alpha Centauri expedition that had crashed. What they told her last time about their role in human history had rattled her enough. Vicki didn't want to talk to them again, but it looked like she wasn't being given a choice.

When they arrived in the city—the same spot where they had entered the first time—they were waiting. The group was small, about half a dozen adults. All tall, slender, with light-colored hair, and slightly elongated skulls. And because of her previous experience as a diplomat, Vicki recognized them for what they were—an official delegation. Apparently, they were going to talk politics.

They all gave each other respectful nods, and Junia disappeared after telling her she'd be back to guide her to the surface once the meeting was over. Vicki was escorted to one of the buildings and ushered into a large room with a central table. It looked like any executive boardroom found at the headquarters of a large corporation, except it was beautiful. Glowing crystal walls. A smooth table made of some sort of natural material. Seating that was too high for her and left her dangling her feet.

She hated it when that happened. And it soured her mood.

"Thank you for agreeing to meet with us."

The speaker was seated across from her. He spoke out loud and moved his mouth, but Vicki was sure that was for her benefit. During her first visit to the city, she had the impression that there was another level of communication taking place. Whether it was telepathy or some sort of unknown-to-humans technology, she didn't know, and it didn't matter. Conversations had been going on around her that she wasn't allowed to hear. And it was obvious to her now that the same thing was happening again. The other five seated around the table had their eyes... focused, but not on anything specific. Every now and then, their eyes would quickly flicker to one individual or another as if that person had made some sort of significant comment.

"That's rude, you know."

Their eyes locked onto her. It was unnerving, but she powered through.

"It's rude to hold a meeting and exclude one person from a conversation everyone else is having. We can do one of two things. One—we can start the meeting over, and everyone speaks out loud so that I can hear what is being said. Or two—I can leave. Your choice."

She thought back to how she jokingly claimed she was the type of diplomat who had mastered the art of telling someone to go to hell, but had never learned the part about having people look forward to the trip. Today it wasn't a joke, and now it was on full display.

While these people were not from Earth, their expressions were much easier to read than those of the Suede Nation. Surprise and consternation showed on all their faces.

"I apologize for all of us, Vicki." This came from the person—a female—seated on the other end of the table. "We haven't been accustomed to—"

Vicki cut her off.

"Despite having received no advance notice of this session, it appears we are in an official meeting between representatives of the Alpha Centauri survivors and a human representative of Earth. So, please address me by my proper title, Counselor Heywood."

Yeah, she was feeling bitchy. And, to be honest, she was scared stiff. Here she was, without warning, being pulled into something way over her head. She wasn't qualified and had no one to consult. And she was terrified that she might say something that all of humanity would be held responsible for at some point in the future.

She had pulled the title of counselor out of thin air. Not as exalted a rank as ambassador—a counselor would need to get ultimate approval from someone of higher rank. At the same time, counselor was a title that was higher than, for example, an advisor, so she was allowed to be bitchy instead of groveling. She was counting on the Alpha Centaurians' remarkable grasp of English to appreciate the difference.

"We apologize, Counselor Heywood." The original speaker was talking. "It was not our intent to offend or exclude."

He then proceeded to introduce himself—Representative Brandori—and his five colleagues, all of whom were also given the title of representative.

Representative Brandori had said they did not intend to offend or exclude. Vicki believed the part about them not wanting to offend her. But the part about not wanting to exclude her from the conversation? That was a lie, and the churning in her gut confirmed it. They didn't want her to know what they were talking about. But now they had been put on notice, and they settled down to discuss why they had called the meeting.

Vicki had only learned about the upcoming shift in vibration a few weeks earlier. She had put it on the back burner because she was still coming to terms with rogue military organizations, ET technology, and impending changes in human DNA. But now she was told that the vibrational shift would have an even greater fallout than that.

"What do you mean your society will now be visible to humans?" If there was a tone of panic in her voice, well... that was correct. This was too much to process.

Representative Lyrith—a female sitting to Brandori's right—was the one who answered. "The vibrational shift will have an effect on all of us who live on and within the planet. But it will have a greater impact on humans due to their current inferior level."

Was her remark meant to be insulting? Vicki suspected it was, but ignored it as Lyrith continued.

"Since humans will now be on the same vibrational level as we are, we will no longer be able to conceal ourselves. And since humans will know about us and see us, there will be no purpose in continuing to live here in the planet's interior. Many of us would like to move to the surface."

Ahhhh. Now she understood. This was a grab for territory, thinly disguised as consultations.

"That would be in violation of your agreement with the Galactic Federation Council," she bristled, speaking through gritted teeth.

"It wouldn't be in violation if humans agreed to it." This was said by a representative whose name she couldn't remember. He sounded younger than either Brandori or Lyrith.

"Why would we choose to welcome the people who nearly exterminated us?"

"That wasn't us; that was the Council forces." Representative Lyrith spoke dismissively.

"The Council forces that were trying to repair the damage to human civilization caused by Alpha Centaurians who willfully defied Galactic Federation guidelines." Vicki glared at her.

"That's enough." Representative Brandori had risen from his seat and was frowning at Lyrith.

When he was sure she wouldn't speak again, he continued, "The issue is that humans will find out we exist, find out who we are, and become aware of our shared histories. How can we handle this in a way that is best for all of us?"

Vicki had balled her hands into fists. Slowly, she unclenched them and took a deep breath. Then, more calmly she replied, "I don't know."

"You don't know?" This was another representative whose name she didn't remember. She needed a list. But the woman seemed genuinely curious, so Vicki replied.

"No, I don't know. Finding out about extraterrestrials will be traumatic for humanity. They will need to know about the Tall Whites, because those are the ones who have been helping the

Partnership develop advanced technology. Humans will also need to learn about the Galactic Federation because Earth will need to establish official relations with it. And since Melly is currently the Council representative to Earth, humanity will be introduced to her people too. It's a lot for us to take in. People are going to be stressed and disturbed and shocked. They'll want someone to blame. They'll need someone to blame."

She paused, realizing her voice had become loud. She looked around the table and continued more quietly. "My money will be on blaming you—the group that nearly caused the extinction of humanity when you had a temper tantrum because you didn't want to go home."

There was a stunned silence. "That can't be true," Brandori said.

"I assure you, it can," she replied, injecting what she hoped was a tone of measured reason into her voice. "It's very possible that when the existence of a colony of Alpha Centauri crash survivors is revealed, humanity will demand that you leave our planet. I believe it is within our rights to do so."

She didn't know if it was true; she was guessing. But no one spoke up to say she was wrong, so yay her.

Lyrith turned to Brandori, and... there was silence.

"Voices, please," she prompted them. Yeah, still feeling bitchy.

The female representative, whose name she'd forgotten, asked the next question. "How did your fellow Guides react when you told them about us?" She was referring to the Four.

"I didn't tell them about you."

Alarm and confusion.

"I did tell them I met you," Vicki corrected herself, "but I didn't tell them who you were. I didn't tell them you weren't from Earth. I didn't tell them you were the ones responsible for nearly killing us off."

"Why not?" asked Brandori.

"We weren't, and we didn't." Lyrith was nearly hissing.

"You were, and you did," she corrected Representative Lyrith.

She turned to address everyone at the table. "I didn't tell the other Guides because I didn't know how to deliver this information without angering them, without making them feel outraged. We have enough of our own problems to deal with right now without trying to fix yours. I need to keep us focused on our mission." She looked at them. "A mission that doesn't include you."

"But it does include us." Representative Brandori's voice was uncertain.

Seriously? They had imagined they could just appear out of the darkest, most broken, disastrous recesses of human history, and—*abracadabra*—they'd be welcomed with open arms? Time to get real.

"I don't feel like I can tell the other Guides until I have a strategy for how to move forward." She crossed her arms and stared at them. "Now, how do you intend to make amends?"

Chapter Twenty-Five

Vicki was floating amongst some trees, watching the sunlight streaming down through the branches and dappling the forest floor. It seemed familiar. She heard the sound of burbling water and came upon a small stream happily flowing between two grassy banks, individual drops of water spraying up on the large rocks that she and Beth had strategically placed as stepping stones. Too bad it had all been paved over for a development more than a decade ago.

Paved over a decade ago. Apparently, she was in the dreamscape again.

She looked around; it all seemed so vivid and sharp. And it felt real.

"Beth?" Her voice was tentative.

Beth appeared out from behind some trees, smiling broadly. "Hey, Vicki."

Vicki didn't cry, although she may have stopped to wipe a speck of dirt from one eye. She smiled back. "We finally figured out the message of the flowers."

"I knew you would. After all that time you spent proofreading the manuscript?" Beth shook her head in disbelief that her big sister might have missed it. Her ponytail swung back and forth with the movement. She looked so healthy, so vibrant, so alive.

"It was always a possibility." Vicki grinned. Then: "Beth, what do you want me to do with your shop?"

Okay, if she had planned things out beforehand, that's not something she would have asked. But her brain wasn't thinking, so she just blurted it out. She should have talked about life and death and missing her, but instead, her mouth took off by itself.

"You're facing aliens and a rogue corporate military organization with superpowers, and that's what's bothering you?" Beth was laughing now. Vicki missed her laugh.

She gave a crooked smile. "I was always the practical one."

"Vicki..." Beth fixed her with her eyes. That look broke Vicki. It always did.

"I don't know what to do, Beth. Everyone thinks I have the answers, but I don't! Everyone expects me to figure out how to resolve all these problems and then actually do it. They're earth-shattering problems—literally! Just when I think I have a handle on one thing, something else pops up. It's too much."

Even in the dreamscape, her body was shaking with stress.

"Vicki." Beth's voice was calm. "Vicki, look at me."

Vicki looked over at her. Beth's eyes were calm and soothing. She missed her so much.

"Mom always said to start with one task, one chore, one problem," said Beth. "And then when you've taken care of that, go on to the next. You don't need to tackle everything all at once, do you?"

"I thought I knew how to deal with the Partnership and the disclosure of extraterrestrials. But now I've found out there's a colony of different aliens living inside the Earth, and they want to move to the surface. The Alpha Centaurians are the reason humanity was nearly wiped out eons ago, so that's not going to go well."

She was whining. She hated the fact that she was whining, but there it was.

"Is it your problem to solve?"

"I actually told them it wasn't." The memory cheered her up, and she snickered a little. No, that meeting hadn't gone as they expected.

"You are part of a team, Vicki. What do they think?"

She looked down, flustered. "I actually haven't told them yet."

"Maybe you should. Stop feeling like it's all up to you. There are a lot of skilled, intelligent people who are trained and ready to do their part. Let them." Beth gave a glum smile. "But then you always insisted on shouldering the entire burden yourself. You should be kinder to yourself."

She was right. When their parents died, Vicki had stepped in to take care of everything. On the surface, that wasn't surprising because she was the eldest by several years. Looking back, however, she could identify a pattern: she was the person who always stepped up to resolve issues in all spheres of life, whether they were related to family, the workplace, or romantic relationships. Maybe she shouldn't have.

"Yes, I'll tell them," she said with shoulders hunched. She felt foolish for having held anything back.

"That's good," said Beth. "It'll go better that way. You need to learn to trust people." She stepped closer and put a hand up to Vicki's cheek.

She could still feel it when she woke up.

* * *

"What the fuck!" Brad's face was white with anger.

James was startled. No matter what the provocation, he had never known his best friend to lose his temper.

That morning, Vicki had told them they needed to skip their tai chi class because they had to talk. James's parents, Mona and Calvin, had also joined them in the studio's back garden. It took Vicki about twenty minutes to brief them all on the meeting with the Alpha Centaurians. She hadn't minced words about how the ACs—yeah, Alpha Centaurians was too long to keep saying—were the descendants of those who had basically butchered humanity's history, culture, and timeline. Not to mention all the dead people. And now they wanted to move in and be neighbors. Everyone was looking at Vicki with various degrees of outrage and shock.

Brad obviously wanted to say more, but whatever angry words came out of his mouth were unintelligible.

Jessica put a hand on his shoulder but didn't say anything. Her expression was equally grim.

"That actually explains a lot," said James slowly. He reflexively raised his hand to push his nonexistent glasses up his nose, then quickly put it back down when he realized what he was doing.

"What do you mean?" His dad managed to get the question out, even though he looked a little sick.

"All the stuff we still can't explain about human history," he said. "Take the Egyptians—they seemed to appear out of nowhere, and their recorded history doesn't line up with what was happening in the rest of the world at the time. Then there are all those giant stone structures scattered around the globe—just sitting there in the middle of nowhere, with no clear past or future. And archaeologists have found all kinds of objects that don't make sense—things that shouldn't even exist in the places where they turned up."

"When the Council forces came to pick up the AC expedition survivors, they erased a lot of history," Vicki agreed. "Actually, from what the ACs told me, it was worse than that. History, people, and places were totally eradicated, and then they tried to take whatever was still left and stitch it back together. Obviously, mistakes were made."

"They have some balls thinking we'd just agree to them moving up to live alongside us," Mona spat out. "As if."

"I'm not sure all of them want to move to the surface," Vicki said, doing her best to accurately reflect the discussion. "And I don't think those who do want to live on the surface want to live among humans. My impression is that they want their own place, their own territory."

"Did they suggest where they wanted to live?" asked Jessica, ever practical.

"Someplace temperate, apparently. They don't like the desert; they don't like frigid temperatures; they like trees and being surrounded by nature. As far as I can tell, it would be some of Earth's best land."

That set off another round of outraged exclamations. Vicki let it go on for a couple of minutes, then raised her hand for silence. When everyone was looking at her, she spoke.

"I told them we'd have them banned from Earth." She smiled.

James was startled to see that Vicki's smile matched Larry's for menace. Good thing she was on *their* side.

"We can actually do that?" he asked. If so, it would solve a *lot* of problems. James knew the ACs couldn't stay hidden forever, but based on what Vicki had said, he suspected many of them saw humans as a "lesser" species. That kind of thinking wouldn't lead anywhere good. And even if they did come forward—how could humans ever forgive them for what their ancestors had done?

"Apparently, we can. I told them they'd probably be kicked off Earth when humanity found out about them. I was just guessing we could do that, but from what I've learned about the Council and its policies, it was a logical assumption to make. And since they didn't contradict me, I'm pretty sure I'm right."

"You are right, Vicki." The impression of bells and gongs. Melly was standing at the outer edge of the clearing. How long had she been there? It was sort of hard not to notice an eight-foot mantis.

"Melly!" Vicki, Jessica, and Brad jumped up and went to greet her. James stood up more slowly and looked over at his uncle, who had been sitting silently all this time. With a smile and a jerk of his chin, he motioned to Melly, and together, they made their formal greetings.

"So, we can kick the ACs off Earth?" Brad was relieved to hear it.

James was relieved his friend was over his mad.

"If that's what humanity thinks is best." Small bells.

"Why wouldn't we?" Brad asked aggressively. "They nearly destroyed us all, and now they want us to hand over part of our planet?"

"Besides," James added, backing up his friend, "it would probably mean forcing a lot of people to leave their homes and relocate—and history shows that never ends well. Just look at the Native Americans, the Palestinians, or all the minority groups displaced in the old USSR. We've seen how badly that goes."

"I think we have a much bigger problem." Larry was speaking for the first time since Vicki began her briefing. Everyone looked at him. "Even if humans order the ACs off the planet, who will enforce it?"

They all looked at Melly. A sigh of soft gongs.

"Larry is correct to be concerned." The polychromatic colors whirled in Melly's eyes. "If the Alpha Centaurians do not wish to leave, the Council will send its forces to compel them."

"Like that worked so well last time," Mona said under her breath. James's mom never minced words.

Larry nodded at her in acknowledgment.

"Exactly. So, if there is any degree of noncompliance, we—those of us standing right here—will be fighting two wars: one against the Partnership and the other against the ACs. There will be a lot of blood—human blood."

Everyone was shocked into silence, finally grasping how desperate the situation had become.

"A further complication," continued Larry, "is the possibility that the Partnership and the ACs could decide to join together should they realize they are fighting a common enemy." As he said, "a common enemy," he motioned with his arms to indicate their little group.

"Is there any way we could inform human governments about the ACs and let them deal with it?" This question came from James's dad.

Larry's expression slid into a frown.

"That's a reasonable suggestion, but it wouldn't work. We have too many human governments that would need to agree on what to do; it would take too much time. Also, informing human authorities about the ACs would start a second Disclosure process apart from the one we are already trying to manage. You can bet someone—probably several someones—would try to cut secret deals with the ACs to turn a profit. It'd turn into a mess we couldn't control."

Vicki sighed. "I figured as much but was still hoping you'd come up with a different solution—some way out of this confusion I didn't see. In the meantime, I told them they needed to come up with a list of how they'd make amends."

"How to make amends for letting them live on the surface and kick us off our land?" Brad was indignant.

"No, how to make amends for having caused the destruction of human civilization all those eons ago. I told them humans would be angry at them, so they'd need to offer compensation before we even started talking about their possible future here on Earth."

"What kind of compensation?" asked James. This was getting interesting.

"I'm thinking technology," she said. "The crystal city I saw was stunning—I'm sure their material and geological sciences are incredibly advanced. Maybe we could also do music exchanges—the songs I heard there were hauntingly beautiful. I don't know what they eat—or if they even *do*—and I have no idea how they handle waste, but I bet they have knowledge and tech that could really help us in those areas."

"Advanced technology that isn't weaponized," mused Jessica. "That would be different."

Chapter
Twenty-Six

Mona, Larry, and Vicki were still sitting back by the pond. Calvin had gone in to teach his morning tai chi classes. James had joined Jessica in driving Brad to the Partnership's offices for his internship.

Vicki had raised her eyebrows when Jess offered to drive after Mona and Larry said they wanted to talk with her. "I thought you didn't know how to drive?"

"And that she was too emotionally fragile to boot," snickered Brad. "She's actually one of the best drivers I know."

Then Jess took her driver's license out of her purse and waved it at everyone. Vicki tossed her the keys and shooed them away, telling Jessica and James to come back to the studio after they dropped Brad off.

She found it unsettling. Jessica had held a driver's license for years—and had kept it hidden from her father the entire time. He had painted a picture of her as someone prone to emotional break-downs—as someone who struggled to handle everyday life. But that was clearly a façade, one she maintained not only for her father but also for the other teens whose parents worked for the Partnership.

Years spent pretending to be fragile, emotionally unstable, and easily overwhelmed.

Frankly, her self-control was a little scary.

Vicki turned to Mona. "Did you know about this?"

"That she could drive? Yes, she let us know a couple of years ago. Here at the studio, she was safe."

Vicki remembered the messages of the flowers—primroses and baby's breath for protection. That now made a lot of sense. She took a deep breath. "How about the part where she has been acting as if she were emotionally and socially incompetent?"

Larry nodded seriously. "We had to lay the groundwork; the kids needed protection. Having people underestimate you is a good strategy when you need to conceal who you are and what you are doing."

"But we're talking about years!"

"Yes, we were waiting for you for years." Mona's response was clipped as if it were Vicki's fault she had been living her life somewhere else.

"Not exactly," Larry said. "The kids were learning and training—and so were you, just in a different way. You needed to gain that government experience. What you told us about your meeting with the ACs proves it. None of the rest of us could've steered the conversation the way you did. I don't know yet what we're going to do about the ACs, but you opened some doors—and bought us time."

Vicki rolled her shoulders to ease the tension building in her neck. Then, she changed the subject.

"What did you want to talk to me about?"

"Chi." Mona's response was prompt.

"Do I need to take more classes here at the studio?"

Larry spoke up. "We think you need to know more about what chi is and what you can do with it."

Vicki looked over at Mona, and she nodded.

"Chi isn't just some abstract force," she said. "It's an actual tool. A powerful one. Especially when we're talking about vibrations and dimensions."

Vicki didn't know what she was talking about, but Mona had her attention. She was in favor of having more tools.

"While we've been talking about moving your chi in class, that's just the starting point. Think of your chi as the energy of your consciousness. And just like your consciousness, it can exist in different vibrations—even in different dimensions—at the same time. It can shift itself into those dimensions. That's how you meet aliens."

"Like how the kids and I meet with Melly in the pocket out-of-time?"

"I understand that's considered a beginning step."

Mona looked at Larry for confirmation, and he nodded.

"Both consciousness and chi energy are similar to scalar energy—a concept based on the work of Nikola Tesla that relates to quantum physics," he said. "The Partnership is working with scalar energy but isn't getting very far because they're using the nuts and bolts of advanced technology without the benefit of chi. They probably won't get very far—at least not by ET standards—but they are doing enough to be causing problems."

"What are they doing?" Vicki asked, but she was pretty sure she knew the answer. She was right.

"They've weaponized it, of course." Mona's voice was matter-of-fact. "They have devices that not only affect us here in our reality but also affect life in other dimensions. They haven't caused much damage yet, but it's starting to be a problem."

In response to Vicki's raised eyebrows, Mona continued, "About a year ago, Melly told us this was an issue we would need to address as part of our larger mission. The Partnership isn't aware of it, but some of their devices are causing harm in the higher vibrations where many extraterrestrials live."

"What kind of harm? And why haven't the ETs themselves put a stop to it?"

"They don't want the Partnership to realize how powerful that technology is," said James from behind them. He and Jessica were walking down the path from the studio. Traffic must have been light for them to have dropped Brad off and returned so quickly. Or maybe Jessica just drove that fast. "Melly said they have it contained for now, but they don't want it to get any worse."

"Okay, that should be resolved if we can take care of the Partnership."

—when—interjected Jessica softly, but Vicki ignored her and continued on.

"If we have an idea of the types of weapons and technology, we'll need to make sure that this information is locked down and not included in the overall Disclosure process."

"I'm already taking care of it," Larry said.

"He's already taking care of it," Vicki repeated back to Mona. "Is there anything else I need to know about chi?"

Both Jessica and James burst out laughing. Vicki just looked at them.

"Sorry," said Jess. "It's just that they haven't even started."

The conversation went long, and eventually they had pizza delivered for lunch. It was a good call—everyone needed the grounding effect of pepperoni and melted cheese after what felt like hours of diving deep into the nature of the universe.

Vicki felt like she'd gone into a study session and somehow come out knowing less than before she started. James tried to reassure her, saying the point was just to get her thinking about what to watch for and which questions to ask. But she couldn't shake the feeling that he was just being kind.

Albert Einstein once said that matter doesn't truly exist; that it's simply energy slowed down enough for us to perceive it. That idea was at the heart of their conversation around the pond—that different realities and dimensions are separated by vibrational frequency, and those living in lower vibrations struggle to perceive beings in higher ones.

Vicki already understood this, thanks to her encounters with the Suede Nation and the ACs. Both groups existed at slightly higher vibrational levels than humans, which made them nearly invisible—even though they all shared the same physical world, the same geography, and the same flow of time.

She hadn't expected to learn that even the most stable parts of reality—objects that seem to persist across vibrational planes—can change dramatically when the frequency shift is large enough. They used the Sun as an example, something that exists across countless vibrational levels.

To humans, the Sun is a life-giving energy source, a massive ball of plasma powered by nuclear fusion. Get too close, and you burn up. Simple.

But from the perspective of someone living at a much higher vibrational frequency...

"A portal? You've got to be freaking kidding me."

"It's true." James' head was nodding so earnestly that it was in danger of becoming detached.

The other three were laughing at Vicki's expression. She looked for any sign they were pulling her leg, but didn't find any.

"Okay, so how does that work? Is the Sun no longer a blazing hot star at higher vibrational levels? Does it transform into some sort of high-tech star gate? Is the Sun—and are other stars—natural phenomena, or are they manufactured?"

She was on her third slice of pizza but realized she had lost her appetite. This was getting too weird. She put the half-eaten slice back in the box.

"That's a lot of questions," commented Jess. But she didn't volunteer to answer any of them.

"We don't know everything, of course," said Mona. "Actually, our knowledge is quite limited. We only know what Melly told us."

"Which is...?"

Larry was the one who finally gave her a clear explanation.

"All stars are portals," he said. "Gateways to other parts of the Universe. I don't know if every star connects to every destination, but this is how extraterrestrials travel huge distances in space—quickly. The key point is, you have to be at a higher vibrational level to use them. And your chi is essential for that. If the Partnership tried flying one of its ships into the Sun, it—and everyone on board—would be destroyed.

Larry paused for a moment, then continued.

"You can't access that higher vibration without DNA activation and chi. And people like me—biologic constructs made with tech reverse-engineered by the Partnership—we'll never be able to travel that way."

He swallowed hard but kept his expression steady.

"So that's the explanation?" Vicki asked, incredulous. "We just change our frequency, fly into the sun—and *poof!*—we're in another part of the universe?"

"It's more complicated than that," Larry replied. "Every destination has a unique frequency tag or identifier. You have to know the exact frequency of the place you want to go. Then the entire ship—and everyone in it—has to match that frequency."

He paused, then added, "The ships the Partnership uses can be tuned to different frequencies, sure. But the people inside them?" He shrugged. "That's the problem. The Partnership can fly at speeds you can hardly imagine within our solar system. Interstellar travel, however, is still beyond them."

"So, how can you tell when you're at a high enough vibration to travel like that?"

"Flying into a blazing hot star and not dying would be a clue," said Mona to no one in particular.

"Are we planning to start flying around in a spaceship?"

"No," said James, looking surprised. "We're just using the Sun as an example of what chi and vibrational levels make possible. The Sun is a gate to our entire future."

"It's also an example of what the Partnership would steal from us." Mona's voice was terse. "We wouldn't be able to shift vibrations if they messed with our DNA. The Partnership would 'gift' us all their upgrades and transhumanist improvements while robbing us of star travel."

"Getting back to the point," Larry said heavily. He waited until everyone stopped talking and all eyes were on him before continuing.

"Chi is what raises your vibration, and that higher vibration gives you access to different abilities. Melly activated specific parts of your DNA on purpose, but to some extent, anyone can do the same thing—by working with their chi and keeping their vibration high. When the planet goes through the vibrational shift, anyone who puts in the effort will be able to access those abilities too."

"But not everyone will want to," said Jessica.

"No, not everyone will want to," agreed Larry, calmly. "But that will be their choice."

Vicki still didn't see the point. "So, what do you want me to do with this information? Yes, it's interesting, but how is it relevant? How will it help us?"

"It's inspirational," said James. "And awe-inspiring."

Vicki made an effort not to roll her eyes. Jessica was less restrained and punched James' shoulder.

"Ow!" James glared at her and rubbed his arm.

"We don't know if it's useful or even relevant," Larry admitted. "But more knowledge is always a good thing. To us, Vicki, you're a wild card. You've got a different background, a different perspective. Maybe this info will just be something interesting to file away. But maybe, at some point, you'll think back on it—and suddenly see a way to use it that none of us ever considered."

Vicki's stomach tightened. "Don't you think you're gambling a little too much on me?"

Larry was dead serious when he replied. "I don't think we have any choice."

Chapter
Twenty-Seven

K iran was coming to dinner.

And if what he'd told Brad was true, Kiran was also planning to plant listening devices. Her brother now had access to some of the Partnership's most sensitive tech, and they wanted to be sure their shiny new intern wasn't a threat. The thought made Jessica laugh—too late for that. The Partnership's security ship had already sailed.

She didn't love the idea of being bugged, of course, but at least they *knew* about it. Oddly enough, that gave her a small—probably misplaced—sense of control in the chaos their lives had become.

"Do you think Kiran is being totally honest with us?" Vicki asked her.

They were waiting in the car outside the Partnership's corporate office building to pick the two boys up. It was on the other end of the same compound where the Family Day event had been held, but it was right on the street and had less security—at least less obvious security. Jessica knew how the Partnership operated—she was sure there was plenty of security they couldn't see.

Vicki continued worrying out loud. "I've come across a lot of people who will tell you the truth, but they don't tell you the entire truth. There could be other things going on behind the scenes Kiran is keeping quiet about."

"Brad thinks he's a good guy—he's pretty good at judging people's characters. And if not?" Jessica shrugged. "You can tell if he's lying by how your gut feels. You just need to be really specific with the conversation."

She could tell Vicki had completely forgotten about her truth-telling-gut ability—the guilt on her face made that obvious. The Four definitely needed to help her practice using it until it became second nature..

Employees started streaming out of the building. Jess spotted the boys and rolled down her window to wave at them. They got into the back seat with their backpacks and, after a brief greeting, continued on with whatever conversation they had been having as they walked out. Their voices were too quiet to hear what they were saying. She knew because she tried.

Supper—once again on the patio because the weather in California is just that good—was more lively than usual. Everyone helped themselves to a big, steaming pan of lasagna in the center of the table while the boys kept her and Vicki laughing with funny stories about people from the office.

"All three of the directors!" Brad was nearly crowing. "All three of the directors came to our photonitron event last week and let us scan their images. They always act so stuffy, and the next day we sent around a company-wide video of the three of them doing the Macarena together."

Brad and Kiran laughed hysterically. Jess offered a brief smile, then quietly returned to her food. The emotionally vulnerable, insecure mask was back in place. Did she need to put it on around Kiran? She wasn't sure. But better safe than sorry.

Brad passed Jessica his phone so she could watch the video. It *was* funny—though a little unsettling, considering it was all part of a simulation. She passed the phone to Vicki.

"Did a lot of people show up to get scanned?" she asked.

"We had people lined up out the door all day," Kiran smiled. "It was great. Our supervisor was thrilled with all the attention our office got from the C Suite. Even my parents stopped by. It was a total success."

Brad cleared his throat, and they turned to look at him. "And right now, in my closet, I have a photonitron and a copy of all the scans we made."

Already? Jessica and Vicki exchanged surprised glances—everyone had expected this to take more time. Jess glanced at Kiran. He looked down at first, then lifted his head and gave them a crooked smile. It was clear this wasn't easy for him.

That's when Jess made her decision—she knew what needed to be done, and she *wanted* to do it.

She straightened, took a deep breath, and flashed him a brilliant smile. "So, you've decided what you stand for."

No longer hiding behind her mask, Jessica focused on Kiran, her eyes clear and full of confidence, looking like a personification of courage and beauty rolled into one.

Kiran warmed under her gaze and gave a more genuine smile. "Honestly, I'm not sure what I stand for. But I do know I can't just stand around and let bad things happen."

Jessica reached out and patted Kiran's hand. He reddened.

"Kiran and I talked about this earlier." Brad, oblivious to the interaction between his sister and his coworker, was helping himself to more lasagna. "It would be best if he doesn't get more deeply involved."

"It would be safer," Vicki agreed.

Brad nodded. "The three of us—we're part of a team. We support each other, and we're together most of the time. But Kiran's on his own. He's surrounded by people—his family, other Partnership employees—who would shut us down in a heartbeat. If he doesn't know certain things, he can't accidentally give them away."

"And he'll have plausible deniability." Jess was still looking at Kiran with approval.

Vicki smiled at him too, then asked Kiran a question.

"You're bugging us tonight?"

Kiran dropped his head a bit and nodded.

"Not something you have control over." Vicki shrugged, making clear he was in a position not of his making, and she did not blame him. "Have you already planted them?"

"When you picked us up, I left one in the back seat near where Brad usually sits, so you shouldn't talk about anything sensitive in the car anymore."

He paused, glanced over at Jessica, then back at Vicki.

"I was there when Brad was dropped off this morning. I saw Jessica—'she who is famously unable to cope with anything'—driving. I don't think anyone else noticed... but still. I don't know why she hides what she's capable of—that's her business. But if she wants to keep up the act, she probably shouldn't drive to the Partnership offices anymore."

How could I be so stupid? Jessica's cheeks reddened in embarrassment. It hadn't occurred to her that she might be breaking cover when she took Brad to work that morning.

"Thanks, you're right," she said. "We weren't thinking, and that was a risk. We'll be careful not to let that happen again."

"There are two more bugs," volunteered Brad. "One in the entertainment room and the other in my bedroom."

"Your bedroom isn't a risk? I know you said you'd fix it, but you do a lot of work there," said Vicki.

"I'm a genius computer expert." His response was nonchalant. "I've already arranged it so I control what sounds it detects. And nothing is ever discussed in the entertainment room, so that's not a problem. We just need to remember it's there."

"Is that all?" Vicki looked at Kiran. "You're not going to put one at the dinner table or out here?"

"They're not intending to bug the whole house—they only gave me three," he explained. "You rarely use the dining room, and out here on the patio, it would be exposed to the elements."

Jessica looked at Vicki for confirmation, and received a nod—Vicki was finally tapping into her truth-sensing ability, and this time it had clearly picked up truth.

Then Vicki asked another question. "Are you and your family being bugged?"

Startled, Jessica and the boys whipped their heads around to stare at her.

"Why would you think that?" Kiran's voice was tight.

"I'm not accusing anyone—I'm just being thorough," Vicki said. "The Partnership is using listening devices to spy on Brad, and they're doing it casually, like it's no big deal. That suggests a few things. First—the Partnership spies on its own employees. Second—they haven't bugged the Martinsson house before now, so the concern is about what happens going forward, not what's already happened. And third—this kind of surveillance is standard practice for them.

She repeated her question. "So... are you and your family being spied on?"

"Not that I know of," Kiran said. "It never even occurred to me the Partnership would spy on anyone in the first place. I was surprised when I was asked to plant these bugs."

Jess saw Vicki relax. This, too, was truth.

"Your parents both work for the Partnership. Have they ever entertained coworkers at your house?"

"Lots of times." He began to look a little green as the implications sank in.

"So be careful about what you say at home, I guess. You need to assume the worst." Brad looked unconcerned as he forked lasagna into his mouth, but he was obviously paying close attention to the conversation.

"But think, even if your family's house is bugged, have you ever said anything that might be considered disloyal to the Partnership?" Vicki asked.

Kiran's eyes shifted upward as he searched his memory. Then he looked at her and smiled. "No, nothing beyond things an employee might say when coming home tired after a long day's work."

"I would assume you're good, then. Even if they have bugged your house, the fact that they asked you to bug the Martinssons suggests they consider you to be dependable and loyal. Not a risk."

"So, keep it up," said Jessica, reaching over to touch Kiran's hand again. "We wouldn't want to lose you."

* * *

After taking Kiran back to his house, the three of them gathered in the kitchen for a late-night snack. The staff had already left for the day.

"Do you think Lucia has plans for these?" Brad was rummaging through one of the refrigerators and pulled out a container of chocolate chip cookies.

"If the cookies are in your refrigerator, I'm sure you can eat them—at least a few. But only if you understand you'll have fewer cookies later on."

Vicki wanted a cookie, too.

"Great!" Brad took three cookies out of the container. They were enormous, with generous chunks of chocolate rather than the small chips more commonly used when making this recipe. Keeping one for himself, he offered the other two to Jess and Vicki. A pitcher of lemonade rounded out their snack.

After a couple of minutes, Vicki brushed some crumbs from her mouth. "I noticed no one talked about the possibility of putting a bug in the media room. I was relieved since that's where Jessica needs to work with Melly."

"I'm not sure Kiran remembered we have one. Or maybe he never even knew? The media room has always been Jessica's thing, not mine, and it's me the Partnership wants to eavesdrop on."

"Does anyone know about the media room?" Vicki looked at Jess.

"I don't talk about it," she said, shaking her head. "I'm erratic and socially awkward, remember? Being good at something would be out of character."

"Besides," mumbled Brad through a mouthful of cookie, "if they knew about the high-quality setup Jess has, the girls would insist on spending a lot of time there recording stuff for their social media posts. Can you imagine what Kiran's sister would do with all that?"

Vicki shuddered at the thought of spoiled little Aija running amok in the room.

"I like Kiran," Jessica announced, pretty much out of the blue.

When Brad and Vicki looked at her in surprise, she added, "While we don't want to put him in danger, I think we can trust him."

"He was telling us the truth, at least as far as he knew." Vicki referred back to the pinging in her gut.

But a big grin spread across Brad's face, and he took his sister's comments in an entirely different direction. "You *like* him! Does he know? Do you want me to tell him you'd be interested in going on a date with him?"

"Don't be an ass, Brad."

Those were harsh words coming from Jess, and her face reddened. Vicki thought Brad hit the nail on the head.

"I'm glad you both agree Kiran can be trusted." Then, fixing them with a stern look, she added, "But his involvement with us has gone as far as it's going to go, remember? So, no talking about Kiran in any capacity other than as a friendly coworker—at least not until this is all over. If he's linked to us, it will put him in danger."

Jessica left first, her face still red. Brad threw one longing glance at the refrigerator where the cookies were stored, then headed off to his bedroom.

Vicki waited a few minutes until she was sure the siblings were out of earshot, then went over to the refrigerator and took another cookie.

Chocolate always helped her think.

Chapter
Twenty-Eight

"**M**elly?"

"Yes, Vicki?" The feeling of small bells.

"I've been working a lot with the Earth's energies."

"Do you have a question?"

"The Earth vibrates; I could feel it when I was exploring. Our scientists called it the Schumann resonance."

"That is a statement, Vicki, not a question."

"Some people say it affects human consciousness because the Earth's vibration occurs in the same frequency range as human brain waves."

Melly waited.

"Does it?"

"How could it not? The lives of humans, animals, and plants are intertwined and inseparable from the planet that makes that life possible." An overlay of gongs.

Vicki took a deep breath—or what passed for a deep breath in the state of consciousness she was in. Then she asked about the thing that was worrying her.

"You've said that not all humans will make the shift when the vibration increases. What will happen to these people? Will they die?"

There. She had finally put her fears into words.

"Some will." Melly was unperturbed. "Others will not. The Earth exists on many vibrational levels. While it's likely the majority of humans will make the vibrational shift, those who do not—and yet still do not die—will continue on the lower vibrational version of Earth."

"I'm trying to understand what that would look like."

"The vibrational shift will not occur all at once but over several years. During this time, the two groups—those who will make the shift and those who will not—will begin to live in different realities."

"What does that actually mean, Melly?"

"Those who stay at a lower vibrational level will face more hardships—violence, economic collapse, natural disasters, toxic work environments—because that's where their energy is focused. People who are bound to make the shift will still live through the same global events at first, but their attention will be on the joy of loved ones, the beauty in daily life, and the wonder of being alive, even during hard times."

She continued. "Both groups will still live on the same planet, but they'll interpret reality so differently that, before long, they'll barely interact. Many won't even realize the shift is happening—because they simply won't notice the absence of people they've stopped connecting with."

This explanation was accompanied by the sound of Tibetan singing bowls. Apparently, it was important.

"So, whether individuals make the shift or whether they are left behind depends on where they focus their attention?" Vicki thought this sounded suspiciously woo-woo.

"That is an overly simplified explanation, but it is basically correct."

"I want everyone to make the shift, Melly."

"We do too, Vicki. We do too."

* * *

Surprisingly, life settled into a comfortable rhythm for Vicki. Early mornings started with tai chi, followed by dropping Brad off at his internship. Then it was coffee and strategy sessions with Larry, James, and Jess—sometimes joined by Cal and Mona—back at the studio. After lunch, she'd spend a few quiet hours on her own, exploring and practicing with Earth energies.

Meanwhile, James and Jessica used the afternoon to work in the media room, refining Jessica's programming. They were polishing the first fourteen episodes of the *Melly Speaks* series and, now that the Council had signed off on it, drafting scripts for a new weekly half-hour show featuring Melly discussing different topics.

After picking up Brad and having dinner, the Four—because James would stay late—would sit together and talk.

Larry didn't always join their evening conversations. Vicki suspected it was intentional—his way of giving her and the kids space to fully grow into a team. She wasn't entirely sure about that, but she didn't ask the others, especially not his nephew.

She didn't know exactly what he was doing, but she knew Larry was taking more risks than any of them. And even though he now moved with a lighter step and more confidence than when they first met, she sensed something deeper—he didn't expect to survive this. Not really.

He needed the Four to become a skilled, cohesive unit that could do the job without him.

"How's it going with the listening devices?" Vicki asked.

They were on the Martinssons' back patio. Lucia and Mateo had cleared away the supper dishes, and now they were drinking coffee and eating cookies as they watched the sun go down. Except for James, who was drinking lemonade.

"Like I told you, not a problem," Brad replied. "Before dinner, James and I played video games in the entertainment room just to give someone something to listen to. I'm not sure if anyone is actually reviewing the tapes. Planting bugs was probably just a 'cover your ass' measure so that they can report to upper management they took all possible precautions."

"Have you and James been playing video games a lot before dinner?"

"Yeah, every day this week. As I said, something for people to listen to."

"Maybe..." Vicki said, feeling uneasiness rising inside her and hating the fact that it did. "Maybe you shouldn't be using James as the other person in your conversation so often. He's not part of the household, and his parents aren't Partnership employees. We don't want to give anyone a reason to look more closely at James, his family, or the tai chi studio."

"Do you think the Partnership would go after James and his family? Everyone already knows James and Brad are best friends." Jessica's face was pale.

"Yes, everyone knows they're best friends, but they don't realize James is spending hours every day with Brad outside of seeing each other at the studio. If the Partnership catches even a whiff of anything, standard procedure would be to dig into all of Brad's friends—especially anyone who hasn't already been cleared."

She looked at their startled faces and added, "I am not suggesting that James spend less time here. I'm just saying his voice shouldn't always be the one the folks on the other side of the listening devices hear talking to Brad. That needs to be diversified: me, Jessica, or any of the staff. It's best not to arouse curiosity. You only have to keep it up for another month or so, and then everything will be OBE."

"OBE?"

"Overtaken by events."

Brad and James both nodded.

"Vicki," Jessica said slowly, "we've spent so much time talking and planning how to stop the Partnership—how to expose what they've done and reveal the truth about extraterrestrials. But the thing is, there are *two* different issues The first is the Partnership. They're going to make some kind of power move near the end of summer, so we have to be ready to counter them by then. But the other issue is the vibrational shift. And honestly? I don't think we have any real sense of when that's going to happen."

"I don't either. I've talked with Melly about it, and her response has been pretty vague, just that it will be sooner rather than later. Or at least it will start sooner rather than later. Supposedly, the shift will take place over several months or a few years?"

"What does 'sooner' mean to a star-faring alien from a race that's over a million years old?"

Once again, James casually dropped a random factoid into general conversation that showed he had been in contact with Melly—and having in-depth conversations with her—for far longer than the rest of them.

Vicki shrugged, then turned back to Jessica as she continued talking.

"Let's assume everything works out perfectly—the Partnership is defeated, humanity is introduced to the idea of aliens and the Galactic Federation, some sort of solution is found for the ACs, and the shift happens. What will life be like then? What do you think we're really fighting for?"

"Besides not being enslaved to the Partnership?" Brad was dismissive.

"Jessica asked a good question. Social and political movements are more successful—and gain more support—if they're fighting for something rather than just opposing current conditions. People need to see the possibility of a better future. And they need to know what the better future looks like."

She looked at Brad. "Political Science 101."

Brad reddened. "Sorry, Jess."

"So, what does that better future look like?" Jessica took a sip of her coffee. "When you put it that way, I see we've spent the last couple of years getting ready to oppose something—the Partnership.

But we haven't spent much time visualizing a life without them, a future at a higher vibration. What does that look like?"

"I don't think anyone knows for sure. Not us. Not Melly. Not even the Council. There are too many variables. But there are a few things we know for sure."

Vicki looked at the three young people encouragingly.

"For the first time, we'll have neighbors—extraterrestrials," volunteered James. "Maybe not on our planet if we decide to kick out the ACs, but we'll know about aliens and their technologies. Maybe even have a formal agreement with the Galactic Federation."

"Right," Vicki agreed. "That will be a big change in the mind-set for most of humanity. It will completely transform how we think about ourselves and our place in the universe."

"Most people will probably get DNA activations," ventured Brad. "Even if it's just some weak activations, that'll be a change."

"More than just a change," Vicki said, her voice picking up speed. "Think about how fast technology will advance if people can tap into whatever universal knowledge bank is out there. Imagine what they'll be able to do if they can access science and tech the way you do with computers. We're talking a complete revolution in science. In transportation. In energy. In..."

She caught herself—she was getting carried away.

"A total revolution in medicine," Jessica added quietly.

Vicki nodded, not trusting herself to speak.

"So, it looks like all of us will end up being winners when the vibrational shift happens. There shouldn't be any problems in getting people's support," said Brad.

He then took the last cookie even though he had already had three. It made Vicki feel less guilty that she regularly stashed cookies in a Tupperware in her room to eat later—with Brad around, no one got their fair share of cookies unless they planned ahead.

"Incorrect." The others looked at her as she poured herself another cup of coffee from the carafe. "Plenty of people will see themselves as losing a lot if our world goes through a vibrational shift. The same people who now enjoy wealth and privileges the rest of us don't."

"Ah," said James in sudden understanding. "The people who own all the oil and stuff."

"And transportation, industry, all of it," Vicki agreed. "But the wealthy? They're adaptable. A lot of them will probably find a way to hold on to their status and their wealth, even after the shift.

She continued, "But there's another group that won't—governments and politicians. Have you ever thought about what happens to them when humanity shifts? They'll lose their relevance. People won't need big, powerful governments in a world where all their needs are met. What's the point of a massive military when there's no more scarcity, no more conflict? What happens when citizens don't need to rely on the system—because they can do incredible things on their own?"

"Vested interests," said Jessica. "I had forgotten about those."

"This is why it's so important to deal with the Partnership before they launch whatever they're planning to do before the end of this summer," said Vicki. "If the Partnership is able to use their photonitrons to simulate an attack by aliens..."

She looked over at Brad.

"...it would be easy to justify larger militaries, more societal controls, price increases, and food shortages," he finished up. "People would be scared and do whatever they are told is necessary."

Vicki turned to his sister.

"So, your videos, Jessica, are critical to our success. They need to be ready to broadcast. They need to not only address Disclosure and what the Partnership plans to do but also paint a picture of how life could be when living a higher vibrational existence."

"They need hope," said James.

"Yes," Vicki smiled at him. "We all need hope."

CHAPTER TWENTY-NINE

Jessica sat on the edge of her bed, her phone in her hands, the soft light from the screen illuminating her face. She stared at the latest message from Kiran, his words appearing one after the other like puzzle pieces clicking into place.

> I know there's a lot more going on with the Partnership than you're telling me. Brad has admitted it to me, but doesn't want to say anything more. Please don't leave me in the dark. I've made my decision—whatever it is. I want to be a part of it. K

Jessica let out a slow breath, her fingers hovering over the screen. The message was bold—maybe too bold—but that was Kiran. In person, he was all about manners and being polite. Behind a screen, though, he didn't hold back. She typed a reply quickly, not overthinking it, just keeping things light—for now.

> You've got a wild imagination, Kiran. What makes you think that? J.

She read the message after she sent it and winced. She didn't want to lie to him, but she couldn't let him in on everything yet. Not when the Four were still figuring things out. Not when everything might explode at any minute.

> My imagination? When I had supper with you, Brad, and Vicki last week, we were literally talking about this—about how I shouldn't get more involved because it would be safer for me that way. But I've thought about it, and safer isn't a path I want to take. I want to make a difference. K.

Jessica winced again. How could she have forgotten that? She already knew the answer—she'd been distracted by *Kiran*. At twenty-two, she was far too old to be getting sidetracked by something that felt like a schoolgirl crush. She'd worked too long and sacrificed too much to lose focus now. The real goal was defeating the Partnership. She didn't have time for distractions—especially not this one.

> You don't need to be part of this. It's too dangerous, and we're still trying to piece everything together. There's too much on the line. We all agreed—it's safer if you stay out of it. J.

> I don't think I could live with myself if you went into danger and I stayed safe on the sidelines. K.

She must have been taking too long to respond because this was swiftly followed up.

> You don't have to protect me, Jess. I'm not some kid who can't handle it. K.

The words hit harder than she expected. She wasn't trying to protect him. She was trying to protect herself. And if she let him in—let him *really* in—it would change everything.

Her thumb hovered over the screen again. Why did he have to make it so difficult?

> It's not just you who could get hurt. This could impact your whole family. They could lose everything they've built—everything they've worked for. J.

The text lingered on the screen for a few seconds longer than it should have before she sent it, knowing full well the effect her argument would have.

A few months ago, the idea of starting a relationship with Kiran would've been laughable. But now? Now that she was done hiding behind her carefully crafted mask, the connection between them was impossible to ignore. Still, it wasn't the right time. It couldn't be.

Not when the world was hanging by a thread and everything they'd been fighting for was on the line.

Would there ever be a right time? The question lingered in Jessica's mind. *Maybe they could have a relationship*—just think about it. She and Kiran, together, like normal people. They could go on a date, sit in a quiet café, laugh about trivial things, and not have to worry about anything more serious than which movie to watch. It seemed so simple, so... normal. A life that felt just out of reach, something she could grasp if she only let herself.

But what if we make a mistake? What if, in trying to have something normal, they let their guard down at the wrong moment? What if their vulnerability was exactly what the Partnership would use to tear everything apart?

She put her head in her hands, feeling the strain of it all. It wasn't fair to Kiran, but she couldn't drag him into her mess. Not when things were this unstable.

Several minutes passed before Kiran's next message came through.

> I get it, Jess. I do. But I'm not going any-where. When you're ready, I'll be here. K.

Jessica stared at the screen as his message came in. *When you're ready.* The phrase echoed in her mind. But... when? Her question remained unanswered. There was no right time. Maybe there never would be.

* * *

Junia could barely contain her excitement as she paced back and forth in the quiet, softly lit grotto. The walls around them were speckled granite, the air thick with the familiar scent of earth and the slight, metallic tang of the underground. But in her mind, she wasn't here. She was with Vicki, guiding the human through the inner world paths to meet with Alun or with the Alpha Centaurians. Everything felt like it was moving so fast, and Junia loved it.

She couldn't stop smiling. She had never felt this kind of thrill before—this mix of anticipation and the electricity of something *new*.

Her cousin leaned against the stone wall, arms folded, his expression unreadable. Bowen was only a few years older than Junia, but his calm, deliberate presence always made him seem much older. Where Junia overflowed with energy and excitement, Bowen was reliable and thoughtful, always weighing the consequences before he spoke or acted. It was one of the things she loved most about him—even if sometimes it felt a little like he was trying to keep her from jumping off the edge of the world.

"You look like you're about to burst," Bowen said dryly, his voice steady but with a hint of affection in it. "What happened with Vicki this time? Did you *really* have to take her all the way to the Alpha Centaurians' chamber? I'm sure she knows the way by now."

Junia stopped pacing, practically bouncing on the balls of her feet.

"Of course! But she's learning, Bowen. And *I'm* the one who gets to show her everything—*everything*—about us. She can't just meet with Alun and the ACs without understanding how we live or where we come from. It's so exciting! She's starting to get it. She's starting to get *us*."

Bowen pushed off from the wall, studying her with a mixture of curiosity and concern. "I get that you're excited, but this is big, Junia. Meeting Alun is one thing. But showing a human our people and communities—that's a whole other matter. We've lived underground for thousands of years for a reason. We don't just—*let*—humans in."

"I know, I know," Junia said, brushing a hand through her dark, coppery hair, the strands falling wildly around her face. "But Bowen, everything's *changing*. The vibrational shift is happening. Sooner or later, the humans are going to *see* us. They're all going to know we're here. That's so *exciting*! We can't hide forever. And if we don't start talking to them, we might get left behind. I want to be part of it. And I want to be there when it all happens."

Bowen frowned a little. "I know you're excited, but it's not that easy. The humans—they're not like us. They've been cruel in the past. Our ancestors had good reasons for hiding, and those reasons didn't just go away. You can't be sure they'll like us, Junia. We've stayed hidden for a reason."

"But that's just it! What if we don't have to hide anymore? What if we can *change* things? Vicki's different. You saw her. She's open to us. I can see it in her eyes—she *wants* to understand us. She's not like the others."

Junia stopped and smiled at her cousin. "This is our chance to make the future different."

Bowen crossed his arms over his chest, tilting his head as he watched her. "You've always wanted something different. I get that. I just don't want you to get hurt. The humans—even Vicki—they don't understand everything about us. They're still just humans. We can't let our guard down. What if she's just like the others?"

Junia's excitement dimmed for a moment, but only for a moment.

"What if she's not?" she challenged. "What if she's the key to everything changing? What if *we're* the key to everything changing? What if, for once, *we* choose the future instead of letting others choose it for us?"

Bowen uncrossed his arms. "It's not that I don't want things to change—I do. I just think you're rushing in without thinking it through. Change always comes with risks. You've always believed the future will be better, but it's not that simple. People are complicated. Humans even more so. I just don't want you to get caught up in something that could hurt you."

Junia gave him a little shove. "Why so careful? You're serious, but usually not *this* serious. Come on, Bowen—let's have some *fun*! We finally get to do something that matters! The humans are going to see us, and then they'll have to change, too. We'll show them we're not bad guys. We're not scary. We're... something more! And if Vicki can help us get there, help us finally be seen..."

She paused to throw her arms in the air and spin around. "Then I say yes!"

Bowen smiled at her then, though his eyes still held a hint of caution. "You make it sound so easy. But nothing ever is, Junia. I know you want to make the world better, and I want that, too. But don't rush. Not everything has to happen right away. Things will come when the time is right."

She smiled back at him, her energy as bright as ever.

"That's just it! The time is *now*, Bowen. This is it. The vibrational shift—whether we're ready or not, we'll have to face the surface world. Whether we like it or not, the humans are going to know about us. It's going to be *fun*, don't you think? For once, we'll get to decide what happens next."

Chapter Thirty

Larry told the young people they were going on a date. He wished it were actually true, but he couldn't let that happen.

He and Vicki arrived at an out-of-the-way Italian restaurant that was definitely upscale. Discreet lighting, soft music, and generous spacing between the tables. The hostess greeted him by name, then seated them in a secluded alcove on an outdoor patio. She left them menus and promised to send a waitress with a couple of glasses of wine. Large urns with blooming roses, shining softly, surrounded them. Vines trailed down from a trellis, partially obscuring them from anyone else walking by.

"A date?" Vicki demanded.

"You said yes." Larry grinned. "With barely any hesitation."

"I only said yes because I could tell there was something else going on. I wouldn't have accepted otherwise."

He was pretty sure she was lying—at least a little. But he didn't have her truth-telling ability, so he let it go.

Larry nodded. "Saying it was a date made sure the kids didn't ask a lot of questions about our outing. I chose this place because I know the owner—he and I go way back. He's former military intelligence who prides himself on being paranoid; he does a daily sweep for bugs. We can be confident there's no one listening in on us here, at least not using electronic devices. You can check the people."

Vicki did so, reaching out with her energy to sense those who were nearby. The patio, while spacious, held only half a dozen tables. The three nearest them were empty. At the fourth table, an elderly couple was quietly discussing medical appointments. At the far end of the patio, a trio of young women were drinking wine, celebrating an engagement.

"All clear. Normal people, all of them. No biological constructs—except for you. We can talk."

But then she gave a quick frown. "But why did we need to come here? We could just as easily—actually, more easily—talk at the Martinssons' or in the back garden at the studio. I'm pretty sure either of those places would be more secure than here."

They both fell silent as the waitress arrived with their wine and a basket of bread. After taking their orders, she departed with the menus. Larry could see Vicki studying him as she took a sip of wine, waiting for him to respond.

"We're meeting someone here," he said after a pause. "Two someones—they work for the Partnership and aren't happy with what's going on. It would be too risky for them to go to either the studio or the Martinssons'; we had to meet in a public place."

"But why just me?" she asked. "Why didn't we bring the rest of the Four? We're a team, so they'll need to know what we talk about."

"Too many people," he replied. "And too young. At least for my contacts to speak freely. They'd be reluctant to do so in front of what they consider a bunch of kids. The truth is things are heating up fast, and we can't afford to spend more time gathering information. If we want to be ready by the end of summer, we need to step things up. I suspect the guys we're going to meet with will not be available for a second meeting anytime soon. If they don't feel free to tell us everything tonight, we might not get another chance."

He tried not to worry the others more than necessary, but the urgency was real. He felt lucky that his two contacts had been willing to meet so soon. Later might have been *too* late.

"Then why bring me? Wouldn't your contacts talk more freely if it was just you?" asked Vicki. "And if we're meeting with two more people, why are we sitting here at a table set for just us? It'll be awkward when they come, and we're in the middle of eating dinner."

Amusement showed in Larry's eyes. "They're not coming for another hour; we'll be done eating by then. But I need to brief you first on a few things so you can be a part of the conversation—you're our strategy expert. And while I trust these guys, I'm not giving them more information than necessary, both for their protection and ours. I told them you were my girlfriend."

He could see that Vicki was startled to hear that he had referred to her as his girlfriend. Larry felt a little guilty that he had done that—it was a self-indulgence they couldn't afford.

"Like I said, this might be the only time we get to talk with these guys. So, you'll need to be figuring out on the spot how we can use their information and how we can use them. You'll need to tell them tonight what they can do going forward to help us from the inside. We don't have the luxury of taking the info back to discuss it among all of us first, so decisions will need to be made without input from the rest of the Four."

The waitress returned with their meals—gnocchi with shrimp for him and risotto for Vicki. She filled their wine glasses before leaving. Larry took a sip of wine and then started talking.

He had said he would do it—that he would get inside information—and now he delivered. He sat across from Vicki, presenting a summation of all the advanced technology devices developed by the Partnership and how they were being used.

Vicki had never heard of CAT—Consciousness-Assisted Technology—which uses human consciousness to operate a device. He described how CAT could control the artificial limbs—even an entire exoskeleton—of amputees and paraplegics, allowing them to lead independent lives once again. While studies were already being carried out in research institutions, the current technology was both crude and prohibitively expensive compared to what the Partnership had.

Then he described the flip side of CAT. The Partnership had weaponized it, of course. Missiles could be launched and guided with a thought—even from a distance. Mind-interface weaponry. Psychotronic disrupters that could disrupt an individual's thought processes, induce tinnitus, and even cause brain damage. To Larry's surprise, the disrupters turned out to hit uncomfortably close to home for Vicki.

"Do you remember Havana Syndrome?" he asked. He had finished his gnocchi and poured himself another glass of wine—his fourth. Luckily for him, biologic constructs weren't affected by alcohol.

"Very much so," she nodded. "I had a friend who was serving at the U.S. Embassy in Cuba during that time. She told me people were falling ill, and no one was taking them seriously. The State Department refused to investigate until someone released the story to the media. Even then, they were going to chalk it up to mass hysteria until reports started coming from other countries' embassies reporting the same thing."

"That was psychotronic disrupters."

"The Cubans have psychotronic technology?" she asked in disbelief.

He shook his head. "What your colleagues experienced was the equivalent of 'friendly fire.' The Partnership shared a watered-down version of this technology with the U.S. military, which then used it against Cuban government and military officials. Unfortunately, U.S. Embassy personnel were working and living close to the targets. Since the Cuban government never publicized that its own people were getting sick, too, it looked like it was an attack on the diplomatic corps."

"So, U.S. diplomats were collateral damage in an attack by our own government?" She looked a little green.

"Pretty much," he said with a shrug.

It wasn't that he didn't care; it's just that there were far worse things out there. He continued down his list.

"We've already talked to you about scalar energy."

"The NikolaTesla energy that causes weapons to go off in multiple dimensions? The thing Melly told us we had to stop?"

"Exactly," agreed Larry. "But we told you only about the negative effects. Scalar technology can be an amazing tool if used correctly—water purification, soil remediation, the wireless transmission of energy over large distances."

He stopped talking as Vicki abruptly stiffened—he realized she had sensed three people coming toward them. As the hostess and two men approached, he stood up and quietly commented, "These are the guys who can help us isolate the dangerous technology from the good."

Larry felt a wave of relief. He hadn't said anything to Vicki, but part of him had worried that they might not show up. Knowing that they were on their side—even quietly, from the shadows—made success feel a little more possible.

Kyle and Graham were visibly nervous, slightly nerdy, and very much a couple. Larry introduced Vicki, and they waited quietly as the waitress cleared off their dinner dishes, then left them with two more glasses and another bottle of wine. Vicki passed, but Larry poured generous amounts of wine for his contacts and himself.

"Kyle and Graham are both in the Product Development Office—the PDO," began Larry. "It's the same office where Brad is doing his internship, but in a different section. For the last decade, they've played a role in nearly every significant new technology produced by the Partnership."

They smiled nervously. The short one—Graham—was in his late forties, Kyle a bit younger. The two men shared a glance consisting equally of worry and determination, then Graham began to speak.

"We're glad you're giving us this opportunity to help. We didn't realize what the Partnership planned to do with the technology and devices we helped develop—at least not during the early years—but by the time we did, it was too late. We want out, but we're stuck."

Vicki took a sip of water. "Stuck? How?"

Apparently, Graham had said all he intended to say and hunched down in his chair. Kyle took up the narrative.

"I've been with the Partnership for nine years, Graham for seventeen. It's the only professional job either of us has ever had. We've worked directly on about half the technologies the Partnership has developed; we have a working knowledge of the designs and capabilities of almost everything else. We won't be allowed to leave; we know too much."

"The only way any of us will be able to leave the Partnership is if it implodes upon itself," agreed Larry.

"But that's not the only reason we want to help," clarified Kyle. "What's happening is wrong. Disastrous, actually. It's not hard to predict what the future will look like if the Partnership continues down its current path. We hope to have kids one day, but not if the Partnership keeps doing what it's doing."

Graham and Kyle were amazing. Painstakingly thorough in their analysis, they detailed which technologies and devices were too dangerous to be released and which could be made available. They had also come up with a technical compromise for those devices that straddled the line.

"We can embed safeguards that will automatically crash and destroy the devices if certain parameters are breached. Total DNA upgrades, for example, would be out. There are just too many ways that could go sideways. We're already seeing that." Kyle didn't look at Larry, but he was referring to the Partnership's biologic constructs. "But boosting certain DNA sequences for medical reasons? Tens of thousands of people would benefit."

"When would you embed the safeguards? And how would you do it without endangering yourselves?" asked Vicki. "Seriously, we'd prefer it if people didn't die."

Graham and Kyle shared another glance, and then Graham pulled up a backpack that had been lying on the floor beside him.

"The designs and schematics are in here. We've already embedded the safeguards in the technologies that require them. You'll need someone who is good with computers to make sense of it all."

"We have someone," said Larry without expression.

"Wait—how about all the tech that's too dangerous to release? Are those designs in the backpack too?" Vicki was trying to keep track, but there were too many balls in the air.

"No," said Kyle, a little defensively. "We thought distributing that information was a bad idea, even to people who are on our side."

"Logical," Larry nodded.

"Is it all stored in one place, in one building?" asked Vicki.

Kyle started to nod, then shook his head. "Not in the same exact building, but it's all located in the research facilities section of the compound."

"You mean the facilities with all the experimental and engineering labs?" Larry asked. From the way Vicki was asking her questions, he could tell she was starting to draw up a strategy.

Graham nodded. "Is that going to be a problem?"

"Don't worry about it," said Vicki. "Leave it there. You two have been magnificent, but you needn't risk yourselves anymore. You've done enough."

"We have?" Both Graham and Kyle wore identical expressions of surprise.

"They have?" Larry felt surprised too.

"They have," Vicki affirmed with a smile. "We have other people working on this, and they can do the rest."

CHAPTER
THIRTY-ONE

The next morning, all of them—the Four, Larry, Mona, and Calvin—were in the studio's back garden drinking coffee. Larry and Vicki gave a debrief of the previous night. People fell silent as they considered what had been said.

Brad spoke up. "I'm the computer guy; do you have something to give me?"

Larry handed over Graham's backpack without comment.

"Who made our coffee today?" Vicki asked, because her café au lait was just that good. It seemed like every time they made her coffee, it got better and better.

"I did." James was sitting by the edge of the pond with Brad.

"But you don't even drink coffee!" His drink of choice that morning was hot cider.

"It doesn't mean I can't follow instructions," he said and smirked. "The internet has recipes for everything."

Jessica was watching Brad rummage around in the backpack. "So now we have the designs for all the technology?"

"All the technology that's safe to release," Larry reminded her. "The dangerous stuff that can't be embedded with a self-destruct trigger is still at the Partnership's compound. My contacts felt re-leasing copies—even to us—was too dangerous."

"I don't understand," said Calvin. "How can we defeat the Partnership if they still have all the most powerful, destructive tech-nologies... and we don't?"

Larry glanced at Vicki. "Vicki seems to have it under control."

That was a total vote of confidence she hadn't expected. But the eyes of everyone else turned toward her for clarification.

"It's better you don't know the specifics right now," she replied. "But if it makes you feel better, I received some DNA ac-tivations from Melly that the rest of the Four didn't."

"The Kick-Ass Quartet," corrected Brad. They ignored him.

Vicki continued, "The destructive tech isn't going to survive the next few weeks."

Calvin persisted. "All the tech and all the devices that are currently in operation? Much of it is at sites far away, including off-planet. How can you knock out all of that?"

"Most of the off-planet facilities are temporarily mothballed until whatever asteroids or moons they're on get closer to Earth." Larry drained the last of the coffee from his mug. "Even with all its money, power, and technology, the Partnership doesn't have limit-less resources. So, this is actually one of the better times of the year for us to act."

James stared into his cider. When he spoke, it was as if he was thinking out loud.

"Even if we had the schematics for all the dangerous stuff, there isn't time for us to build it ourselves. And if we were suddenly able to get our hands on some already-made devices? We don't have enough people to operate them. We're not an army. We'll just have to do without—we always knew there would be risk."

A beat of silence. The youngest member of the group had just verbalized the very thing they were all trying to avoid thinking about.

"But assume we're successful and the most dangerous tech-nology *is* destroyed." Mona was carefully picking her words as she thought it through. "Shouldn't we at least have copies of it so we'll be able to defend ourselves against similar weapons in the future?"

Vicki already knew how to respond to that question. "That's a mindset that has driven actions in the past. More than once, a serious disease has been eradicated, only to emerge again when it escapes from a lab. Only worse. Researchers often tinker with virus samples, making them stronger 'just in case' they mutate. Their real goal is to make their careers by coming up with future vaccines. Instead, they end up unleashing a stronger version of those diseases on the world."

"Technology can't mutate," stated Brad. It looked like he was totally engrossed with the contents of the backpack, but he was clearly following the conversation.

"The desire for power and riches is a powerful motivator," said Larry. "It's unreasonable to believe that someone, or many someones, wouldn't move heaven and earth to get ahold of that technology. Best that it no longer exists."

Now, the touchy part—something Vicki had given a lot of thought to. "We've finally come to the point where we're ready to start discussing specifics." She looked over at Mona and Calvin. "You two need to bow out of our group—at least temporarily. You don't have roles that can't be carried out by someone else, and the more people involved, the riskier it is. Being uninformed is the best way you can help us."

As she expected, both Mona and Calvin exploded in protests.

Who did she think she was—this involved them as much as any of them, and their tai chi classes were the reason they had been able to get this far in the first place. James was their only child, and if she imagined they'd allow him to take part in this scheme without them, she had another thing coming.

Vicki didn't listen. She heard it, and she actually agreed with what they were saying. Along with Larry, they had been the main drivers behind the effort to put a stop to the Partnership and its activities. It was their tai chi classes that led to Melly's initial contact with the kids. And yes, James was only sixteen.

But it didn't matter.

It didn't matter because this was the path forward. She had been brought in as a strategy expert, and as that strategy expert, this was the only way she could see to get from here to there. Of course, there would be bumps and detours along the road, but this was the one best path. There were too many ways their entire plan could go sideways. Being able to take Mona and Calvin out of the equation would simplify things.

The arguments and outcry swirled around her, but she had retreated inward. Mona and Calvin were giving voice to their fears. The young people were watching, confused, clearly having been taken by surprise by the request. And Vicki? She was wondering what it would be like to be dead.

It wasn't as morbid as it sounded; she had been thinking about death a lot lately. Really hard not to, having talked with Beth a couple of times during the past few weeks. Really hard not to, having experienced existence on several different vibrational planes.

Melly had once quoted Einstein—energy cannot be created or destroyed, only changed from one form to another. Vicki used to think that was all about how a person's body, when dead, disintegrated, became compost, then gave rise to other life. But that was before she had learned about consciousness, about vibration, about reality. She wondered what life would be like when not tethered to a physical body. She wondered what life would be like when she didn't need to breathe. She wondered if she was going to find out the answer to that question sooner rather than later.

"ENOUGH!"

Larry yelled loudly enough to bring her out of her reverie and shock Calvin and Mona into silence. The young people had retreated a few feet to watch the grown-ups in safety. Larry looked at his brother.

"We always knew it would come to this someday. I'm sorry. I'm sorry to tell you Vicki's right; you need to step back. I'm also sorry to tell you James needs to continue with us." Larry wearily rubbed the back of his neck.

Mona drew in a sharp breath. "But he'll be in danger!"

"Everyone is in danger. Even if he wasn't involved with us, James would be in danger. Just like everyone else in the world. What makes James different is that he has a critical role that can help change that."

Calvin said nothing. His eyes looked old. He took his wife's hand and pulled her back toward the studio. She resisted, then gave in, her expression stormy.

Larry turned back to Vicki. "As you were saying?"

Vicki took a deep breath. "You told me the Partnership has scheduled you for an upgrade in two weeks? That it's no longer optional?"

Larry nodded.

"Good—that means the Partnership still considers you to be one of them. And they'll want you to be fit for duty for what they're planning to do. From an operational standpoint, the Partnership will want to make sure you have several days to integrate your upgrade—and to reintegrate with your fellow biologic construct soldiers—before you're pressed back into service. So, if we add up the two weeks for your upgrade plus another week or two for the integration, we can anticipate the Partnership will strike in three to four weeks."

Larry nodded again. "When Dave and CJ stopped by our table when we were all having supper last month, they were insistent I needed to get an upgrade by the end of August. This timeline would track with what they said."

"Then next week—we launch next week. The Partnership will be about three weeks behind us. We'll catch them off guard. I don't expect we'll be able to head them off entirely, but we can at least change the conversation."

The young people watched the exchange with wide eyes, both understanding and not understanding what was being discussed. It was Jessica who asked for clarification.

"What, exactly, is the Partnership planning to do?"

"Just like we thought, it'll be a false-flag attack," growled Larry. "A couple of their own reverse-engineered ships, plus a whole lot of photonitron-generated flying saucers."

The young people didn't show surprise; this was what they had expected.

Larry continued, "From what Graham and Kyle told us, this UFO invasion will cause real damage for the first day or two. Then, the Partnership will swoop in out of nowhere to save the day. Humanity will shower it with gratitude, and those who question how the Partnership actually got the weapons used to rescue the world will be called ungrateful. Humanity will give the Partnership whatever it wants to ensure our safety from the 'bloodthirsty aliens.'"

"When you say, 'real damage,' what exactly does that mean?" Brad was no longer absorbed in the backpack.

"They'll attack cities—at least two in the U.S., another in Europe, one or two in Asia."

"And we can stop this?"

"We're going to try." Vicki's voice was grim. "The Partnership's 'real damage' includes real deaths—and they don't care."

"So, what do we do?" This from James.

She let out a breath. Smiled. "Brad, in that backpack, did you see the schematics for free energy?"

Brad's grin was her answer.

"First thing, as soon as I do my part at the Partnership's headquarters, that gets posted on the internet as widely as you can manage—all countries, and as many sites as possible. I'm talking thousands of sites if you can manage it. Graham and Kyle gave us a design version that's scaled for home use—a system simple enough for someone with a mechanic's background to build."

She looked at the three young people. They were scared, but they were determined. She quietly added, "If we are able to do nothing else, getting information on free energy out to the public will prevent the worst of the future the Partnership has planned for us."

"And my interviews with Melly?" asked Jess.

"On the first day also. Immediately after Brad posts the free-energy schematics. I'm not a computer whizz or a media expert, so I have no clue how long it will take or what it might involve—you guys take care of it. If James isn't busy, he'll be running between the two of you, lending a hand where he can."

James nodded his agreement.

"What about preventing the false-flag attacks?" Larry's brow furrowed as he considered the schedule Vicki was outlining.

"Graham and Kyle said that was being coordinated here in LA at the Partnership's main property. That first night, I'll need your help. We'll need to go in person."

Larry didn't ask any more questions. None of them did. They trusted her, and that scared her. It scared her more than the Partnership, more than super-soldiers, more than weaponry that could cause mass destruction in multiple dimensions simultaneously. It scared her more than aliens who had nearly wiped out humanity and now wanted to live among them.

They trusted her, and they were family.

Loving people was the scariest thing of all.

Chapter Thirty-Two

The next morning, Vicki woke up early. There was a three-hour time difference between Los Angeles and Washington, DC, and she needed to make a phone call. She grabbed a coffee from the kitchen and then returned to her room. She needed to take notes and be focused—not something she could do if someone interrupted her on the patio.

When Vicki was hired as a diplomat by the Department of State, she went through orientation with thirty other new officers. After training, all of them were sent to U.S. embassies overseas for two years to process visas—no matter what their official job titles were. Vicki had been hired as an economic officer, and expected to spend her career on commerce, finance, business, and environmental issues. But the "needs of the Service" came first, and that meant everyone—whether they were public affairs, consular, economic, political, or management officers—started out on the visa line.

Some new diplomats were frustrated at having to "waste" two years doing visa work that had nothing to do with their long-term career goals. Vicki wasn't one of them. Yes, processing visas could be brutally monotonous—but it also provided a crash course in essential skills they'd use for the rest of their careers—and lives.

Even though she was an introvert, she learned how to speak to two hundred strangers a day. She learned how to make quick decisions and move on, instead of second-guessing herself for weeks. She learned how to say no—and be okay with someone believing she had just ruined their life.

The best part of visa work was the camaraderie. Vicki had gone through orientation and her first tour with Jerry Smith. Though they were both economic officers, they never served in the same office again. Still, she trusted him completely. If Jerry told her to lie down on train tracks with a train speeding toward them, she would—and she knew he'd do the same for her. Shared hardship had that effect.

They were nominally the same type of diplomat but ended up specializing in very different areas. Vicki held several positions focusing on commercial and environmental issues, while Jerry immersed himself in the finance side of things. It was because of his finance experience that she was calling him now.

"Vicki!"

They chatted a bit about personal matters. His wife, Anne, had just given birth to their second child, another boy, and was halfway through her six-month maternity leave from the law firm where she worked. He once again encouraged Vicki to come back to the State Department after her year's leave of absence was over. She demurred, saying she hadn't yet made any decisions. Jerry was the one who finally got to the point.

"You're calling to follow up on your other phone call?"

Yes, yes, she was. Three weeks prior, she had called him up, asking for advice. Jerry had never suggested she was imagining things or making stuff up. He trusted her. Shared hardship had that effect.

"Did you find out anything?"

He had. She had given him the names of four aerospace and defense corporations—all of them turned out to be publicly traded companies that fell under SEC jurisdiction. Anne had helped him by browsing through Dr. Greer's online archives, and she found substantial documentation that rose to the level of credible evidence.

"Oh my god, Jerry. I never suggested you get Anne involved!"

While Vicki had told him this was sensitive information, she hadn't expected him to keep it secret from his wife. All the same, she had assumed that it wouldn't occur to either of them to interrupt Anne's maternity leave.

"I had nothing to do with it," he protested. "The new baby is amazing; he sleeps through the night and half the day, which means Anne is going stir-crazy. She was already deep into it before I found out. Here's the thing—Anne was able to get in touch with Dr. Greer himself, and he provided her additional evidence that hasn't yet been digitalized."

Vicki was stunned into silence. Anyone searching online for reliable information about ET technology would eventually come across Dr. Steven Greer. A former emergency room surgeon who left medicine to focus entirely on lobbying the U.S. government about UFOs, Dr. Greer had built an extensive archive of evidence showing that the government was well aware of the extraterrestrial presence. Of interest to Vicki, however, was the documentation proving corporations were involved.

Jerry went on. Anne had been shocked by what she'd seen. There was a lot of testimony from credible sources—mostly former military personnel and defense contractor employees. And they were surprisingly open about the ET technology they'd received from the government. All of them claimed that corporations were given full permission to reverse-engineer the tech and were even encouraged to develop commercial products from it. If even half of what they said was true, those companies had access to things most people couldn't begin to imagine.

"Actually, I would believe it," said Vicki. "I've seen it myself."

"Ha!" said Jerry explosively. "This is going to be great—these companies haven't declared any of their ET technology–derived products as assets, so they're in violation of SEC rules. The antitrust angle brings in the Federal Trade Commission. And Anne said that deliberately holding back technology that would save lives and heal the environment is an action that might constitute a crime against humanity—and that could land the corporate executives in the International Criminal Court."

Vicki's head was whirling. This was better than she had hoped. The problem was the timeline.

"How long would filing with the SEC and the FTC take?" she asked. "We're on a tight schedule. We're moving forward next week." She didn't bother asking about the International Criminal Court—even she knew that was a long shot; its pace was glacially slow.

Jerry's wife was on the ball. Anne had already contacted her firm about it—but she'd been clever. She didn't ask the partners to file lawsuits directly. Instead, she suggested it as a practical exercise for the interns—half a dozen law students who mostly did grunt work. Starting with the SEC would be easiest, and filing by next week shouldn't be a problem. Of course, the cases would take months or even years to move forward.

"What exactly are you looking for?" Jerry asked.

"Publicity," said Vicki. "Lots and lots of publicity. The noisier, the better."

She could hear the smile in Jerry's voice when he replied. "I think we can manage that."

* * *

It was game night at the Martinssons' house again. Like last time, Lucia and Mateo had made mini quiches and a fruit and veggie platter. And, like before, dessert was the star of the night. This time, Lucia tried something new—brownies instead of cookies. They turned out to be gooey, chocolatey bombs of deliciousness that no one could resist.

There would be fewer guests than last time. Jessica had explained it to Vicki beforehand.

"It's August—a lot of people are taking the month off before school starts up again. Europe, yachting, the Cape, family estates on private islands—that kind of stuff."

"That's a little beyond my pay grade," Vicki had replied, dryly. "I guess crime *does* pay."

And there was one person who would be coming for the first time.

"Kiran said he'll be coming tonight." Jessica's voice was studiously noncommittal, but her cheeks reddened slightly.

"Brad works in his office, and they've become pretty good friends, so it won't raise any questions," Vicki said. "And, honestly, Kiran is probably eager to spend more time with people he doesn't have to hide anything from."

Jessica let out a breath and nodded.

"But if you think the rest of them won't notice about you and Kiran, you're kidding yourself." Vicki continued, her voice kind. "You'll still need to be the same socially awkward Jessica they've known all these years. And since the entertainment room is bugged, you'll need to keep in mind you have yet another audience. The Partnership will be listening, too."

"I know my job," Jessica snapped. Then she paused. "Sorry, it's just so... much."

Vicki sighed. "Me too."

It could have gone much worse, but it was still bad.

Jessica sat with James and two others as they played a video game, her fingers moving as she and James coordinated their next move against the zombies. She could hear Brad and Kiran laughing by the pool table as they played. Kiran's voice tugged at her attention, but she tried to ignore it. It was so stupid, really. She didn't have time for distractions—especially not this kind. Still, she caught herself listening for his laugh even as she launched another attack on their opponents. James nudged her with a grin, and she forced a smirk in return, pretending she wasn't keeping track of everything Kiran said.

Aija, the little brat, once again held court with her two blonde friends by the food board. And—whether by accident or on purpose—her voice carried. When she mentioned Kiran, Jess started paying attention.

"I don't know why Kiran came today; he's never come before." Aija's eyes shot daggers at her older brother. It seemed this was the continuation of an ongoing argument.

"Does it matter?" One of the blondes popped open a compact to peer at her lips.

"He's helping Brad, I know he is. I'm his sister, but I was told I had to take two years of college before joining the Partnership. Brad, however, is going to be hired as soon as he turns eighteen. It's not fair. I'm sure Kiran is pulling strings somehow—strings he's refusing to pull for me."

"It's not fair," agreed the second blonde. The first one didn't respond; she had gone from inspecting her lips to examining her eyebrows.

The pool game ended, and both Brad and Kiran wandered over to watch the video game. As Kiran casually took a seat on the arm of the sofa by Jessica, she tried not to react. It wasn't much, but it attracted Brad's attention, and he raised an eyebrow.

Only briefly, but it was enough to draw the notice of the ever-vigilant Aija.

"Kiran! What are you doing so close to *that*?" Aija's voice was mocking. Her blonde friends tittered with laughter.

Jessica and her brother both put on their blank faces—they had lots of practice controlling themselves.

Kiran? Not so much. Kiran was angry.

"Aija! Shut your mouth! You're speaking rudely about one of your hosts!"

Conversation halted, and James paused the video game. Aija was now in her element, the center of attention, all eyes on her.

"Come on, we all know Jessica is limited. She can't help it, poor thing. But you don't have to go out of your way to pretend otherwise." Aija actually preened.

Kiran stood up, livid. Brad put a restraining hand on his shoulder. Aija's eyes were sparkling. Everyone's eyes were riveted on the drama.

Then Jessica fled the room. It was her best option.

Years. For *years*, she had pretended to be less than she really was. But now that the end was in sight, it was harder to keep up the act. They were getting so close, and the cracks in her façade were getting bigger every day. This was exactly the wrong time to be interested in anybody.

She could have chosen to do something else—she knew she could have. She could have verbally ripped Aija to shreds and allowed her intelligence and strength to shine through. She could have made the others wary, made them feel respect, and reached out to the young man she was interested in. Instead, she kept her head down and played the fool.

She did her job.

But it was getting harder to pretend to be something she wasn't, especially now that she couldn't stop thinking about Kiran. For the longest time she didn't care when the Heirs cracked jokes at her expense. She could just shrug it off because it was all part of the act. But now, for the first time, she felt embarrassment. Because now Kiran was watching, and *his* opinion of her mattered.

More than it should have.

She didn't regret any of it. This was what it meant to be one of the Four—to do whatever it took, even if it meant hiding her true self. Playing her part was necessary if they were going to stop the Partnership and keep humanity from falling under its control. It wasn't always easy, but she believed in what they were doing. She believed the future was worth fighting for. And if pretending to be weak or broken helped protect their mission, then she was more than willing to do it.

That didn't mean she never wished she could be normal.

Jessica was still sitting in her bedroom with the lights turned off when there was a knock at the door.

"Jessica?" It was Vicki.

She didn't answer.

Chapter Thirty-Three

This time, Vicki hoped she was prepared for what she was getting into. She told the young people she'd be unavailable for a few hours, locked the door to her suite, and then went into meditation to raise her vibration. Being detail-oriented, she had done a deep dive into international agreements but hadn't found anything that seemed helpful.

So yeah, she was totally winging it.

She had considered doing nothing. She had no authority, no legal background, and zero experience with treaties. Maybe it was better to just let things unfold. But then she pictured the worst-case outcomes. While things might not go the way she hoped, the odds of disaster were a lot higher if she stayed silent than if she stepped in and got the conversation started.

Junia was waiting in what Vicki had come to think of as her grotto. She was delighted to see Vicki and chattered nonstop.

"Everyone has been impressed that I'm doing so much! They thought I was only going to guide you once, just to the Earth crystal and back, but now I'm your guide for everything." Junia was spinning around enthusiastically as she spoke, her arms outstretched, her dark coppery ropes of hair flying.

"You're literally the Guides' guide," Vicki replied with a smile.

That stopped Junia short, her topaz eyes widening. "I'm a guide squared? I had never thought of it as that."

"Maybe that should be what you call yourself from now on," Vicki suggested. "Junia, Guide-Squared. It has a nice ring to it, and it sounds responsible. Are you the first one to hold that title?"

Junia's grin was answer enough. She kept that grin the entire time she led Vicki through earth and stone to the crystal city. She was still smiling when she left her with the Alpha Centaurians.

Representative Brandori was the only one waiting to meet her, but when they arrived at the conference room—the same one as before—the rest of the AC delegation was already seated. There were seven in total this time—two were new, and one from last time was absent. Unfortunately, Representative Lyrith was still part of the delegation. Also unfortunately, the seats were still too high, and Vicki's feet again dangled.

Brandori made the introductions. He also laid down some ground rules. "Communication in this room must be conducted out loud only; no speaking mind-to-mind."

This made Vicki smile. Apparently, they didn't want a repeat of the ill-tempered mood she had brought to the table last time. Brandori even provided her a list with the names of the AC delegation's seven representatives, a brief description of their areas of expertise, and a diagram of who was seated where. The ACs really, really wanted their talks to go well.

She could use that.

She could also use silence. She nodded at each member of the delegation as they were introduced, then looked expectantly at Representative Brandori, silently willing him to make the first move. He did.

"Counselor Heywood, we have had many discussions with our people about what you said during our last meeting regarding the possibility humans might view us with hostility when we make ourselves known."

"*Will* view you with hostility," she corrected him gently, but firmly.

"That's not a certainty." Lyrith's tone was both aggressive and dismissive.

"Oh, but it is," Vicki assured her in her most serene voice. "After all, *I* view you with hostility, and I am one of those you refer to as the Guides. I am one of the very few humans who not only know that extraterrestrials exist, but have spoken with members of different species. I am one of the very few humans who are able to reach higher vibrational levels. I am also a human who has worked in diplomacy her entire career and understands the advantages of peaceful relations between neighbors. If *I* still view you with hostility, please accept my assurance that the opinions of other humans will be much more negative."

Okay, she laid it on a little thick, but not much. She didn't want to deal with them. She was annoyed and angry they were taking up her attention when time was running short on the surface. But her approach was effective. All the ACs around the table—even Representative Lyrith—blanched.

"I assure you everyone in our three cities is aware of the delicate situation we find ourselves in," said Brandori. "After our first meeting, we have been educating and informing all our people about what's at stake. We've been having discussions about what we are able to offer humans in recompense for the actions of the original Alpha Centauri settlers."

"I believe you are," Vicki said. "And I believe you're trying your best. But it's curious—right here at this table, one of your own representatives still denies the reality of your situation." She kept her eyes on Representative Brandori, though she could feel the others turning toward Lyrith. Her voice sharpened. "Are you sure you speak with *full* authority for your people?"

Shock. A quick intake of breath. Now *that* had been seriously rude.

One of the other representatives ventured to speak. Vicki snuck a quick look at her list. This was Representative Qixal, who was responsible for mining.

"Counselor Heywood, please accept our apologies for whatever rudeness has been offered to you here today," he said.

It was an effort to keep from laughing. Aside from Representative Lyrith's initial comment, she was the one being rude. Deliberately so. She didn't regret it—their reaction showed her how desperate they were to reach an agreement with humanity. Now, she knew how far she could push them and what boundaries she might establish.

Representative Qixal continued, "We truly do want to create an agreement with humans. Despite any minor squabbling you might hear, we are very aware that establishing good relations with humans is the only possible way for us to remain in a place that has been our home for thousands of years. We understand our initial introduction to humanity will be difficult, but we are willing to work to make it as smooth as possible."

It was a nice speech—just what she wanted to hear. But while Qixal was talking, Vicki took a quick glance at Lyrith. She was sitting ramrod straight, staring at nothing in particular. Representative Brandori was staring at her, a frown on his face. Vicki had the impression Brandori was reaming her out mind-to-mind, but she didn't call him out on it. She had made her point and brought them to a good jumping-off point. She didn't need Representative Lyrith to be publicly humbled for them to work together.

She briefly inclined her head in acceptance of Representative Qixal's apology, and then they got to work. Qixal went first. He offered maps of the planet with details of resource deposits—minerals, petroleum, crystals, salts, water, and a few other things Vicki wasn't familiar with. He also pledged to provide mining technology that would be low-polluting and have a minimal impact on the planet. Then he brought up an issue she hadn't thought about.

"The documentation isn't entirely complete. We've avoided cataloging resources near the cities in which we live. We also reached out to the Suede Nation and have come to agreement on what data we can release concerning resources where they live and work. We are trying to avoid any misunderstandings between humans and those of us who live in the interior. Our maps are complete aside from the exclusion of those areas."

Huh? She was so startled by his use of "Suede Nation" for Junia's people that she almost missed he was waiting for her to respond. How could the ACs even know that nickname? If Junia's people had told them about it, they must like it more than she'd thought. She shook off the thought and refocused.

"This is a very good start," she said encouragingly. "I'm curious, why are these included?" She pointed to a couple of minerals she didn't recognize as valuable.

"These are materials humans will begin to work with as you adopt higher levels of technology. Although the maps include all the petroleum and coal deposits within the planet—at least the ones that can be accessed without causing severe environmental damage—your people will only extract a fraction of them before they start employing other sources of energy—other technologies—that will make them obsolete. These materials you are asking about will be important in the production of the new technologies."

She hadn't even thought about that. She hadn't brought up-coming changes in technology into her calculations. Like she said, she was out of her league. Qixal had just handed her the biggest Christmas present ever.

"Thank you, Representative Qixal," she said warmly. "This is exactly the type of restitution that will help frame the introduction of the Alpha Centaurian survivors to humans as a positive event."

There was more, of course. One representative who worked closely with Qixal—Representative Lacino—specialized in materials science. Working with him, humans would soon be able to build their own crystal cities and create thin sheets of metal as strong as thick girders. Earth's architects were going to have a field day.

Medicine would also need a complete overhaul. The AC's medical technology was far more advanced than anything the Partnership had provided. Some people—especially those who made money from pharmaceuticals—wouldn't be thrilled. But for most of humanity, it meant better health and longer lives. Representative Juthin had already put together a summary of how the AC's technology could be adapted for human use.

It was more than she had hoped for. This was easier than she had anticipated. Of course, there were a couple of snags.

"Disclosure will happen next week—humanity will find out about extraterrestrials," she said. "The other Guides and I—and Melly—have an educational program ready to broadcast. We'll also introduce them to the concept of the upcoming vibrational shift and what that means for our evolutionary development. The Council is aware of what is happening on Earth and has agreed with how we are choosing to move forward."

She stopped and looked at the seven representatives. "The survivors of the Alpha Centaurian settlement are a wild card. I suggest a six-month delay from when humanity finds out about extraterrestrials before we introduce you."

Of course, the ACs disagreed with that. They felt the sooner, the better. They eventually compromised on four months.

"The delay is important," she said. "It would be best if you are not associated with what will happen during the next few weeks. The Partnership is on a course to pretty much enslave the whole of humanity. The Tall Whites have unwittingly facilitated their plans. You would benefit from having a certain amount of distance put between the upcoming events and yourselves."

"After four months, we'll be able to make our homes on the surface?" Of course, this was from Representative Lyrith. She was speaking politely, however, so Vicki replied in kind.

"Four months would be ambitious. We need to evaluate how the rollout goes first and only then make plans." She sensed some unhappiness with her answer. She smiled at everyone and added, "I say 'we' because I will be right there, arguing for you. I will be supporting your request to live on the surface. I will be defending you against being condemned for the actions of your ancestors thousands of years ago."

There was a stunned silence. She would be on their side?

"What about selecting the area where we want to live?" asked one of the representatives. "Shouldn't we have that information already prepared?"

She didn't bother to look up his name. "Absolutely not."

Everyone looked at her.

"You won't be allowed to choose a region to populate. The surface does not belong to you. If—and I stress the *if*—if everything goes well, those of you who wish to live on the surface will be able to visit the surface and see what's available. You will need to find vacant land that you can purchase, then build your dwelling."

She didn't suggest they find a human house or building to live in—after seeing the buildings in the crystal city, human-built structures would be laughingly uncomfortable.

"But what if we all want to live together in our own city?" This question came from the unnamed representative again.

She went back into bitch mode. "All of you living together, maybe building a separate crystal city on the surface? It won't happen. Ever. Earth does not have that amount of territory available. You will need to spread out in various communities. You will be living with human neighbors."

She looked at their faces; several of them reflected apprehension. Perhaps, at least in the case of Representative Lyrith, a touch of distaste.

"Representatives, you need to get over it. Earth's surface belongs to humanity. You will never be able to replicate what you have down here. And you shouldn't even try. If you end up on the surface, you will not be living the same type of life you have lived down here in the Earth's interior for thousands of years. You will be creating something new. Maybe what you're really looking for isn't a place to live, but a chance to change and grow. Maybe what you want is expansion."

She could see the change in the expression on some of their faces. Curiosity. Interest.

She continued, "This city is a breathtakingly beautiful place. I'm sure many of you will choose to remain here. But for those who wish to make a life on the surface? You will have the opportunity to create, to dream, to emerge. That's what change is. You will have the chance to find out who you really are."

Chapter Thirty-Four

"**Y**ou told them what?" Larry nearly spat out his coffee. His voice was incredulous.

It was early morning, and Vicki and Larry were sitting on the back patio at the Martinssons'. Their special tai chi classes and talks in the studio's garden were now a thing of the past. Mona still felt offended that she and Calvin were no longer allowed to be involved, and apparently, she could hold a grudge. The first tai chi class after the two of them had been officially disinvited from the planning had been... uncomfortable. It was easier just not to go back. Now Larry was bringing his nephew to the Martinssons' so they could continue to move forward. Vicki felt bad Mona was angry, and she felt bad they were no longer going to tai chi. But this would only go on for another week or so before everything changed.

For better or worse.

"I told them a lot of things. What specifically are you referring to?"

She took a sip of her latté. Brad had taken it upon himself to use his own funds to buy a top-of-the-line espresso machine, then sequestered himself for several hours in the kitchen with Lucia as they taught themselves how to operate it. They were drinking so much more coffee than before; it would be worth it, he had explained. His father wasn't a coffee drinker and wouldn't have approved the purchase as a household expense.

Larry's eyes narrowed. "The part where you were talking about how they could eventually live with us on the surface."

"Oh, that." Vicki set her coffee down and tore off a piece of croissant. Lucia had been warned there would be breakfast guests all week, so she had stocked up. This morning's spread included pastries, eggs, and sausages.

"What would you have had me tell them?" she asked. "That they couldn't? We need the ACs to have something to look forward to on this planet because they one hundred percent don't have any desire to return to their original star system. It's not like they'll be able to stay hidden—the vibrational shift will take care of that. Even if we told them no, I'm sure many of them would end up living on the surface anyway. We might as well have a voice in how that happens."

"Uncle Larry," said James, putting down his fork. "Didn't Melly say that if humans decide to kick the ACs off Earth, the Council would send its forces to make sure our decision is enforced? Wouldn't the same thing happen if we told the ACs they had to stay in the interior, and they moved up anyway?"

"Probably," said Larry. "And if it followed the same pattern as what happened before, it would be a disaster for Earth. There would be all-out war, and humanity would pay the price. But I just don't like it. I don't like the idea of humanity sharing Earth with extraterrestrials."

"Cheer up," said Vicki. "I've started them thinking. Not about how and where they can live, not about their own self-interest, but about what they can do and be. Imagine if the ACs opened a school for engineers, builders, and architects. It would be a dream come true for those fields. People all over the world would compete to have an AC school in their region. We could even hold global conferences with the ACs giving talks on things like wastewater systems, mining, and medicine. If we help shape how Disclosure happens with the ACs, this could spark a real renaissance across many industries."

"The ACs would be living a different life here on the surface—one that's less privileged," Jessica pointed out. "Do they want to change their way of life? Are they all so adventurous?"

Vicki shrugged. "Those ACs who want to live life exactly as they do now can stay in their subterranean cities. It's not humanity's responsibility to make them happy. It's their responsibility to make us happy. I told them that."

"You said before not all humans would be happy if there were changes in our current technology," said Brad. "That they would fight against losing profits and status."

"Yeah, we're already talked about the vested interests. Pharmaceutical companies won't welcome new medical techniques that might make their products unnecessary. The oil and gas industry will fight against new energy sources. I'm sure you can think of dozens more examples. That's why the rollout is so critical. We want to make sure the new technologies aren't kept a secret for the benefit of a few select individuals. That's what the Partnership has been doing."

"Kiran wants to join us," said Jessica suddenly.

They all looked over at her in astonishment, even Brad, who was both Kiran's friend and his coworker.

"He knows we're up to something; he wants to help," she said defensively. "Ever since that night he gave us the photonitron, and planted listening devices in our house, he feels like he doesn't fit in any longer—either at work or with his family."

"He left a bug in my car too," said Vicki under her breath. She was still a little sensitive about the Bentley.

"What are you even talking about? My parents have been involved with our group since the beginning, and we just kicked them out." James's voice was disbelieving. "And now you're suggesting we should bring in someone totally new?"

"It would be useful to have someone who has a bit more familiarity with the photonitron," admitted Brad. "I can operate it, I can make the holo reels, but I'm slow. Kiran helped design it. He's way speedier than I am—the fastest in the office. Besides, I really need to focus on the computer stuff—I'm the only one here who can do that."

Larry was looking at Jessica. "How is it you are the one bringing this up rather than Brad? What exactly have you been discussing with him? And didn't we agree to limit contact with him for his own safety?"

Vicki leaned forward. She wanted to know, too.

"I like him, okay?" Jessica's face was flushed, her body stiff. "And he likes me too. There's nothing wrong with that!"

Larry looked over at Vicki. She nodded back at him—her gut pinged truth. She turned back toward Jess.

"But if we bring him into our group, he will be the one who is most at risk," she said softly. "He'll need to be involved in the most dangerous part of our work, and he'll be totally defenseless. He hasn't had training in reaching higher vibrational levels; there's no time for a DNA activation. Even if Melly did give him an activation, there's no time for him to learn how to use it."

She laid it out bluntly, "Kiran will be the person most likely to die."

Jessica's face was as stone. She took a deep breath, let it out, and then seemingly came to a decision. "Aren't ordinary people allowed to fight for their own futures? We're the Four. We say we're giving humanity information. We say we're giving them the opportunity to make choices. But when they want to have a role in deciding their own future, we pat them on the head and tell them it's too dangerous for them—to go away and play nicely?"

She had a point.

"Kick-ass Quartet," said Brad through a mouthful of eggs. "But it would be helpful to have Kiran working with me."

Larry looked over at Jessica, then nodded sharply. "I will help protect Kiran."

"I cannot believe this is happening." James shot them all a furious glance. "My parents were kicked out."

"James." Larry's voice did not have the tone of uncle to nephew. Instead, it was general to soldier.

James looked at him, still scowling.

"Your parents—my brother and his wife—have played an indispensable part in this project."

"Then why..." started James. But Larry held up his hand, and James fell silent. When Larry was sure James wouldn't interrupt him, he continued speaking.

"Your folks were critical players at the start of this project, but now, when it's time to carry out our offensive, they no longer have a role. Just like Kiran, they would be the most likely to die. But unlike Kiran, they would be risking their lives needlessly. They would die for no reason." Larry's voice was implacable. "Do you understand?"

James nodded. But his expression was still mutinous.

* * *

"Melly." Vicki smiled. She went to steeple her hands over the alien's forelegs in greeting, focusing on Melly's whirling iridescent eyes. How did the world look with eyes like that? Did Melly see life as humans did while on this vibrational level? Or something else?

They were meeting in a tree-sheltered area in the back of the Martinsson property. And they were in normal, everyday reality. Vicki needed the physicality to ground her, to be sure of what she was doing. It was just the two of them—she didn't want to air her doubts in front of the others.

"The Four are getting close, Vicki." Melly spoke fully—there was a trifold overlay of bells, gongs, and Tibetan singing bowls.

"I know. I'm scared of what's going to happen. I'm afraid we will fail."

Melly laughed—the feeling of small bells. "You are a true child of your system."

"What do you mean?" Vicki was tempted to feel offended, but there wasn't any time.

"Those who control the political and economic life on your planet benefit from the population believing they are power-less—that people are less than they truly are. Your media advertises ways to change yourself, suggesting you are not whole and need to be fixed. If something in your country is broken, the citizens look to the government for a solution instead of looking to themselves."

The part about the media being bad for self-image was old news—something everyone already knew. Vicki didn't bother bringing up the issues of resources and funding for problems on a nationwide scale. Besides, weren't they already tackling these sys-temic problems by holding elections and having their governments address them? She had been involved in that work herself, as a diplo-mat handling issues that crossed international borders.

Melly continued, "Would you like to outline your current plans to me? I can be..." At this point, Melly paused as she sought the right word. "I can be a sounding board. Would this help?"

Yes, yes it would. While Melly and the Council were generally aware of what they were proposing to do, they had kept themselves at arm's length. Probably to ensure this wasn't seen as some sort of alien plan to take over the world. But now? Now Vicki seriously needed someone to tell her their crazy scheme would work. So, she talked to Melly—an eight-foot-tall mantis being who was a Galactic Federation Council representative—and Melly listened.

Vicki told her everything. They would kick off their plan early the following week with the SEC filings. A couple of days later, Brad would upload the free-energy schematics to the internet and then immediately air the first interview between Jessica and Melly. The daily broadcasting of the fourteen segments would take place over the following days. She told Melly about the defensive measures they would be taking with the photonitron device and her own individual contribution for dealing with the advanced technology and devices stored at the Partnership's compound. She ended with the tentative arrangement she had reached with the ACs.

It seemed like Melly stood there, eyes whirling, for a long time after Vicki stopped speaking. Maybe she thought their plans were rubbish and didn't know how to break the news. Nonetheless, Vicki felt relief, as if a horrible burden had been removed from her shoulders.

"Do you have any feedback or suggestions?" she asked.

"If you successfully complete even the first step, you will have achieved success." Soft gongs. "It will be enough to change the direction in which the Partnership can move forward. It will be enough to make people start questioning what they've been told about reality and to start looking for answers within themselves. The change in vibration will come, whether or not the Partnership is completely stopped. But implementing your first step will ensure that more people are ready for it and will benefit from it."

Huh, Vicki hadn't realized the SEC filings would be so decisive. She mentally filed this away.

"Vicki." There was a serious gong overlay, and Vicki looked up at Melly in surprise. "Do you think you can kill another human being?"

"I..." Her mind stuttered. WTF? But she came up with an honest answer. "I'm actually pretty sure I could. If someone was attacking me or one of the Four? Definitely."

"Would you be able to take the actions you just outlined to me if you knew that innocent people would die?"

Vicki fell silent.

"It would be better for you to answer this question before you set your plans into motion, rather than when you're in the middle of them. Whichever path you choose is the correct one, but you need to be prepared. Indecision would be disastrous."

They talked for a long time. Sometime during the conversation, Vicki came to the realization that when Melly talked about the scenario in which they "would succeed even if they *only* completed the first step," she was implying that Vicki—and everyone she now loved—would probably die. They would die if she wasn't able to take actions that would result in the deaths of innocents. Would she kill to prevent her friends from dying? Would she let innocent people die?

Maybe she was finally on the road to figuring out who she really was.

CHAPTER THIRTY-FIVE

O ver the next few days, Vicki found herself thinking a lot about death. Melly's question—whether she could kill someone—had shaken her. On the bright side, her connection with Beth was helping her see death differently. Maybe life and death were just different vibrational states? It was an intriguing thought, though she hadn't had time to explore it fully.

She'd become a diplomat to help people—both Americans and others around the world—and felt proud of the work she'd done. What she hadn't expected, though, was how much violence diplomats could face when posted overseas.

Fun fact: more U.S. ambassadors had died in the line of duty than American generals.

Their training reflected this violence. "Crash and Bang" was the unofficial name of a course that taught diplomats both defensive driving ("Crash") and how to handle weapons ("Bang"). Another three-day course covered a variety of things to know if an embassy was attacked—from dealing with a flailing chest wound to deciding who should be evacuated first. So yes, she was aware of death.

But killing was another matter entirely. And planning something that could lead to innocent people dying? That was never something she thought she'd have to consider. Yet Melly had made it clear—if Vicki couldn't face hard choices, their plan wouldn't even get off the ground. From that point on, things were only going to get more violent.

So... she could either kill innocent people or she could allow the Partnership to take over the world.

Her choice.

* * *

On the Sunday night before their launch week, Vicki found herself sitting with the young people on a large sectional in the media room. They would have gathered in the entertainment room, but... bugs. James and Jess had been making final edits to the fourteen-segment interview series with Melly. The two of them were reading excerpts out loud from the disclosure book that Melly and the Council had provided.

"I'm not sure this book is going to be as useful as Melly thinks it will be," said James. He had overcome his previous bright anger and was now the complete professional. Fairly impressive for being just sixteen years old. Really impressive for being the son of a woman who held a grudge.

"Listen to this." He started reading from a document Melly had given him. *"What happens when the road you were going down suddenly disappears? You find yourself in the middle of the unknown with no map or GPS. Moving forward or backward is pointless. But a third option relies on neither geography nor time—you can turn inward. Despite the great rewards, for most people, turning inward is the proverbial road less taken. This is regrettable because that's the road we recommend."*

He looked up at them. "I'm pretty sure a lot of people will think this is nonsense."

Vicki tended to agree. The vocabulary was too ornate, and the information would only appeal to a limited audience. Thankfully, they had the interviews with Melly and the free-energy schematics to share. Much more practical.

"Here's another one," said Jessica. She was seated beside Kiran because, yes, he was now included in their little group. *"The power structures of your society depend on people believing life is dangerous and that if they do as they are told, they will be safe. Safety is never guaranteed and should not be high on your list of life goals. Consider all the possible benefits of giving yourself permission to live your life rather than remaining paralyzed by fear of events that may never come to pass."*

"Yeah, that's cryptic," commented Brad.

"Maybe not so much cryptic as not actionable," Kiran said a little tentatively.

Kiran was still unsure where he fit in, and they weren't sure either. But he had spent the weekend at the Martinssons', coming home with Brad on Friday night to stay through Wednesday. The two of them had received permission from work to take off a few days for "summer vacation activities." Their office had been happy to approve it—they hoped it would sway Brad's decision about where to work when he turned eighteen. The boys had spent the entire weekend working with the photonitron.

"How are you guys doing with your holograms?"

Brad glanced at Kiran. "We're pretty much done. We have scans of all of us and of lots of people at the Partnership. Then we created holo reels of them."

Vicki raised an eyebrow in question.

"We have scans of people in our division, some of the head honchos, several guards, and random office staff," he clarified. "We took most of them when we were having our office event. Kiran and I have been combining them into reels these past couple of days. Let us show you."

She expected the boys to go and get some bulky equipment from Brad's room, but no, he just pulled a small metallic cylinder—about the size of a stick of butter—from his pocket, pointed it to the middle of the floor, and pushed a button. Up from nothing sprang a full-sized image of two men in business suits talking. After a few moments, the men paused to look at them—one man actually gave them a quick wave—before returning to their conversation.

"Holy crap!" Vicki jumped out of her seat and went to examine the image, walking around it and viewing it from all angles. It was perfect; there were no cracks in reality.

Correction—reaching out with her chi, it was easy to tell they were not real.

"They're hoping to add audio to the next generation of the photonitron," said Brad. "But until then, it's totally silent."

"It still has its uses." Vicki was thinking furiously. Brad pushed another button, and the image just... collapsed. Creepy.

"We have scans of flying saucers." Kiran's quiet comment was met with exclamations, Vicki's included. "While I said flying saucers, they're really ARVs—Alien Reproduction Vehicles. The Partnership made several of them after taking apart and reverse engineering a real flying saucer handed over to them by the government. The saucer was in bad shape—it had crashed—and a couple of the aerospace companies belonging to the Partnership were much more capable of piecing it back together than anyone in the government. And they did."

"So why aren't we using flying saucers in daily life?" asked Jessica. "If it was our government who gave them alien saucers to work on, whatever they discovered, whatever they were able to develop, belongs to the taxpayers."

"You'd think," snorted James.

"I'm sure the Partnership framed it as being too dangerous to release to the public—a threat to national security," said Vicki.

Kiran nodded. "I also made copies of the holo reels they created of the ARVs—flying, landing, and taking off. The Partnership doesn't have many ARVs yet, but in one of the reels, they spliced together several of the individual images to make it look like there was an entire squadron."

"False-flag event," they all chorused. The Partnership was ready to stage an alien invasion if they felt threatened.

Brad cleared his throat. "Much more boring but maybe more useful—we also took scans of complete strangers, which wasn't easy. Normally, we can scan a person in a minute or so. Secretly scanning people in public without looking like perverts? It took us half a day to get a couple dozen scans."

"How did you do that?"

"We spent a lot of time in coffee shops," answered Brad. "It's a place where people stay still for a relatively long time, and it doesn't look weird if you stand close to them."

"Why bother?" James asked, genuinely curious.

"Crowd scenes," replied Kiran. This was the first time he had spoken to James directly. He must have heard about James's initial reaction to allowing him to work with them. "Depending on how we need to use it, a crowd made up of only people who work for the Partnership might look out of place. A crowd of strangers will give us more flexibility."

"Flexibility for what?" Jessica tucked a strand of hair behind her ear.

Both Brad and Kiran looked at Vicki.

"Defensive purposes," she said. "It's going to be extremely dangerous. At some point, we will likely need places to hide. If we can create a holographic crowd of people at will, each one with their own heat signature, we can hide in the middle of it or behind it—the holos are solid to human eyes. And although the Partnership may be able to tell the difference between the holos and actual flesh and blood people in a laboratory, I'm betting they don't have the resources to do that on the street—or anywhere outside the lab, for that matter."

She looked at Brad and Kiran, and they both nodded their confirmation.

"You think it will get that bad?"

"It will get worse," she said, refusing to sugarcoat the danger for her team. "People will die. Probably lots of them. Maybe us." For the first time, she wasn't disturbed to admit this.

All eyes were on her. She took the opportunity to bring up something she had been thinking about for a few days.

"We need a fallback base."

"What do you mean?" asked Jessica.

"A fallback base of operations," Vicki explained. "Right now, we have this house, the media room, and Brad's computer setup in his bedroom. What would happen if, for whatever reason, we're prevented from being here? What if it gets destroyed?"

Pale faces all around. She didn't think Jessica was aware she was clutching Kiran's hand. Brad and Jessica had once talked with her about accepting the possibility that they might fail—or even die. But thinking about it in theory was very different from looking at the practical aspects.

She didn't mention that Melly had asked her whether she could kill someone. That was a burden she had to carry on her own.

"What would a fallback base of operations involve?" Brad got straight to the point.

"Everything we need to continue our work. If, for whatever reason, we cannot use this house, how do we still carry out our plans? We need you to be able to upload stuff to the internet—to websites worldwide—without anyone being able to trace it back to our location. While we don't need a recording studio—at least not in the short term—we need copies of Jessica's interviews with Melly."

She looked at Kiran. "We also need copies of all the holo images and videos you and Brad have created—we can't risk having them in just one place."

"We'll need medical supplies too," James said.

She looked at him in approval. "I had forgotten all about medical stuff."

"I'll take care of getting together medical supplies," volunteered Jess. "I got a crash course in nursing when Mom was sick."

Brad had been silently doing calculations. "I could create a duplicate of my computer setup in less than a day—I built my current system myself, and I have plenty of extra equipment. Setting up a rudimentary recording studio for Jess wouldn't be hard either—as long as we have a physical space and connection to the internet."

"I think I know of a flower shop that's empty." For the first time, thinking about Beth's shop didn't stress her out.

Vicki stayed quiet while the young people talked among themselves about how best to set up a fallback base. She hoped it wouldn't be needed. After several minutes, they came to agreement on what they needed to do.

"Tomorrow. We can do everything tomorrow," said Brad.

* * *

Outwardly, James looked calm as he worked with the others to set their plan in motion against the Partnership. He had been the first one Melly contacted, so he had been at it longer than anyone. And he *was* excited—excited and happy and scared. He didn't know if they'd succeed, but after all the years of preparation, it felt good to finally take action.

But inside he was stewing. It didn't make sense. His parents had been in this fight from the beginning—risked just as much, maybe more. Now, suddenly, they were sidelined for their own good? He didn't buy it. Larry and Vicki said it was about keeping them safe, about timing. But if safety was the priority, why was Kiran being brought in now? Kiran, who still worked at the Partnership, who hadn't risked anything yet. And now everyone was acting like he was some critical piece of the plan just because he could operate the photonitron. Well, James couldn't deny that part—Kiran *was* good. But that didn't erase the fact that he was stepping into the space James thought his parents had earned.

And the way Jessica and Kiran were looking at each other didn't help. Probably nothing had happened yet, but James wasn't clueless—he saw where this was heading. They had all worked hard to build a team based on trust. How would bringing in someone new change that?

He really hoped that Larry and Vicki knew what they were doing.

Chapter Thirty-Six

It was Monday evening, late. They were having dinner on the Martinssons' back patio, the table lit by a few strategically placed lanterns. To the surprise of everyone but Vicki, they weren't talking about how they had just spent twelve hours setting up a fallback base at Beth's flower shop. Or even about the holo reels Brad and Kiran had made with the photonitron.

"They're picketing the SEC?" Once again, Larry was incredulous. He had seen the stories on the news shows—lots of well-dressed, angry shareholders holding signs and shouting at SEC personnel entering and exiting the building.

"And the individual aerospace and defense corporations that we have proof are holding back reverse-engineered ET products," said Vicki, happily munching on grilled hamburgers, potato salad, and sweet corn. Hamburgers and sweet corn always made her happy.

"I... don't see how that can help us," said Jessica, confused. She and Kiran were sitting side by side.

"These are *rich* people picketing the SEC and blowing up the phones," Vicki explained. "These are major shareholders who have just learned the corporations they have invested in are not declaring assets, and therefore, they—the rich people—are being shorted a significant portion of their dividend earnings. No one likes being cheated out of money; rich people, less than most."

"One of the reasons why they're rich," contributed Brad. He reached across the table and took another hamburger.

"You're rich," James pointed out. Brad just grinned and took a bite of his burger.

Jessica frowned. "Most of the coverage was on the side of the protesters, but I read a couple of negative stories... by someone with the last name of Riley? She said something about—and understand I'm paraphrasing—'modern defense technology cannot be reduced to chants on a sidewalk.'"

Kiran nodded. "Yeah, I saw that too. And then she poked fun at financial fraud being mixed up with aliens—implied that it wasn't professional."

Vicki shrugged. "Doesn't matter. Even if the protesters don't have a clue, the money behind them does. And that's what's getting attention."

"So, this is all based on the records of the witness testimonies about UFOs and stuff that that doctor collected? I thought regular people wouldn't talk about UFOs because they'd look crazy. They'd be ridiculed." Jessica's brow was furrowed.

"They're not talking about UFOs—they're talking about *money*. And fraud. And because they're talking about money and fraud, the story has been picked up by all the major news outlets."

"What I don't understand," said Larry, "is how you got that law firm to file with the SEC so fast. And why they would even do it in the first place—UFOs and aliens aren't something reputable law firms are eager to take on. They have their own concerns about looking crazy."

He didn't have a plate in front of him. The first time that happened, Vicki had been worried until he reminded her that as a biologic construct, he didn't need to eat as much as regular people. He always ate a meal when they were out in public. He always drank coffee whenever it was offered. Meals in private with just them? About fifty-fifty.

"I have friends," she said, smirking. Everyone except Kiran rolled their eyes. "One of the attorneys at the law firm is the wife of my friend Jerry from the State Department. She's on maternity leave, bored, and thought this sounded interesting. She pitched it to her firm as a practical exercise for their interns."

"But how did they come up with this strategy so fast?" asked Larry.

"Because they've done it before. Several times before. The law firm where she works has brought several cases against oil and gas multinationals that are running roughshod in the Amazon. What they did today—the filings with the SEC and getting stockholders involved—they've done that in their cases against the fossil fuel industry."

"That's clever," said Kiran.

"Very clever. Lawsuits like this generally take years, and this one will too, if they pursue it to the end. But all we need is a lot of attention-grabbing, splashy publicity that will get the issue in the public eye in a credible way. Money is always credible." Vicki took another ear of corn and started buttering it. "For what it's worth, Melly told me that if we were able to complete the first step—that's the SEC filings and the publicity surrounding it—we should consider ourselves successful."

"I don't feel successful—not yet. I think there's a lot left to do." James pushed some potato salad around his plate with a fork while he thought.

"You're right. But Melly said the publicity will change how the Partnership moves forward. People aren't going to be as gullible as they were before."

"People will always be gullible," countered Larry.

"True. But now that people are starting to realize the Partnership has been hiding advanced technology—technology that could save lives, clean water, and end poverty—they'll feel cheated. From now on, whatever the Partnership does, people will be looking for the cheat. They'll expect a trick. So when the Partnership suggests replacing human bodies with biologic constructs, fewer people will agree. And that means more will be able to benefit from the natural DNA upgrades that come with the vibrational shift."

"I'm familiar with the idea of a vibrational shift," said Kiran. "It's not that different from the tradition in Hindu cosmology of yugas—cyclic ages in which humans pass through different levels of evolution. But what do you mean when you say that people will benefit from natural DNA enhancements? How does that happen and how will we benefit?"

"Biologic constructs don't have any junk DNA," explained Jessica. "If you're a biologic construct, the vibrational shift will have no effect on you."

The rest of them carefully avoided looking at Larry.

"Effects? What kind of effects?"

James started talking. He was the one who had originally explained it to Vicki in the back garden of the tai chi studio those many weeks ago.

"Humans have a lot of DNA. Scientists say that somewhere between seventy-five and ninety-five percent of it is junk—just sitting there, not doing anything. But what they're starting to realize is that genes can be switched on and off. When people live at a higher vibration, some of that inactive DNA—DNA they say is junk— starts to turn on. And when that happens, new abilities appear—things we used to dismiss as woo-woo or hocus-pocus."

"Things like suddenly becoming a computer genius, being able to understand schematics with no training, and coming up with solutions to IT system problems that no one else can," said Brad in response to Kiran's unasked question.

"Oh, so that's why you..." It looked like a lightbulb was going off in Kiran's head.

"But that's the least of it," said Jess. "The supernatural stuff is more interesting—telepathy, teleportation, thought forms, levitation—"

"Disappearing out of a closed room," added Vicki. She realized she was more like Mona than she had thought—she, too, could hold a grudge.

Kiran's expression cleared. "You're talking about the siddhis!"

The rest of them looked at him in confusion.

"My family immigrated from India a decade ago," he explained. No one said anything; they already knew that. "In the Hindu tradition, siddhis are divine abilities people can achieve through advanced yoga or meditation. All human beings have the potential to access these powers; they just have to be unlocked."

"That is... exactly what we are talking about," said Larry. "And despite everything the rest of us have learned about human potential over the past couple of years—and even experienced firsthand—I've never heard of siddhis. Can you be more specific? Can you explain them to us?"

Kiran did so, happy to have finally found a place in the group.

The word "siddhi" in Sanskrit meant "attainment" or "accomplishment." While a person might be the one in a million who was fortunate to be born with these abilities, they were usually the result of an intense meditation or yoga practice. Kiran explained that these abilities weren't meant to be goals in themselves; rather, they were just by-products on a person's path to enlightenment.

"Spiritual teachers warn their students that these powers are a distraction; they could even be dangerous, and you shouldn't seek them out. But of course, we all dreamed of having them."

"You do yoga?" For some reason, Brad seemed surprised.

"Not anymore. My grandfather was a very dedicated yoga practitioner—he's the reason I started in the first place. But I didn't have the self-discipline to continue when we moved to the U.S. I liked being in a class with my friends. But I kept up with my meditation."

"When did you start?"

"I was seven years old."

Seriously? Vicki was pretty sure any robust meditation practice involved reaching higher states of consciousness. And Kiran had been meditating for around seventeen years? Maybe he would fit in better than any of them had realized.

They spent the rest of the evening discussing the siddhis. The lower siddhis were ESP, clairvoyance, intuition, and the ability to heal others. Higher siddhis included levitation, materialization, and the ability to travel between dimensions. There were others, as well: invisibility, super strength, and knowledge of the outer universe. Kiran told them tales of holy men who were known to be able to bilocate—they could be teaching a class in one location while at the same time eating dinner with friends a hundred miles away. There were sages in the Himalayas who speed-traveled on their journeys, covering hundreds of miles in a day on foot. Different traditions had additional siddhis; Kiran said he knew of more than thirty.

"The siddhis sound similar to the abilities Melly has told us could be activated by a vibrational shift," said Brad.

"Identical," agreed Larry.

"Who's Melly?" Kiran whispered to Jessica.

She patted his hand. "I'll tell you later."

Larry wanted to explore the strengths and capabilities of their newest recruit. He looked at Kiran. "Everyone here—except for you—practices tai chi. That's how we reach higher levels of vibration and higher levels of consciousness."

Well, technically, Larry didn't, but they weren't going to call him out on it.

He continued. "Are you able to do this with meditation?"

Kiran looked like a deer caught in the headlights, but he did his best to respond honestly. "I believe I do—there really isn't an easy way to measure it, is there? But when I meditate, I fall into a state where I feel very present, if that makes any sense. I'm calmer; the world inside my head feels larger like it's no longer confined within my skull. Sometimes, I get a... floaty feeling? And my body feels like... maybe the feeling you'd get if you were a bedsheet that had just been taken out of the dryer—a staticky feeling."

"Sounds like he's able to move the chi energy," commented Jessica.

"Prana," corrected Kiran. "I can feel the prana moving."

"My mom says tai chi is like moving meditation," said James.

Yes, Mona did say that.

"It seems there isn't as large a gap between us as I had feared," said Larry. "I'll need to think about how we can use that."

After that, they didn't have anything specific to discuss, but they stayed out for another hour just talking and laughing together. Vicki was the happiest she had been since before Beth died.

* * *

A noise woke Vicki up. The alarm clock said it was 2:30 a.m. Something was... not right. She heard a car door slam. Who was here at this hour?

She stayed in bed but reached out with her chi. She found the person and identified the energy. It wasn't hard because he had entered the foyer and was stomping upstairs, heedlessly broadcasting his emotions. Kurt was home. Kurt had returned without giving them advance notice. He was angry—*furious*. And he was scared.

And that scared her. What could have happened to frighten this unaware, self-important man? She was paranoid it had something to do with them, that they'd been discovered. But racking her brain, she couldn't think of how. Kurt's presence at home, however, would make it more awkward to carry out their plans.

She followed him energetically as he went down hallways and then to his bedroom. When it was clear he was settled in for the night, she took her phone and texted the group to warn them.

One last good night's sleep.

Chapter Thirty-Seven

*T*hank goodness Kiran is staying with us.

That thought repeatedly ran through Jessica's head at breakfast the next morning. They were in the dining room because that's where their dad preferred they eat. It was obvious to everyone that the man was in a foul mood, but he kept it tamped down in the company of a guest—a guest who not only worked for the Partnership himself but whose parents both worked for the Partnership. Their dad went out of his way to engage Kiran in conversation.

"You've been at the Partnership for how long now? Three years? How do you like it?"

Kiran put down his fork. "Actually, it's been six years—I was hired as soon as I got out of high school. And it's been amazing. There is so much room for advancement, so much opportunity to work on groundbreaking projects that truly don't exist anywhere else in the world." He glanced over at Brad. "He's just an intern, but Brad has become the superstar of my section. He'll have a brilliant career if he decides to hire on with us. It's pretty clear that he'll be the second person—after me— that the Partnership hires with only a high school degree; they're just waiting for him to become a legal adult."

Kiran then snorted. "Frankly, there will probably be a bidding war between my office and the Human Enhancement Division. Of course, I'm here trying to convince him to join my office."

The next half hour was a pleasant three-way conversation between their dad, Kiran, and Brad about career possibilities in the Partnership. Their dad was clearly pleased with Kiran's bright prognosis of Brad's prospects.

She and Kiran weren't sitting together. Of course not. They even avoided looking at each other. Kurt was at the head of the table, with the two boys sitting on one side and the two women on the other. Jessica once again put on her emotionally vulnerable, socially awkward mask. But inside...

Inside, she was *seething*. Feelings of outrage and scorn were bubbling up, all combining to make a toxic stew that threatened to burst out at any moment.

Keep a lid on it, Jessica, keep a lid on it, Jessica, keep a lid on it. She wasn't sure whether she was giving herself a command, or whether she was praying.

It came to a head when Lucia came in to see if anyone needed more coffee. Yes, yes, please. When she accidentally over filled Jessica's mug and spilled some coffee onto the tablecloth, Kurt went ballistic. As in erupting in a foaming-at-the-mouth rage. He ripped Lucia up one side and down the other. The poor woman just stood there, head bowed, taking it.

"I can't do this anymore!" Jessica slammed down her fork and rushed out of the room.

They were so close and it was getting so hard—she hoped she hadn't ruined it for all of them.

* * *

A couple of hours later, Vicki was in Kurt's office, giving her report on his kids' activities. But first she updated him on Jessica.

"She's been doing pretty well, but you know how erratic she it. I checked on her and she'll be fine."

Kurt's expression cleared as Vicki supplied the prism through which to view his timid daughter's angry outburst. Vicki noticed how quickly he dismissed it from his mind—his child's distress was of no importance.

As they moved on to other subjects, Kurt was surprised to hear the kids were no longer going to tai chi class. Although he didn't mind.

"Just a short break," Vicki told him. "A lot of people are on vacation, and Brad is so busy with his internship at the Partnership..."

That made him smile. He was obviously a man who intended to climb the corporate ladder through his son.

"I wasn't sure the internship was a good idea at first," she continued. "It's the last few weeks before the beginning of his senior year, and his tutor has already sent him a list of books he should read."

"But this is his future." Kurt was very sure.

She nodded. "I was glad to find out he would be interning in Kiran's office. I know they knew each other beforehand, but since Brad started interning, the two of them have formed a strong friendship. It's good for him. Kiran is another young person and a good role model."

Kurt nodded in agreement.

Now came the tricky part. Vicki leaned slightly forward and arranged her face into an expression she hoped looked approachable and friendly.

"Kurt, I saw that you're upset, that something's wrong. Is there anything I can help you with?"

A whole series of emotions passed over Kurt's face—panic, dismay, frustration, worry—one after another in a matter of seconds. Then his face smoothed out into a neutral expression. He was wavering between keeping his manly self-control and letting it all out. Vicki decided to give him a nudge .She reached out and placed her hand on his arm.

"I would really like to help," she said softly.

And that's all it took.

Seriously? She'd have expected that a rogue criminal group like the Partnership would be more careful in sifting out weak links. Because when Kurt spilled, he spilled it all.

Something was wrong at the Partnership; he didn't know what. It began with the shareholders picketing the SEC, but there was something going on behind the scenes that he wasn't privy to. Everyone was being called in from their satellite offices. Serious discussions were taking place behind closed doors. The top brass were walking around with thunderous expressions. Rumor had it that one of the division heads had left for lunch and not returned.

"Really? Something is happening that's so bad one of the top executives just up and left?"

In this, Kurt was honest. "We don't think he left... we think he was prevented from returning."

"He was fired?" Vicki wanted to press the issue. She needed confirmation.

"The Partnership doesn't fire people when they reach the highest levels in the organization." Kurt swallowed. "They eliminate them."

Remembering what Kyle and Graham had said about not being allowed to leave, she was half expecting the words. Still, it was shocking to hear, and she let that shock show on her face.

"You told me the Partnership works on Top-Secret projects. So, this man must have done something wrong—he must have leaked information or something."

"There has to be something more." Kurt ran his hand through his hair. "This isn't the first time a high-level person hasn't returned from lunch."

She heard quotes around "returned from lunch" when he said it.

"In those cases," said Kurt, "things get back to normal—fast. Like within an hour or two fast. And then, everyone goes about their day pretending nothing happened. But now? The top brass is still angry, going around barking at people and huddling in their offices in secret discussions. Employees are still being called in from distant locations."

Vicki patted his hand reassuringly. "If this trouble had anything to do with you, you'd know it by now. I'm sure it will be resolved within a few days. You should try to relax because there's nothing you can do."

Kurt took her hand and squeezed it. She pasted a smile on her face.

No, there was nothing Kurt could do. But there was something the rest of them *had* to do.

* * *

That evening, they had an early supper. Larry arrived afterward with his nephew. Kurt was still in a bad mood and had retired to his bedroom, complaining of a nasty headache. This relieved Vicki no end, because she had been wondering how she was going to get him out of the way. Kurt's headache was a welcome coincidence.

But... was sending a headache to an inconvenient human one of the abilities aliens have?

She was seated with the young people on the back patio. "Do you have your go-bag?" she asked James as he and Larry approached.

Wordlessly, he held it up. The go-bags for the rest of them were already piled at the end of the table.

There wasn't a whole lot of conversation. Time was short, and there was no need. Vicki had already passed on what Kurt had told her about the uproar taking place at the Partnership's offices. She didn't think they were the cause of what was going on, but they all agreed they needed to act immediately.

She looked at Brad. "One of us will contact you when it's time to upload the free-energy schematics. As soon as you finish that, broadcast the first of Jessica's videos. James will give you whatever help you need."

She tossed Jessica a set of keys. Jessica raised an eyebrow in question.

"They're the keys to the flower shop and to Beth's old Toyota. I would tell you to drive the Bentley, but it's bugged." Vicki had asked Kiran about removing the listening device, but he told them if they did that, a remote signal would be sent out, indicating someone was tampering with it. "The Partnership will probably not be looking our way, but it's best not to risk it."

Jessica nodded. Vicki continued.

"Put all the go-bags in the trunk, then park the car in a place that's not easily visible. Is there a service entrance to this property?"

"The grounds people use a gate at the back. It's locked with a keypad, but both Brad and I know the code."

"And the street?"

"Not the same street as the main entrance."

Vicki nodded. "Good. You three use your best judgment. Don't wait for the bad guys to come knocking at the gate. If anything seems off at all, fall back to the flower shop."

Brad and James nodded, but Jessica looked startled. "Three? Not four?"

"Kiran needs to come with Larry and me."

She could see the panic in Jessica's eyes, then watched her quickly shove it aside and nod again.

"Larry? Kiran?" Larry and Vicki got into his vehicle. Kiran gave Jess a quick, awkward hug, then scrambled into the back seat a moment later.

The car Larry was driving tonight was a dark gray SUV, one that was dirty and dinged up.

"What happened to your cute little Corvette?" Vicki asked.

"Too flamboyant," he grunted. "If we need to run, the SUV will blend into traffic more easily. I bought this for cash off a guy on Craigslist last week, but I still haven't filed the paperwork to change the registration—it can't be traced to us." He continued down the highway.

"We'll need to run?" Kiran's voice sounded hesitant. Not as if he was frightened or having second thoughts, just that he wanted a more concrete idea of what would be happening.

Unfortunately for him, Vicki hadn't told anyone the extent of what she would be doing tonight—they were all operating on trust—just that it would involve one of the abilities Melly had activated in her. She didn't answer Kiran's question. Instead, she looked back at him and asked one of her own.

"You brought the photonitron?"

He brought the metallic cylinder out of his pocket and waved it at her. "It's just the transmitter, of course—it's not like I'd be able to create new reels on the spot. But this holds everything we've done so far."

"That's a pretty compact device to contain all those holos." She was impressed.

Kiran smirked. "ET technology."

Twenty minutes later, Larry crossed two lanes of traffic and took the off-ramp to the neighborhood where the Partnership's compound—with its offices, labs, and research facilities—was located. It was late, but the long summer days provided some amount of daylight until after 8:00 p.m. He pulled to the curb on a side street and looked at her. "This okay?"

She nodded, pulled out her phone, and placed a call. Jessica answered.

"Vicki?"

"We've arrived; everything looks quiet. All good with you three?"

"Beth's car is on the other side of the fence with our go-bags. Brad is all set to begin uploading the schematics. He'll broadcast the first Melly video when that's done. We're ready."

"Then tell Brad to start. Now. We'll be doing the same."

She put her phone in her pocket and looked up to see both Larry and Kiran watching her.

She smiled. "Time to get going."

Larry led them to a section near the fence that he swore was not under camera surveillance. Both Kiran and Larry stood protectively by her while she removed her shoes and sat down on the grass.

The sun was just setting. Would she still be alive when it rose again? Would any of them?

She didn't know.

CHAPTER THIRTY-EIGHT

Vicki sat on the grass, bare feet and bare hands connecting with the Earth. She sank deep into meditation, finding her way through gravel, dirt, concrete, and rock. Several days earlier, she had consulted Google Earth and identified the boundaries of the Partnership's property—all 15 acres. Larry had pointed out where the labs were located, and where the tech, the schematics and the devices were stored.

He hadn't been able to tell her how deep it all went, though—maybe he hadn't known. Vicki discovered the buildings were much deeper than they were tall. Not just the parking garage. The subterranean levels of a couple of the lab buildings reached down seven floors, with a network of underground tunnels leading from one structure to the next. Like a giant concrete spider web.

She continued her way down through the Earth, her skin noting the differences between the materials. Clay felt calm and dense; granite was bright. Junia would have argued against letting her wander through the interior of the Earth without her by her side. But by now, Vicki could do it herself, and she didn't want Junia involved—not in this.

Ahhh. Here was a small river that had been cemented over several decades earlier—a fate suffered by many of waterways as the population skyrocketed and new developments were thrown up. What an unexpected gift. She dipped her hand in its silent waters and asked how it was feeling. Melancholy, cramped, closed in. A feeling of wrongness. Would it like to play with her? They could change that. The eagerness of a young puppy presented with a new game. This would be fun. As she left, she promised to send a signal for when to start.

She toured the perimeter of the property. She wouldn't have put it past the Partnership to expand their tunneling underneath the properties of their neighbors, but they hadn't. Given the water shortage in California, it was probably too big a risk that one of those landowners might try to drill a well. While they hadn't done so yet, if the landowners ever decided to see what was down there, they'd find a relatively profitable oil and natural gas deposit at a surprisingly shallow depth.

She had nearly finished her circuit when she realized what had been niggling at the edges of her awareness. She could feel the energies of people in the buildings—many more than Larry had anticipated. She stopped. She paid attention.

Then she felt nauseous.

Melly had once asked her whether she'd be able to kill other human beings. She had thought Melly was referring to some sort of modern-day gunfight involving not only those who were attacking her but also a number of innocent bystanders who were in the wrong place at the wrong time.

But no, *this* was what Melly had been hinting at. Instead of the dozen or so guards they were expecting, there were roomfuls of employees working overtime tonight because their bosses were panicking about something. Roomfuls of human beings whom she would deliberately kill.

She spent a few self-indulgent minutes feeling disgusted with herself. She called it "self-indulgent" because she had already made her decision. She might die carrying this out, or she might survive. It didn't matter—no one in the compound would be left alive to blame her.

So, she spent those few minutes punishing herself. She reached out with her chi and explored the energies of the people who were about to die. She owed it to them to know who they were. Mostly middle-aged, some younger. Tired, worried, unaware of what was going on. They wanted to call it a night and go home to their families. They had dogs to walk and kids to hug. Overwhelmingly men, a smattering of women. Maybe a dozen or so biologic constructs.

She didn't feel bad about the biologic constructs because Larry had explained that the Partnership had searched out literal psychopaths in choosing who they would make into super-soldiers—men who lacked morality, empathy, and remorse. Men who would kill and torture without a second thought. The world would be safer without them.

She shook her head and started pulling her chi back into herself when it lightly brushed against something unexpected.

"Lyrith!" she spat out.

"Who's Lyrith?" asked Larry.

The shock of sensing Lyrith had knocked her out of meditation and back into physical reality. Darkness had fallen, and she could hear crickets.

"Lyrith is the Alpha Centaurian who seems to despise humans and believes we don't have any rights. I sensed her in one of the buildings." She swallowed. "In a room full of super-soldiers."

Larry's eyes widened. He turned to bark out an order to Kiran. "Call Jessica and tell her they need to evacuate immediately!" He turned back to Vicki. "How much longer?"

"Give me ten." She sank back down into meditation.

"Hello, little river."

The response was joyful and frisky. "Is it time?"

"Follow me."

She didn't know how to explain what she did next. She moved through the Earth, plunging a little deeper than the lowest level of the Partnership's buildings. And as she went, she carved an enormous passageway through the rock, sand, and granite. All around the perimeter of the Partnership's property, then crisscrossing underneath it. The little river happily burbled in her wake.

"No more?" The river halted when she did, disappointed.

"Now the real fun starts," she promised. "There's going to be a big earth shift, and when that happens, you should push up to the surface however you can, as hard as you can, as fast as you can." She paused for a moment. "The moon is out tonight; it's beautiful."

She opened her eyes on the surface. Larry and Kiran stood close, tense.

"The others have evacuated?"

Larry nodded. "They're en route to our fallback. They should be there within twenty minutes."

She turned to Kiran. "Hide us now. Maybe in a crowd of people who appear to be looking at what's happening on the Partnership's compound?"

Kiran took the metallic transmitter out of his pocket and pressed a button. A whole crowd of people sprang up around them, concealing them from anyone searching with eyes or radar. The holo showed the people gesturing at something beyond the fence, their faces worried. Kiran had positioned the holo so carefully that it even hid Larry's vehicle. That was something Vicki hadn't thought of.

She smiled up at the two men from her seated position, then closed her eyes and slammed her hands to the ground—hard. And she yanked.

Melly had strengthened her Earth energies when she activated portions of her DNA. Her visit to the Earth crystal had taught her how to use them. Although she might have felt bad about basically disemboweling a portion of a conscious planet, the Earth crystal itself had shown her how, and she took that as blanket permission to do what was needed.

She could feel the rock and earth as she pulled; she could hear it moaning. She shoved harder, and it began to move, the river waters rushing upward in glee. Everything convulsed. The ground shook and rippled. She could hear people screaming and car horns blaring. The smell of gas and sewer lines filled the air as they were ripped asunder.

And then? Then, the Earth shook, and all the buildings on the property collapsed.

She came back to physical consciousness with Larry gripping her arm and pulling her into a standing position. He was saying something to her, but she couldn't hear. It was as if she were surrounded by a blanket of silence, a bubble of peacefulness. And she looked at what she had done.

At first, there wasn't much to see because of all the dust in the air. She waved her arms back and forth to clear it away, but even after the dust settled, her logical mind couldn't make sense of what lay before her. The buildings were gone. Totally gone. As was the property itself. Everything had collapsed into an enormous 15-acre sinkhole that was rapidly filling with water.

Yes, she had planned this, she had done this. But it was still a shock. She slowly turned her head and looked at Larry in confusion. He was talking to her urgently, but she couldn't hear him. She shook her head back and forth a couple of times, and the sound came rushing back in.

"Vicki! We're done here—we need to leave now!" Larry's eyes showed fear. But he wasn't afraid of the Partnership. He wasn't afraid of what had just happened.

He was afraid of her.

She was still moving slowly, uncertainly. She let Larry bundle her into the car where Kiran was already waiting. With his hand on the gearshift, Larry pulled out onto the road, careful not to drive in a manner that would attract attention. Kiran was leaning over the back seat, keeping an eye out the window with his transmitter pointing at his holographic crowd image. When they had gone about half a block, he pushed a button, and the holo collapsed.

"Worked perfectly." Kiran smiled. She was surprised he sounded so calm. She had spent a couple of months getting used to this, Larry had spent years, Kiran only a few days. Yet here they were—Larry scared, Vicki shocked, and Kiran serene and laid-back.

The traffic was insane, with bumper-to-bumper traffic in both directions on the highways. Emergency vehicles with sirens wailing. Rescue helicopters. Police helicopters with searchlights. Were they searching for something specific or just showing they were on the job?

She must have fallen asleep because the next thing she knew, Larry was pulling into the parking lot in the back of the flower shop. The journey had taken them three times longer than normal. The back door of Beth's shop flung open, and James and Jess burst out.

"You're finally here—we were so worried!" Jessica wrapped her arms around Kiran. James went to hug his uncle. Vicki continued into the shop.

"Brad?" she yelled. His reply—*Up here*—had her mounting the stairs to Beth's apartment. She found Brad in the midst of a complicated computer setup. She didn't understand why he needed so many monitors, keyboards, and cables, but it made him happy. "How did it go?"

Typing furiously and keeping his eyes on one of the monitors, Brad grinned. "It went great—everything uploaded perfectly, and now I'm just playing whack-a-mole, re-uploading the free-energy schematics as soon as anyone takes them down from a website."

"People are doing that?"

"They try; some are more insistent about it than others. An hour ago, Australia cut off internet access for everyone."

"For the entire country?" She was amazed.

"Yep. Sucks to be them."

She looked at him, uncomprehending, but by this time, the others had made their way up, and James answered her unasked question.

"If everyone *except* Australia downloads this technology and builds free-energy devices, where will that leave Australia? In last place."

"Along with North Korea and Belarus," added Brad, happily. "Maybe other countries will try to do the same thing, but it's been nearly five hours. The cat's out of the bag."

"And the broadcast of Jessica's first interview with Melly?"

"It went well—at least from our perspective. Yeah, news pundits were all self-righteous and blustering about their network signals being taken over, but there are so many stories happening now that the interview is sort of being buried in the news feeds. Social media is arguing whether it's a deep fake or real. So far, the deep-fake crowd is winning. I'm pretty sure they'll change their minds over the next couple of weeks as we broadcast the other episodes."

"Larry told us you were successful with the Partnership," said Jessica. "What actually happened? We saw news reports about a disaster, but Larry wouldn't explain."

Vicki glanced at Larry, but he was looking away. "Earth energies." She kept it short. "Melly gave me stronger connections with Earth energies when she activated my DNA. I triggered an earthquake, which, in turn, created an enormous sinkhole that swallowed the entire property."

"But I saw from the news coverage there was flooding?"

"A subterranean river. One that had been cemented over decades ago—it was happy to escape its prison."

But something was bothering her. She turned to Kiran. "Why are you so calm? I'm still freaked out. I even scared Larry. And you're acting like it's no big deal?"

"So, you know my family is Hindu," began Kiran. "I've already told you we have the tradition of siddhis—abilities that humans access at higher levels of vibration. That's not so different from what all of you are doing. So, I'm good with it." He shrugged.

"Opening the earth and swallowing an entire 15-acre compound?" growled Larry. "How does that fit in?"

"Kali is known as the Hindu goddess of death and destruction."

"You got that right," said Larry under his breath. Vicki flinched.

"People often forget that Kali is also the goddess of time, change, and creation. You cannot have life without death. You cannot have change without destruction. What Vicki did..." Kiran stopped for a moment, then corrected himself. "What all of us are doing is dancing Kali's eternal dance. The dance of the never-ending cycle of creation. The dance of life and death. The dance of all things in the universe."

Okay, that was more philosophical than she expected—and probably more accepting than she deserved. She hoped one day she would believe it.

Chapter
Thirty-Nine

They spent the rest of the night catching short naps in between watching the news and helping Brad with his whack-a-mole game against various internet censors. The media had shifted from speculating about the origin and authenticity of Jessica's first interview with Melly to excitedly reporting on the "disastrous earthquake in Los Angeles" in catastrophic terms. It wasn't until the next day that the full extent of the damage to the Partnership's property became visible, and that's when it became clear they hadn't been exaggerating. One of the network news shows flew a helicopter over the property to film the destruction in the early morning light. The entire property was... a lake, its edges precisely and bizarrely following the property lines. But not a serene lake—not even close. Much of the evidence of what had been destroyed was floating on top—pieces of buildings, cars, uprooted trees, and...

Vicki felt the bile rise in her throat and rushed to the bathroom.

It was Larry who came knocking a few minutes later. "Are you all right?"

She flushed the toilet, rinsed out her mouth, and opened the door. Larry was standing there, blocking her way and preventing anyone else from seeing in. He looked at her searchingly, then gave a sharp nod as if concluding that she'd be all right.

"My first time in battle, the first time I killed a man, it was the same way," he said. "The bodies were everywhere, both ours and the enemy's. I puked my guts out."

"There were bodies in the lake," she whispered. "I could see them. They said they expected the death toll to reach nearly two hundred people."

"It's war," said Larry.

"Not war," Vicki protested. "Those people weren't soldiers. We're not soldiers. This is…"

Larry interrupted. "Just because you're fighting on a different kind of battlefield doesn't mean you're not a soldier."

"But you were afraid of me! You've been on battlefields, and it still scared you to see what I'd done. You looked at me as if I were some sort of freakish mutant—as if you didn't want to have anything to do with me."

There it was, finally out in the open—she cared a *lot* what Larry thought about her, and now he knew it. She lowered her eyes.

Larry gave a wry smile. "I always knew I was a monster."

When she winced, he reached out and lifted her chin so that she was looking into his eyes.

"Vicki, I've spent a decade believing I was 'less than'—thinking that I was a badly distorted version of a human being. But seeing you last night made me understand that I've been putting myself in a box—I've been putting humanity in a box. I'm kicking myself for wasting those years. I had such a limited view of what it means to be alive."

He paused for a moment, searching through his pockets before pulling out a handkerchief and handing it to her. As she wiped her eyes, he continued:

"Yeah, I was scared. I was scared because I realized that human potential is impossibly immense. Humans—and I'm finally including myself in that group—are more amazing and powerful than anything we can imagine. Thank you for that."

Larry leaned forward, his lips lightly brushing her forehead. Then, stepping aside, he allowed her back into Beth's apartment. No one looked up as she sat on the sofa; she was still sniffling a little. Everyone was watching the news coverage.

"Do you want us to turn it off?" asked Jessica. The program was now interviewing a first responder.

"No, we need to hear what they're saying about it."

After a couple of minutes, the show cut to a commercial and then returned. This time, there was a breaking story about a luxury mansion that had just been destroyed by a gas leak. Jess gasped as the camera panned over the scene.

"That's our house!"

It was. The mansion was now a smoking ruin—firefighters were still spraying water on sections where small flames threatened to re-erupt. Everyone came over to watch.

A reporter was interviewing one of the gardeners with emergency vehicles in the background. No, he didn't know anything; the police were already on the scene when he and the other workers arrived, and no one was allowed any closer. He didn't know if anyone was at home when the explosion happened but volunteered that a family of three lived there.

Vicki's blood went cold. "Lucia?" While she didn't live at the Martinssons' place, she had a bedroom there for when she had to stay late.

"Both she and Mateo left the house last night before we did; I made sure of it," said Brad. Then he added, swallowing, "So, it was just our dad."

The siblings both had their stone faces on.

"How'd they track us down so fast? Where was the leak? And who was able to do this?" Larry barked rapid-fire questions at them.

James was the only one not intimidated by his uncle's tone. "When Brad uploaded the free-energy schematics, he did it anonymously. There are lots of employees who would've had access to the data, so tracking down the guilty party would be time-consuming. But the broadcast of Jessica's first video came right after both the data upload and the compound's destruction? The timing would have made anyone from the Partnership suspicious. Jessica wasn't anonymous; her face was all over the video. Anyone could see it was all connected."

"But what I can't understand is who did it," said Jess slowly. "Didn't they all die last night—at least the most important ones? So, who else would be left alive to retaliate? Who would have had the resources to do so? And who was left that would even care?"

"And did they realize you weren't at home when they destroyed it?" Kiran asked.

Everyone stopped and looked at him. That was a good question.

"If they think you're dead..." began Larry.

"They might wonder whether you're still alive when Brad broadcasts the second interview today, but they won't know for sure because it's a pre-recording," said Vicki. "But airing the next episode will tell them that *someone* is still alive—someone who is involved with all of this. Everyone needs to make sure their go-bags are ready."

"How would they be able to track you here?" Kiran had put his arm around Jessica's shoulders but addressed Vicki. "As far as the Partnership is concerned, you're the hired help. You're nothing—not important."

Harsh words, but true.

"So, they probably aren't aware of this place," he continued. "Maybe we won't need to run again." He sounded like he was trying to convince himself.

"What if the people who destroyed the mansion went in first?" Brad was staring straight ahead, eyes unfocused. "Think about it; they'd want to know exactly what was taken. They'd want to remove any evidence and recover whatever they could. They'd want to be sure we'd die."

Kiran began to argue. "But that doesn't mean they would know about this place."

"They would have questioned our dad before they killed him," interrupted Jess in a flat voice. "They would have questioned him about where we might have gone. We left last night without saying anything to him, but our dad would know Vicki was with us; he knew about this flower shop. No one would have had to force the information from him. He would have volunteered it."

Yeah, Kurt would have tripped over his feet to ingratiate himself with anyone in power. He wouldn't have hesitated to put a target on his kids' backs. Even if it was likely he'd be dead a few minutes later.

If possible, Larry's face became even grimmer. "Brad, you need to broadcast the second interview now; we don't know when we'll have the equipment to broadcast more. Everyone else—pack up. We're leaving!"

Vicki had never unpacked her bag, so she watched as everyone flew about the apartment, making sure they had what they needed: Jessica, her interview tapes; Kiran, the photonitron and its transmitter. James was going through the backpack Kyle and Graham had given them, making sure all the schematics and designs were still there. He had to gather some of them from the kitchen table, so she assumed he and Brad had been going through them the night before.

"Ha!" Brad pushed himself away from his computer setup and turned to grin at them. "All done." They turned to the television and watched as Jessica's second interview with Melly came on the air. They flipped through channels; the only show available was theirs. Jess was sitting across from Melly, who was explaining the vibrational shift and the benefits it would bring to humanity. Seen on a television screen, Melly looked much less scary than she was in person.

"My computer equipment?" Brad looked at his electronics as if calculating how quickly he could break down his system.

"No time," said Larry. He was looking out the windows that overlooked the street. Then, he uttered an expletive. "They're here."

They all rushed to the windows to look—and were greeted with the most surreal sight any of them had ever witnessed. Three—*three!*—flying saucers had landed about fifty yards away at the nearby intersection. It was still early; the shops had not yet opened, and traffic was light. But there were still passersby who, depending on their individual temperaments, were gawking, fleeing, or taking photos with their phones. Nothing happened for a moment.

"Why aren't they doing anything?" murmured Jessica. "And why did they land so far away instead of right in front of us?"

Larry was studying the scene with the eye of a professional. "One of those saucers is larger than the others—it wouldn't fit in the street, so they landed near the intersection so they could stay together. Vicki, you're the strongest at this—could you reach out with your chi and take a look?"

She blinked in surprise; the possibility hadn't even crossed her mind. She did as he asked. "Ah, I see what you're getting at, and you're right—two of the saucers are holos. Only the larger one is real."

"And inside?"

"That's easy. Three biologic constructs, Lyrith, and... Kurt!"

"So, the Partnership didn't kill my father after all. He must have volunteered to lead them here so they could murder us." Brad's voice was bitter.

"But how?" Vicki stammered. She didn't understand how Lyrith was alive and well when she was pretty sure she'd killed her the night before.

"Biologic constructs are super-soldiers: strong, able to go for extended periods without breathing, and hard to kill," said Larry. "At least three in the group you sensed last night survived, and they protected your Alpha Centaurian. Since these men are psychopaths, hurting and killing are more important to them than escaping—not that they'd be easy to catch."

He went over to his own go-bag and took out a gun, but not a kind of gun Vicki had seen before. Then he pocketed one of those slender flashlight weapons she remembered from the Partnership's Family Day.

Taking a quick look out the window, Larry observed, "They're sending Kurt in first to try to talk Jessica and Brad into coming out. This is better than I had hoped." He threw her the keys to his vehicle. "Everyone out, now!"

They all shouldered their bags and ran down the stairs. Only when they were heading out the back door did the young people realize that Larry wasn't coming with them.

"Larry!" James' cry was anguished.

"Do your jobs!" thundered Larry. But seeing his nephew's face crumple, he took a couple of steps forward and crushed the boy in his arms. Looking over James' head, Larry's eyes sought out Vicki's. "It has been a true honor to serve with you," he said.

Releasing his nephew, Larry rushed out the front door, slamming it behind him.

They should have left through the back door right then, but no force was strong enough to keep them from watching. Larry was lightning-fast, reaching Kurt within a couple of seconds, not slowing down as he took the flashlight weapon and discharged it against the man's chest. He was already at the saucer when Kurt began to scream.

"Well, that's that," Jessica said indifferently. She and Brad linked hands.

"What's Larry doing? What's everyone in the saucer doing? Why aren't they coming out and attacking?" asked Kiran.

"They're probably trying to turn Larry off, and now they're finding out they can't do it," said Brad. Vicki remembered when he had told her how he'd deactivated the kill switch during his first internship at the Partnership. "But even though the Partnership can't do anything via his programming, Larry can..."

They saw the blast a few milliseconds before the sound—a giant, flaming torch erupting toward the sky. And then the sound struck; it was deafening.

"Out the back!" Vicki shouted amidst the screams, some of them her own. She didn't want to wait to see if anyone had survived. She didn't want to risk that other biologic constructs might be coming. She rushed everyone ahead of her out the door—then bumped into them as they came to a sudden halt.

Why had they stopped?

"Oh shit." There was another flying saucer in the parking lot.

Chapter Forty

"Vicki?" Jessica asked quietly.

The saucer resembled the ones that had landed out front, but it wasn't quite the same. For one thing, it hadn't landed—it was hovering several feet above the pavement. The second thing was... Vicki reached out with her chi.

"This one feels different," she said.

The saucer was real, not a projected hologram, but the craft itself gave off an energy of being alive. It was beautiful to look at—metallic silver-gray—but she had to squint to see it. It seemed a little fuzzy, as if her eyes were having trouble bringing it into focus.

"This is not a flying saucer that was reverse-engineered by the Partnership," she said. "This is the real deal."

They all just stood there, staring. What else could they do? The saucer was blocking the parking lot exit, so having the keys to Larry's vehicle didn't help. They could have taken off running through the streets, but there was no point. So, they stood waiting when a door opened and a stairway unfolded.

"There should be three of them," Vicki told the others. "But my chi doesn't recognize their energy. Not human, not biologic constructs, not ACs. They're something I haven't come into contact with before."

What came down the stairs were two little alabaster-white beings, each about four feet tall, totally bald, and wearing cream-colored jumpsuits. The third being remained standing at the opening of the craft.

"Those aren't the Tall Whites," Brad said, surprised.

Vicki was surprised too. The Tall Whites were the extraterrestrial race that had helped the Partnership reverse-engineer the alien technology. If anyone had been expected to come for them in a spaceship, it would have been them.

The little beings marched over. They reminded her of Kewpie dolls, but as soon as they opened their mouths, the illusion was broken. These beings were nothing like the sweet, charming Kewpie dolls of her grandmother's youth.

"Why are you standing here—get on the ship!" the first being snapped. He didn't snarl, but it was close.

"Your enemies will be here soon, and the Council is waiting," added the second.

The young people looked at each other and mentally shrugged. Getting on a flying saucer with aliens claiming to act on behalf of the Galactic Council was better than waiting around for the Partnership's next attack. They went over to the craft and mounted the stairs.

The inside of the spaceship was not what Vicki had expected. The floors and furniture were made of a material that was yielding and warm. Alive, maybe? The little beings directed them to a group of chairs, and when she sat in one, it felt like snuggling next to her childhood dog, minus the fur and the doggy smell. The space inside the craft was twice as large as it appeared from outside. This was good, since this crew of three now had five human passengers who were both unexpected and unwelcome.

But were they truly unexpected? The number of human-sized chairs was exactly five, and she doubted ships like this were habitually outfitted with human furniture—especially not in the exact number needed. That said, they were certainly unwelcome. The beings made that very clear.

"We are not a delivery service," one said aggressively. Vicki couldn't tell which—she couldn't tell them apart. They hadn't volunteered names, nor asked for theirs.

"But we will do our duty. When the Council calls, we serve."

James was the only one who wasn't cowed. He had knuckled away the tears that had started spilling when Larry rushed out the door and was now totally focused on the experience. How did a kid his age get such resilience?

"How long will the trip take? And when will we get there? We don't want the Partnership to catch up with us."

One of the beings scoffed. "You humans are unobservant. We left your planet before you sat down."

They had? Everyone looked up in surprise. Seeing this, one of the beings pushed a button, and a section of the wall became clear. They were flying—through outer space! They all jumped up to look out the windows. The stars were so clear it almost hurt to look at them.

"There will be twenty minutes of your time before we pass through Sol Gate. You are permitted to look out the window or sit in your chairs—nothing else."

Vicki was content to gaze out the window, but Brad had a question. He asked it politely. "Do humans need to do anything specific to pass through the gate?"

A good question—one that wouldn't have occurred to her.

"Of course," one of the beings said dismissively. "Like all species, you must raise your vibration in order to pass through the gate unharmed."

All eyes turned to Kiran.

"What?" he asked.

"Kiran," Jessica said urgently. "We're going to go through the Sol Gate—we're going to fly into the sun! But the sun only works as a portal in higher vibrational space. If you can't raise your vibration, you'll end up flying into a ball of flaming lava. Anyone on this ship who hasn't raised their vibration when it goes through the portal will die. The four of us have a lot of practice doing this. Can you?"

"If he can't, it'll be a short trip for him," James said, not very helpfully. Jess shot him a glare.

"Maybe we can turn back," Jessica began.

"Impossible. The Council has requested your presence," one of the beings said. Vicki hadn't realized they were listening.

Kiran reached out, took Jessica's hand, and smiled. "After seventeen years of meditating, my grandfather would be ashamed of me if I couldn't reach higher states of consciousness."

There wasn't much to say after that. They remained silent. The ship had passed the moon before the viewing window was activated. They saw Venus go by, but not Mercury—perhaps its orbit wasn't near their path.

But the sun—Earth's sun—loomed larger and larger. It was a hypnotic view.

Vicki heard a noise behind her and turned to look at the Kewpie crew. The three had left the control panel and now stood around a small lump embedded in the floor—one that hadn't been there before. It was growing. When it reached the size and shape of a two-foot pillar, the beings stepped back. One placed an enormous cut crystal on the top—an octagonal capstone. "Almost ready," a second one said quietly.

"Excuse me."

They all turned to scowl at her.

"Could you tell me what that is?" she asked politely, knowing they wouldn't want to be interrupted.

There was a pause. Then, one of them answered. "This is our navigation stone. Once in Sol Gate, the stone will choose our path to the Council."

"The navigation stone will choose? How does that work? Is it alive?"

"Everything is alive, Victoria Heywood."

They hadn't made introductions, so she had no idea how they knew her name. Every alien species she came across seemed to know who she was.

Not comforting.

The being continued, "Every object in the universe resonates at its own specific vibration. This crystal has encoded within itself all possible vibrations. When we are at a gate, we ask the crystal to vibrate at the specific vibration of our destination. When our ship and the destination vibrate at the same frequency, they cannot help but be at the same place."

"That's how interstellar travel works?" Brad asked incredulously. He had left the window to listen in.

More glares. "While we are required to treat with Victoria, we do not need to do so with you," came the haughty reply.

What? She didn't understand that comment.

"Now, you humans must make your preparations."

The Kewpies ignored the humans as they gathered together—sick with worry, sick with hope. Kiran squeezed Jessica's hand, then went to sit in one of the chairs, which self-adjusted to better fit his cross-legged position. Vicki wanted to think more about that, but James had started doing cloud hands, and the rest followed his lead.

Of course, they were doing it for her. The three of them could quickly reach higher vibrational levels just by meditating like Kiran. That told her they were afraid for her.

But she wasn't afraid. For several minutes she swayed from side to side, making the familiar circular motions with her arms. Soon she felt the prickly static begin in her hands and move through her body. Warmth on her skin, ribbons of energy running up her spine. She was there—she knew it. She opened her eyes.

She was the last. The others were already at the viewing window. Kiran's arm was around Jessica's shoulders. They all looked solid, felt solid—just like when she journeyed in the inner Earth. Did it feel different? Hard to say—she hadn't felt normal in a long time.

But the view had changed. No longer stars, but sparkles. A pulsing, velvety darkness filled with sparkles. She joined them at the window.

"So, this is what a portal looks like from the inside?" The others smiled and made room for her. They watched the mesmerizing sparkles, the shades of undulating blackness.

Then she looked around for the Kewpies. She really shouldn't keep calling them that. They were sure to object if they found out the origin of the nickname—but she had nothing better to call them.

They were still around the crystal, pressing their hands against it rather than their foreheads. Now their expressions were positively beatific. Finally—proper Kewpie dolls.

Vicki was still smiling when they looked up and noticed her watching. They scowled.

She smiled bigger.

They glared.

She snickered.

The young people turned from the window to observe the odd standoff. Rolling their eyes, they returned to admiring the view.

Vicki felt calm and relieved—even joyful. The Partnership's compound had been destroyed. The Four had survived. Kiran looked to be a great addition. Disclosure had begun—and no matter how loudly people cried "deep fake," that genie wasn't going back in the bottle.

She didn't let herself think about Larry's sacrifice—not yet. That grief would come later. Nor did she think about the lives she had taken. That, too, would come later. For now, she let a small sense of peace wash over her—the most she'd felt since before Beth fell ill.

"We're almost there, aren't we?" she said, as the beings did something that caused the pillar to sink back into the floor. Correction: the floor absorbed it. Maybe that was how they'd created the chairs. It would explain a lot.

Another glare. "Yes, we are finished with you. When we arrive, Representative Melly will take you."

"Melly will be there?" James' face lit up.

"Yes. We will be well rid of you." All three turned and stalked to the control panel.

Vicki laughed.

CHAPTER
FORTY-ONE

The five humans watched out the window as their ship exited the portal and snapped back into physical space. The sight was amazing—like the Star Wars bar scene, only with different types of spaceships rather than different kinds of aliens. Saucer-shaped craft like the one they were in, black pyramids, glowing spheres, triangle boomerangs, and trapezoidal ships in every possible combination—all clustered around a central spaceport. At least, they assumed it was a spaceport.

They remained at the viewing window as their Kewpie hosts deftly piloted the ship into position and locked it into place. A whooshing sound announced the bond was complete.

"This is the end of your journey. Our obligation has been fulfilled," said one of the Kewpies, maybe a little defensively. He was standing stiffly nearby while his two companions worked the controls to open the exit.

They all moved to the door, but Vicki stopped to address the first Kewpie. Being formal and showing respect couldn't hurt. "Yes, your obligation has been well and truly fulfilled. We thank you."

For a moment, he looked startled and gratified, then recovered himself and motioned them toward the exit.

The young people had waited for Vicki, so she went down the steps first. She admitted to feeling nervous and waited for the others to descend before turning around to face...

Someone was waiting—alien, of course. It was Melly. Relief washed over Vicki, and she broke into a smile.

"Melly!" She went over to the being and steepled her hands over Melly's forelegs. James and the Martinsson siblings did the same.

Kiran trailed behind, eyes wide. He hadn't met Melly before. Honestly, he had handled the entire "being rescued by little aliens and escaping in a spaceship through the Sol Gate" situation so well that Vicki hadn't expected him to have a reaction at this point. But Melly was at least four feet taller than the Kewpies—and she was a bug.

Jessica, noticing that Kiran had stopped, reached out her hand and dragged him forward. "Melly, this is Kiran. He has joined our team and become an essential part of our group. Kiran, this is Melly. She is the one who made everything possible."

Swallowing and keeping his gaze down, Kiran took a tentative step forward and steepled his hands over Melly's forelegs like he had seen the others do. Melly nodded, then quickly stepped back, clearly trying not to spook him.

"I am honored to meet a friend of the Four." An overlay of soft bells.

Startled, Kiran looked up, noticed her whirling, iridescent eyes, then quickly lowered his gaze and stepped back. Better than Vicki had done when she first met Melly.

"Thank you for sending someone to bring us here," Vicki said. She chose "someone" carefully—didn't want to say "Kewpies" and have the nickname get back to them. "It was a very timely rescue. We are grateful."

The feeling of bells and gongs. "That was no rescue. You had already triumphed, Victoria. The Four had already triumphed. Your enemies will not pursue you further at this time."

Vicki's eyes welled up as she remembered just how they had triumphed. Larry had sacrificed himself. Melly seemed to understand.

"Your companion made his choice. He was both courageous and honorable—an example for all humans."

Larry would have appreciated that—he would have appreciated hearing an alien use him as an example for other humans, even though he himself was a biologic construct. Behind her, Vicki heard James give a quiet sniffle.

"We asked you to come here to introduce you to members of the Galactic Federation Council, and also to discuss the process of moving humanity forward. The others are waiting."

Vicki had never seen Melly walk more than a dozen feet. But now she could see how fast Melly moved—skittering, even—as befitted a giant insect with four hind legs. The humans were nearly trotting to keep up, which was both a shame and a blessing.

A shame because there was so much to look at—a variety of alien species, views out the windows, strange art on the walls. A blessing for the exact same reasons—they were moving too fast to freak out about how *un*human everything was.

They arrived at a medium-sized conference room that reminded Vicki of the boardroom where she had met with the Alpha Centaurians in their crystal city. But this table was longer, with room for more than a dozen, plus additional seating behind each place. Now it really was the Star Wars bar scene—there were several different species: some cute, some bland, and some terrifying.

Vicki hoped no one in the room was telepathic. Her thoughts wouldn't help humanity's reputation.

Melly seated her at the end of the table with the young people behind her. Apparently she was now the de facto spokesperson? Melly had once told her that her government experience was one reason she had been selected as a member of the Four. Vicki sat up straight, took a deep breath, and tried to focus.

Melly introduced the beings, giving their names, species, and roles in the Council. Vicki retained none of it. Her mind was too frazzled. An individual who looked exactly like a tall human—except with a beak instead of a mouth—stood and addressed them. The beak did not interfere with his speech.

"On behalf of the Council of the Galactic Federation, I would like to thank you for your assistance in addressing the issue of extraterrestrial technology being used on your planet. It was against our rules, and we failed in our duty to prevent it. We are pleased that you could resolve the problem without needing to call for our assistance. It's always preferable for the people of a planet to settle their own affairs."

Vicki swallowed. "Thank you for those kind words, but I'm afraid we were not entirely successful. There is evidence of extraterrestrial involvement. When the Partnership attacked us, they arrived in spaceships that had been reverse-engineered from actual ET craft. I saw many people taking photos."

The man made a quick side-swiping motion that seemed to indicate insignificance. "There were no extraterrestrials in view, only humans. When you return to your planet, you will be able to make another one of your films to explain what happened."

He looked at Melly, who nodded.

"We would also like to introduce you to the Council's representatives for Earth," he continued. Two individuals behind him—one man, one woman, both with light-blue skin—stood and nodded.

"Wait, Melly won't be our representative? We've worked with her for a long time already." Vicki felt a small wave of panic bubble up inside her. She really didn't want to start over with a new alien.

Melly responded. "Vicki, you yourself had difficulties with my appearance."

Vicki flushed. True, but... "We've already introduced you to humanity in the videos," she protested.

"There is a significant difference between seeing an alien—one who resembles an insect from your planet—on a screen and meeting one in person, especially when that alien is much taller than you are. Even in the videos, I took care with the seating to appear to be the same height as Jessica." The tinkling of bells—Melly was laughing. "Besides, I do have other work; I cannot devote myself to Earth only."

Vicki sighed. Melly was right—and she was acting like a spoiled child. She turned to the blue-skinned pair. They didn't seem upset by her preference for Melly. If anything, they looked... understanding. That somehow made her feel worse.

The blue woman spoke. Vicki made a mental note to learn their species name. Handing out alien nicknames like candy on Halloween was a bad habit.

"The Council selected us to be its representatives to Earth because we closely resemble humans. It will be difficult enough for your people to accept the existence of interstellar civilizations. Someone who looks like them, except for an odd-colored skin, will not cause too much alarm."

Now the man spoke. "Actually, those of our species have many different skin colors. Some individuals look exactly like humans. But the Council felt it best to establish a visible difference so humans wouldn't fear that aliens walked among them in disguise."

"They've seen the movies!" Brad whispered from his seat behind her.

Apparently, those at the table had better hearing than humans—they all burst out laughing. Melly's bells joined in.

Vicki ignored them. She inclined her head. "Thank you. I'm sure the Council made the correct decision, and I am delighted to have the opportunity to work with you."

Then a thought struck her. "In a few months of our time, we will introduce humanity to the survivors of the Alpha Centauri crash who have lived in our planet's interior for thousands of years. We had reached agreement on how this would proceed, but there was an Alpha Centauri individual in the group that attacked us. Will this affect the Council's decision on how to move forward with Earth?"

The blue pair had sat down. Now, an AC at the far end of the table stood. At least she assumed he was an Alpha Centaurian—he resembled the ACs from the crystal city with his tall stature and elongated head. He waited until he had everyone's attention, then he began to speak.

"We apologize for the problems our distant cousins have caused you," he said, voice radiating controlled anger. "Please rest assured we have taken care of the situation. The one who attacked you is no longer living. The ones who have settled underground will remain there, causing no problems. We have spoken with them, and they will wait until you are ready, Victoria Heywood."

He gave a shallow bow and sat down.

Well, that was... final. More than she had hoped for.

The meeting continued for another couple of hours. Vicki learned the blue people were called Pleiadians. They came in shades of green, black, brown, red, and white. Some humans had called them "Nordics" because of their Viking appearance. She must have looked skeptical because they explained that past expeditions to Earth had used white- or brown-skinned personnel to blend in. But now, the blue skins were meant to be a marker—alien yet familiar—to help acclimate humanity.

That sounded like a good idea. Humanity needed time before being introduced to some of the species seated at that table. A couple of them looked straight out of horror movies. Again, she hoped no one could read her thoughts.

Then the Council representatives presented Vicki with a gift.

Correction—they gave her a gift that she, as Earth's representative, accepted on behalf of all humanity. It was a complete history of everything that had happened on Earth over thousands of years—events humans knew nothing about.

They said they wanted humanity to learn the truth—about its history, and about its relationship with extraterrestrials.

Finally, Vicki thought, *we'll have proof whether our myths were real places and real events.* Would this be a good thing for humanity? Or would it throw them into a collective depression once they realized how much of what they believed was wrong?

She just hoped that what was in those records didn't blow human civilization apart.

Chapter
Forty-Two

T hey were back at Beth's flower shop before nightfall. Vicki's mind was numb. How could their lives—and the lives of everyone on Earth—have shifted so much in less than a day? Just a week ago, humanity had several options open to it. The events of the last twenty-four hours had resolved those possibilities into a single, glowing path stretching out before them into the future.

Was the path ahead glowing because it was hopeful, or because it was slick as ice and would launch them into danger before they could stop? Vicki didn't know.

Instead of being delivered by the Kewpies, Melly had personally escorted them back. The Council craft had several features the Kewpies' spaceship lacked, including some amazing cloaking technology. The crew set them down in the back parking lot, waited for them to disembark, and then took off without anyone being the wiser.

Not that there were many people around to see. The entire area had been shut down. Businesses were closed, and there were no customers or passersby. But even if there had been, they couldn't have gotten close. Out front, a lot of very *official*-looking people were keeping gawkers away and cleaning up the street. Among them were more military personnel than Vicki would have expected; most of them seemed fixated on retrieving whatever wreckage survived the explosion.

Brad joined her at the front window of the shop.

"I suppose they've called out the military because the regular emergency responders have their hands full at the Partnership's compound," he said. "They're probably still continuing rescue operations and trying to figure out how it happened."

Kiran came up beside them. "I don't think so. I'm sure the military is here because someone reported a spaceship blowing up. Probably several someones—there were more than a few people making videos with their phones. The government wouldn't want civilians to get their hands on anything resembling advanced technology."

"Look," Kiran pointed to a few well-built men dressed in black who looked dangerous and vigilant. "Mercenaries—probably former Marines or Special Forces."

Vicki took a quick step back. "You're right. Everyone away from the windows; let's not attract attention. I assume they've already gone door-to-door ordering people to evacuate. We don't want to have to explain how we're here now, even though we weren't here before. It wouldn't go well since we all have connections to the Partnership and the Martinsson mansion—and both were destroyed last night. Too many connections to be a coincidence."

They made their way upstairs to Beth's small apartment. There was food only because the young people had thought to stash some in their go-bags when they evacuated from the Martinssons'. Vicki was thankful for their foresight as Jessica took out chips and salsa. They were all hungry.

Then something hit her. "Brad!" Her eyesight blurred, and tears began rolling down her cheeks. The others looked at her in alarm. "Brad, your beautiful espresso machine—it's gone! It was blown up with the house!"

To her embarrassment, she started to cry.

Jessica came over and handed her a wad of tissues. She cried harder. Vicki could hear Jess explaining to the others that she was just letting out the stress. After a few minutes, she wiped her nose and blotted up the remaining tears. When she looked up, the others were studiously looking in other directions.

"Sorry." How humiliating. She was older than any of them by nearly a decade, and here she was, breaking down in tears.

"No need," said James with a crooked smile. "If you hadn't cried, the rest of us would have had to."

"I think we'll all be crying off and on for a while," she said, dabbing her nose. "Have you reached out to your folks to let them know you're okay? They must be frantic."

"I texted them as soon as we got back. I didn't tell them where we were, just that we were safe. I also told them about Larry." James swallowed.

"And you?" Vicki turned to Kiran. "Your family thinks you were at the Martinssons' house."

He shook his head. "I hadn't thought about it; I'll tell them now."

"Text only. Say you just heard about it because you and Brad were out camping in the mountains; there wasn't a signal, and the connection is still sketchy. You're starting back, but it will take another day."

"Now that we're done with housekeeping," Jessica said, taking another chip, "where do we go from here? What's the plan?"

"We keep moving forward. You still have a dozen interviews with Melly left to broadcast. The setup here is sufficient for that."

Vicki looked to Brad for confirmation, and he nodded.

"But if you think you need a recording studio—which I think you do—we'll need to get more equipment, and you can install it downstairs."

She laughed at the surprised expression on their faces. "I never knew what to do with Beth's flower shop. Now I do. The main floor is big enough to accommodate a recording studio, all Brad's electronics, and whatever office space is needed. The top floor can be your living quarters."

She looked at them. "You'll need a place to live," she reminded them gently.

Their faces briefly turned somber as they recalled why they needed one.

She turned to Kiran. "I'll drop you off at your family's place tomorrow."

She saw Jessica's mulish expression but continued on without giving her a chance to say anything.

"Give it a month—then you can tell them you're moving out. You're already twenty-four, so it shouldn't be too big of a shock. Honestly, it will be better for you, for them, and for us if you live apart from your family. It will be safer for everyone involved."

Kiran nodded. Jessica gave a brief smile.

Finally, she turned to James.

"Tomorrow, I'll take you home, too. But there's something we all need you to do." She handed him the small crystal that had been given to her by the Council; it was no larger than a pack of playing cards.

"You're the historian of the Four. Here's the entire record of Earth—all the history we never knew about. Why don't you take a look at it and develop a plan with the other three about the best way to release it. You might want to consider going century by century, but you four can decide how."

James' expression was rapturous.

Jessica picked up on the comment right away. "The other three? We four?" she said, encompassing the other young people, including Kiran, in her statement. "Aren't you a part of the Four? And you just gave all of us assignments. What about you?"

Vicki smiled at them. "I have a few calls to make, but I think I'll be going back to the State Department after all. They might not know it right now, but very soon, they are going to realize they desperately need a different sort of diplomat."

* * *

Mona could hold a grudge. They were sitting in the back garden of the tai chi studio—Vicki, the Martinsson siblings, and the three Coopers. They had dropped Kiran off in front of his house and pulled away. But not so fast that they missed the front door bursting open and his parents running out to throw their arms around him. They must have been waiting by the window.

Mona and Calvin were beyond relieved to have James back safe and sound. But looking past Calvin's joy at seeing his son again, Vicki could see his grief. No surprise there, since his brother—his best friend—had just been killed.

And Mona? Mona glared at Vicki over her son's head as she hugged him close. Her expression only darkened as she heard what Vicki had to say.

"What? You kick us out, and now you need us?"

Cal was sitting on one of the benches with an arm around James, but Mona was too furious to sit. Instead, she paced back and forth. She reminded Vicki of a tiger she'd once seen at a zoo. Even behind bars, the huge feline clearly radiated anger at the zoo-goers, making it obvious it would gladly turn them into a meal if it ever got the chance.

"Yes, we need you now," Vicki replied calmly.

She didn't respond to the implied accusation that going low contact with Cal and Mona had been a mistake when events became heated—there was no benefit in revisiting past actions. Besides, except for Larry, they were all still alive. Which meant that her strategy had worked.

"The Partnership—the primary danger to us—has been dealt with. There are only a few people here and there who might be threats. Right now, they are lying low."

Hilariously low. Stories about the SEC protests had taken over the airwaves. The screens were full of angry shareholders, effectively crowding out inquiries into the Partnership and its activities. The SEC lawsuits named the aerospace corporations themselves, not the Partnership, so no one was connecting the undisclosed assets to the destruction of the Partnership's compound. At least not yet.

Was this true ignorance or deliberate misdirection by the authorities? It was an open secret that military and intelligence agencies had assets in media organizations to ensure the public learned only what they deemed appropriate. Vicki supposed that was why there was still minimal reporting on the free-energy schematics.

"How about the super-soldiers?" asked Calvin. "Did any of the biologic constructs survive?"

"Melly told us that most of them didn't. The three who came for us in the Partnership's spaceship were destroyed, as were a couple dozen who were in the Partnership's compound when it was demolished. That said, a few of the biologic constructs in other places at the time did survive. While they might be a problem in the future, Melly said that, for the moment, it looks like they are pulling back and considering their options. The Partnership no longer exists, so they no longer have a job. If they wanted, they could melt into the general population and lead normal lives."

Brad snorted. Vicki agreed with the sentiment. No way those psychopathic super-soldiers would be content to live life in the suburbs. But that was a problem for another day.

"Vicki gave me an assignment," James piped up.

"You gave *my* son an assignment?" Mona's outrage was now on full display.

"Chill, Mom. It's really cool. It's history."

"I couldn't do it myself," Vicki interrupted. "I'm leaving."

That stopped Mona cold.

"I'm going back to the State Department."

"You're taking back your old job as a diplomat?" Calvin asked.

This time, all three of the young people snorted.

"Not hardly," Vicki said. "I reached out to the Department yesterday, and after several hours on conference calls, you are now looking at"—she paused dramatically—"the new Deputy Assistant Secretary for the Office of Multispecies Relations. 'OMR' for short." She grinned at him.

"The State Department already had an office for dealing with aliens?"

"No, that's new too. It took about twenty minutes for them to figure out what I was offering, and then they couldn't move fast enough. But even moving fast, making changes in a bureaucracy takes time. Imagine the chaos right now. Offices need to be found. Staff need to be assigned. Actually, I have veto power over my staff, so I need to return quickly so I can select them."

Mona was now sitting on the bench with her husband and son. Vicki didn't expect she'd ever totally forgive her, but at least steam was no longer rolling off her.

"So, if you're in Washington, the Four will no longer exist?"

"They will—just not with me. Kiran, who worked with Brad at the Partnership, has become part of the Four. You'll meet him soon, but believe me, he's a good guy. He brings some pretty incredible talent to the table, and all the kids like him."

Vicki swallowed. "Larry liked him."

There was a moment when nobody spoke; then Mona asked a question.

"You said the State Department couldn't move fast enough after what you offered them. What exactly did you offer them?" Her tone was suspicious, but Vicki could tell her heart wasn't in it.

"Control," Vicki said. "Control over the extraterrestrial issue in the United States. I am, at this moment, this country's only contact with the Galactic Council. That means the State Department will now have the lead over American military and intelligence agencies as Disclosure is carried out."

She smiled, remembering the conversation. "I could hear people drooling over the phone."

Calvin smothered a laugh but asked, "Won't people get upset? Certain powerful people?"

"Our military and intelligence people have had control of the ET file for the better part of a century. Look at what it got us: a population needlessly forced to live with pollution, poverty, and illness while a rogue corporate conglomerate hoarded knowledge and wealth—and nearly took over the world. It's hard to imagine the State Department could do worse."

She turned to address Mona directly.

"So, the Four need you and Calvin to keep training them. The entire world needs you to train other students. Remember, the vibrational shift is coming, and we need to get as many people as possible ready for it."

Brad seemed to be turning everything over in his mind before asking, "Aren't there some downsides to getting the State Department so deeply involved? Didn't you say it's known for leaking like a sieve?"

Vicki smiled.

"I'm counting on it," she told him, thinking of the backpack Kyle and Graham had given them. "I'm truly counting on it."

Epilogue

Have you ever wondered what life will be like after the vibrational shift? The energy is amazing. Communication is a vibration you pluck out of the air when you need it. Interstellar travel is like being a drop of water in a cold, rushing river. And the awareness is so deep and so powerful it makes you feel as if your eyes are finally open after a lifetime of living blind.

—Victoria Heywood
Excerpt from address to the UN

Vicki had never spent much time in New York City, so this was her first time taking its subway. Despite reports of a transit system in decline, she found it efficient—a quick way to travel from the hotel to her exit on 42nd Street. She liked that. The United Nations was only a twelve-minute walk from the station, so she still had an hour. Plenty of time.

The elderly woman seated next to her was hunched over in pain and muttering to herself. Young people wearing earphones bopped along to music no one else could hear. Tired mothers held children in their laps. Businessmen stared blankly into space. So many people trying their best—that's what Vicki sensed from her fellow travelers.

The loudspeaker blared out her station as the train lurched to a stop. She stood up and joined the crowd leaving the train. It was early—maybe she should grab a coffee.

* * *

Eleanor hated the heat—the pain from her lumbago was flaring to unbearable levels. How was she supposed to bear it? As the saying goes, getting old was not for the faint of heart. She slid into the window seat the younger woman had just vacated, being careful of her back. It was going to be a difficult day. About to mutter some more cross words, Eleanor paused. Was the pain gone? She sat up straight for the first time that week.

Jarred left the subway at 42nd Street, hurrying to make his class. There was a test in economics that day, and he had stayed up late studying for it. Majoring in business was the smart choice, and his parents were proud of him. But while Jarred kept telling himself he was doing the right thing, why did he feel so empty?

He took the escalator two steps at a time, bypassing those who preferred to be carried up and muttering a quick apology to the dark-haired woman he jostled in his rush. He passed by the retail shops without looking, then paused after going through the doors to the outside world. He took a deep breath. The air seemed unusually fresh that day. Very clear. Suddenly, *everything* seemed clear. He took another deep breath. Yes, this would be the day he changed his major to theater.

Carmen sat at the bus stop, holding three-year-old Lia. They weren't waiting for the bus, just pausing to rest for a few minutes before going into the hotel kitchen for work. Carmen felt lucky that Lia was so well-behaved; the manager allowed Lia to stay in the staff room during her shift when childcare fell through, which seemed to happen more often than not. Carmen loved her daughter but also envied the professional women she saw walking down the street. She envied them their confidence, their education, their language skills. How would she ever give Lia a better life?

Lia's eyes tracked a professionally dressed woman walking down the sidewalk, holding a cup of coffee. As the woman passed by the hotel entrance, Lia's attention switched to the concrete bollards opposite, poorly disguised as flower pots.

"*¡Mamá! ¡Mira las flores!*"

The flowers were beginning to glow.

ABOUT THE AUTHOR

Nancy Nelson retired after 25 years as a diplomat with the U.S. Department of State, then spent a few more years launching her kids, and traveling the world. Now she lives in California and explores the possibilities of humanity's future paths.

Cloud Hands is the first of the Disclosure Files Series, and is Nancy's attempt to weave a story of people facing the need to choose who they wish to be in a future with many options.